WARLOCK

SELECT EDITIONS

This condensation has been created by The Reader's Digest Association Limited by special arrangement with Macmillan Publishers Ltd.

With the exception of actual personages identified as such, the characters and incidents in this volume are entirely the products of the author's imagination and have no relation to any person or events in real life.

The Reader's Digest Association Limited,
11 Westferry Circus, Canary Wharf, London E14 4HE.

www.readersdigest.co.uk
ISBN 0 276 42594 4

Printed and bound by GGP Media, Pössneck, Germany

WARLOCK

A CONDENSATION OF THE BOOK BY

WILBUR SMITH

READER'S DIGEST SELECT EDITIONS
CONDENSED BOOKS DIVISION

In the ancient lands that border the River Nile, fourteen-year-old Prince Nefer is being groomed by his wise friend Taita, in preparation for his eventual succession to the throne of Lower Egypt.

But behind the loyal faces at court, a traitor lurks. As cunning and as patient as a cobra.

Can the aged Taita, with his wisdom and wondrous magical powers, avert the danger that threatens to destroy his country's hopes of a peaceful future?

CHAPTER ONE

Like an uncoiling serpent, a line of fighting chariots wound swiftly down the gut of the valley. From where he clung to the dashboard of the leading chariot, the boy looked up at the cliffs that hemmed them in. Openings to the tombs of the ancients honeycombed the rock, staring down at him like the implacable eyes of a legion of djinn. Prince Nefer Memnon shuddered and looked away, furtively making the sign to avert evil with his left hand.

Over his shoulder he glanced back down the column and saw that from the following chariot Taita was watching him through the swirling clouds of dust. The dust had coated the old man and his vehicle with a pale film, and a single shaft of sunlight that penetrated to the depths of this deep valley glittered on the mica particles so that he seemed to glow like the incarnation of one of the gods. Even at that distance his ancient eyes seemed to bore into the core of Nefer's being. Seeing all, understanding all. Nefer ducked his head guiltily, ashamed that the old man had witnessed his superstitious dread. No royal prince of the House of Tamose should show such weakness, not now when he stood at the gateway to manhood. But then, Taita knew him as no other did, for he had been Nefer's tutor since infancy, closer to him than his own parents or siblings.

Nefer turned back and drew himself up to his full height beside his father, who flipped the reins and urged the horses on with a crack of the long whip. Ahead of them the valley opened abruptly into the great amphitheatre that contained the ruins of the city of Gallala. Nefer thrilled to his first sight of this famous battlefield. As a young man Taita himself had fought on this site when Nefer's grandfather, Tanus Lord Harrab, had destroyed the dark forces that were threatening Egypt. Taita had related to Nefer every detail of the fight.

Nefer's father, the god and Pharaoh Tamose, wheeled the chariot up to the tumbled stones of the ruined gateway and reined in the horses. Behind them a hundred chariots neatly executed the same manoeuvre. Stripped naked in the heat, the charioteers swarmed down from the footplates to begin watering the horses.

'My lord!' Pharaoh hailed Lord Naja, his army commander and beloved companion. 'We must be away again before the sun touches the hilltops. I wish to make a night run through the dunes to El Galsar.' He glanced down at Nefer. 'This is where I leave you to go on with Taita.'

Nefer opened his mouth to protest. Pharaoh forestalled him. 'What is the first duty of a warrior?' he demanded.

Nefer dropped his eyes. 'It is obedience, Majesty,' he replied softly.

'Never forget it.' His father nodded and turned away.

Pharaoh Tamose's battle plan was bold and brilliant. If it succeeded, it would bring to a close, at one stroke, the war with the Hyksos that had already raged through two lifetimes. Nefer had been taught that battle and glory were the reasons for his existence on this earth. But even at the advanced age of fourteen, they had so far eluded him. He longed with all his soul to ride to victory and immortality at his father's side. Now he felt himself spurned and discarded. His eyes smarted and his upper lip quivered, but Taita's gaze stiffened him. He blinked to clear his tears and took a pull from the water-skin that hung on the side rail of the chariot before turning to the old Magus with a jaunty toss of his thick, dust-caked curls. 'Show me the monument, Tata,' he commanded.

The pair made their way through the chariots, men and horses that choked the narrow streets of the ruined city, past temples and palaces now inhabited only by the lizard and the scorpion, until they reached the deserted central square. In its centre stood the monument to Lord Tanus and his triumph over the armies of bandits who had almost choked the life out of the richest and most powerful nation on earth.

Taita watched the prince as he walked round the monument, a bizarre pyramid of human skulls cemented together and protected by a shrine made of red rock slabs.

'Tata, show me where it was that you captured the leader of the robber barons.' Nefer's voice cracked with excitement and the onset of puberty. 'Was it here?' He ran to the broken-down wall at the south side of the square.

'No, it was here. This side,' Taita told him, and he strode on those long, stork-thin legs to the eastern wall. He looked up to the crumbling summit. 'The ruffian's name was Shufti, and he was one-eyed and as ugly as the god Seth. He was trying to escape by climbing over the wall here. I brought him down with a single throw.'

Even though Nefer knew, at first hand, the old man's strength, he was astonished when Taita suddenly stooped and picked up half a baked-mud brick and hurled it upwards. It sailed over the top of the high wall.

He is as old as the mountains, older than my grandmother, Nefer marvelled. Men say he has witnessed two hundred inundations of the Nile and that he built the pyramids with his own hands.

'You know the story well enough, for I have told it to you a hundred times.' Taita feigned modest reluctance to extol his own deeds.

'Tell me again!' Nefer ordered.

Taita sat down on a stone block while Nefer settled at his feet in happy anticipation and listened avidly until the ram's horns of the squadron sounded the recall.

There was a great bustle and scurry outside the walls of the ruined city as the squadron made ready to go on into the dune lands. The water-skins were bulging again, and the troopers checked and tightened the harnesses of their teams before mounting up.

Pharaoh Tamose looked over the heads of his staff as Taita and Nefer came through the gateway. He summoned Taita to his side with an inclination of his head. Together they walked out of earshot of the squadron officers. Lord Naja made to join them. Taita whispered a word to Pharaoh, then Tamose turned and sent Naja back with a curt word. Flushed with mortification, Naja shot a look at Taita that was sharp as a war arrow.

'You have offended Naja. Some day I might not be at hand to protect you,' Pharaoh warned.

'We dare trust no man,' Taita insisted. 'Treachery tightens its coils around your palace. Until you return from this campaign in the north only the two of us must know where I am taking the prince.'

'But Naja!' Pharaoh laughed dismissively. Naja was like a brother.

'Even Naja.' Taita said no more. His suspicions were hardening into certainty, but he had not yet gathered all the evidence he would need to convince Pharaoh.

'Does the prince know why you are taking him into the desert?' Pharaoh asked.

'He knows only that we are going to further his instruction in the mysteries, and to capture his godbird.'

'Good, Taita.' Pharaoh nodded. 'You were ever secretive but true. There is nothing more to say, for we have said it all. Now go, and may Horus spread his wings over you and Nefer.'

'Look to your own back, Majesty, for in these days enemies stand behind you as well as to your front.'

Pharaoh grasped the Magus's upper arm and squeezed hard. Then he went back to where Nefer waited beside the wheel of the royal chariot.

'It is my command that you go with Taita into the desert to capture your godbird, to prove your royal blood and your right one day to wear the double crown.'

NEFER AND THE OLD MAN stood together beside the shattered walls of Gallala and watched the column fly past. Pharaoh led it, leaning back against the pull of the horses, his chest bare, linen skirts whipping around his muscular legs, the blue war crown on his head.

Next came Lord Naja, haughty and proud, the great recurved bow slung over his shoulder. Naja was one of Egypt's mightiest warriors, and his name had been given to him as a title of honour. Naja was the sacred cobra in the royal crown.

The two were silent long after the last chariot had disappeared and the dust had settled. Then Taita turned without a word and went to where their horses were tethered. He hiked up his kilts and swung up with the limber movement of a much younger man.

Nefer, as he vaulted up onto the back of his favourite colt, cast a last, longing glance at the feather of distant dust left on the northern horizon by the squadron, then firmly turned his back upon it. 'Where are we going, Tata?' he demanded. 'You promised to tell me once we were on the road.'

Taita was always reticent and secretive, but seldom to this degree. 'We are going to Gebel Nagara,' he told him.

Nefer had never heard the name before, but he repeated it softly. It had a romantic ring. Excitement and anticipation made the back of his neck prickle, and he looked ahead into the desert where jagged hills stretched away to a horizon blue with heat haze and distance.

Taita looked on this terrible place with a sense of nostalgia and homecoming. It was into this wilderness that he had retired after the death of his beloved Queen Lostris, Nefer's grandmother. He was a physician and a surgeon, a master of the known sciences, and alone in the desert he had discovered the key to doorways of the mind beyond which few men ever journey. He had gone in a man but had emerged as a familiar of the great god Horus, adept at strange and arcane mysteries.

Taita had only returned to the world of men when his Queen Lostris had visited him in a dream as he slept in his hermit's cave at Gebel Nagara. 'Darling Taita,' she had whispered, as she touched his cheek, 'you were one of the only two men I have ever loved. My husband Tanus is with me now, but before you can come to me also there is one more charge that I lay upon you.'

'I am yours to command, mistress.'

'In Thebes, my city of a hundred gates, this night is born a child, the son of my son. They will name this child Nefer, which means pure and perfect. My longing is that he may carry my blood and the blood of Tanus to the throne of Upper Egypt. But great perils already gather around him. He cannot succeed without your help. Go to Nefer. Go swiftly and stay with him until your task is completed. Do not fail me, Taita.'

Taita awoke, his face wet with tears, gathered up his possessions, then strode away into the western desert, back towards the city of Thebes. That had been over fourteen years ago, and now he knew that the dark powers of which she had warned were gathering.

'Come!' he said to the boy. 'Let us go down and take your godbird.'

ON THE THIRD NIGHT after leaving Gallala, Pharaoh Tamose halted the squadron to water the horses and to eat a hasty meal of sun-dried meat, dates and millet cakes. Then he ordered the mount-up. There was no sounding of the ram's horn trumpet now, for they were into Hyksosian territory.

The column started forward again at the trot. As they went on, the landscape changed dramatically. Below them lay the strip of dense vegetation that marked the course of the Nile. They had completed a wide circuit and were in the rear of the main Hyksosian army on the river. Although they were a tiny force against such an enemy, they were the best charioteers in the armies of Tamose, which made them the finest in the world. Moreover, they held the element of surprise.

It was almost two centuries since Egypt had been split apart. Since then either an Egyptian usurper or a foreign invader had ruled in the northern kingdom. It was Tamose's destiny to drive out the Hyksos and unite the two lands once more. Only then could he wear the double crown with justification and the approval of the ancient gods.

The night air blew cool in his face, and his lance-bearer crouched low behind the dashboard to shield himself. The only sound was the crunch of the chariot wheels over the coarse gravel, the lances rattling softly in their scabbards.

Suddenly a wide wadi opened ahead of him and Pharaoh Tamose reined down the team. The wadi was the smooth roadway that would lead them down to the river. Pharaoh tossed the reins to his lance-bearer and vaulted down. He stretched his stiff, aching limbs as Naja's chariot came up behind him.

'From here the danger of discovery will be greater,' Naja said. 'Look down there.' He pointed to where the dry riverbed debouched onto the plain below. 'That is the village of El Wadun, where our spies will be waiting to lead us through the Hyksosian pickets. I will go ahead to the rendezvous to make safe the way. Wait here, Majesty, and I will return directly.'

'I will go with you.'

'I beg you. There may be treachery. You are Egypt. You are too precious to risk.'

Pharaoh turned to look into the beloved lean and handsome

face, and touched Naja's shoulder with trust and affection. 'Go swiftly, and return as swiftly,' he acceded.

Naja ran back to his chariot. He saluted as he wheeled past where the king stood, and whipped up his speeding horses, down towards the village of El Wadun. When he had gone, Pharaoh walked back down the waiting column, speaking quietly to the troopers, calling many by name, encouraging and cheering them. Small wonder they loved him, and followed him so gladly wherever he led them.

WHEN LATER PHARAOH TAMOSE saw the chariot returning, he knew by the impetuous manner in which Naja drove that something was afoot. He ordered the squadron to mount and stand with drawn weapons, ready to meet any eventuality.

The moment the chariot drew level with Pharaoh, Naja sprang down.

'What's amiss?' Tamose demanded.

'A blessing from the gods,' Naja told him. 'They have delivered Apepi defenceless into our power.'

'How is that possible?'

'My spies have led me to where the enemy king is encamped. His tents are set up just beyond the first line of hills.' He pointed back with his sword.

'What is his strength?' Tamose could barely control his excitement.

'With his usual arrogance he has a bodyguard of fewer than fifty, and half of them are asleep. He suspects nothing. A swift charge out of the darkness and we will have him in our grasp.'

'Take me to where Apepi lies,' Pharaoh commanded.

Naja led them, and the soft, silvery sands of the wadi muffled the sounds of the wheels. The squadron swept around the last bend and Naja raised his clenched fist high to order the halt. Pharaoh drew up alongside him.

Naja pointed up a pathway towards the crest of the hills. 'On the far side is an oasis. His tents are set among the trees.'

'We will take a small patrol with us to scout the camp. Only then can we plan our attack.'

Naja had anticipated the order. He selected a scouting party of five troopers. 'Muffle your scabbards,' he ordered. 'Make not a sound.' Then, with his bow in his left hand, he stepped onto the pathway. Pharaoh came close behind him. They went upwards swiftly, until Naja saw the crossed branches of a thorn tree silhouetted against the dawn sky. He stopped abruptly.

It was here, not half an hour before, that he had met secretly with his cousin Trok, a Hyksosian general. Not even Pharaoh knew that Naja's mother had been Hyksosian. In the decades of their occupation, with a dearth of their own women to choose from, many Hyksos had taken Egyptian wives, and over the generations the bloodlines had become blurred.

Naja held up his right hand for silence.

'What is it?' Pharaoh whispered close behind him.

'I thought I heard voices on the crest,' Naja answered, 'speaking the Hyksosian tongue. Wait here, Majesty, while I clear the path ahead.' Pharaoh and the five troopers squatted beside the path, while Naja went on stealthily. He stepped around a large boulder and his dim figure disappeared from view. The minutes passed slowly and Pharaoh began to fret. As a soft whistle came down to him he sprang to his feet and hefted his fabled blue sword.

'The way is clear,' Pharaoh murmured. 'Come, follow me.'

Pharaoh went on upwards and reached the tall rock that blocked the pathway. He stepped round it then stopped abruptly. Lord Naja faced him at a distance of twenty paces. They were alone, hidden by the rock from the men who followed. Naja's bow was at full draw, a Hyksosian arrow aimed at Pharaoh's chest. The full realisation of what confronted him blazed in Pharaoh's mind. This, then, was the foul thing that Taita, with his clairvoyant powers, had smelt in the air.

'May you live for ever!' Silently Naja mouthed the words as though they were a curse, and he loosed the arrow, which took Pharaoh high in the centre of his chest, throwing him against the red rock of the boulder. For a moment he clung to the rough surface but the flint arrowhead had pierced him through, and he began to slide down, his legs buckling under him. Naja sprang forward with a wild cry, 'Ambush! Beware!' and he slipped one arm around Pharaoh's chest below the protruding arrow.

Supporting the dying king he bellowed again, 'On me, the guards!' and two stout troopers appeared round the rock wall, responding to his cry. They saw at a glance how Pharaoh was struck and the unmistakable bright fletching feathers on the base of the Hyksosian arrow.

'Carry Pharaoh back to his chariot while I hold off the enemy,' Naja ordered, and whirled around, pulling an arrow from his quiver and loosing it up the path towards the deserted summit, bellowing a challenge, then answering himself with a muffled counter-challenge in the Hyksosian language. He snatched up the blue sword from where Tamose had dropped it, then bounded back down the path and caught up with the small party of charioteers who were carrying the king away.

'It was a trap,' Naja told them urgently. 'The hilltop is alive with the enemy. Hurry! The king must not fall into their hands.'

The troops below had heard the wild cries in the dawn, and the regimental surgeon was waiting for them beside Pharaoh's chariot. He had been trained by Taita, and, though lacking the old man's special magic, might be capable of staunching Pharaoh's terrible wound. Lord Naja would not risk that, so he ordered the surgeon away brusquely. 'The enemy is hard upon us. There is no time for your quackery now. We must get him back to the safety of our own lines before we are overrun.'

Tenderly he lifted the king onto the footplate of his own chariot. He snapped off the shaft of the Hyksosian arrow that protruded from the king's chest and held it aloft so that all his men could see it clearly. 'This bloody instrument has struck down our Pharaoh. Our god and our king. He wrapped the arrow in a linen cloth, and placed it in the chariot. He would need to deliver it to the council in Thebes to substantiate his report on Pharaoh's death.

'A good man here to hold Pharaoh,' Naja ordered.

While the king's own lance-bearer came forward, Naja unbuckled the sword-belt from around Pharaoh's waist and carefully stowed it in his own weapons bin.

The lance-bearer jumped onto the footplate and cradled Tamose's head, as the chariot wheeled in a circle then sped back up the wadi with the rest of the squadron.

Facing forward so that none could see his expression, Naja laughed softly, the sound covered by the grinding wheels. Leaving the wadi, they raced on towards the dunes.

IT WAS MIDMORNING, and the blinding white sun was halfway up the sky before Naja allowed the column to halt and the surgeon to come forward again to examine the king. It did not need his special skills to tell that Pharaoh's spirit had long before left his body and started its journey to the underworld.

'Pharaoh is dead,' the surgeon said quietly. A terrible cry of mourning ran through the column.

'The state is without a head,' Naja told his captains. 'Egypt is in dire peril. Ten of the fastest chariots must take Pharaoh's body back to Thebes with all haste. I shall lead them, for the council may wish me to take up the duties of regent to Prince Nefer, who must be found and informed of his own succession.'

He unrolled a papyrus scroll, a map of the territory from Thebes down to Memphis. 'You must split up into your troops and scour the countryside for the prince. I believe that Pharaoh sent him into the desert with the ancient eunuch to undertake the rituals of manhood, so we will concentrate our search there, around Gallala, where we last saw him.'

Naja held them with a final command: 'When you find Prince Nefer, bring him to me. Give him into no other hand but mine.'

He ran back to his chariot and seized the reins, 'Onwards!' he cried with a clenched fist. 'Onwards to Thebes!'

FOLLOWING NAJA'S SECRET ORDERS, a full legion of the Phat Guards, his own special regiment that was oath-bound to him, were waiting for him at the oasis of Boss, only two leagues from Thebes.

The guards' pickets saw the dust of the approaching chariots and stood to arms. The colonel, Asmor, and his officers turned out in full armour to meet Lord Naja.

'Lord Asmor!' Naja hailed him from the chariot. 'I have dreadful news to take to Thebes. Pharaoh is killed by a Hyksosian arrow. Egypt is without a father.' He raised his voice so that it carried clearly to the rear ranks. 'Prince Nefer is a child still and not ready to rule. Egypt stands in desperate need of a regent to lead her.' He paused and stared meaningfully at Colonel Asmor. Asmor lifted his chin in acknowledgment of the trust that Naja had placed in him.

Naja raised his voice to bellow: 'If Pharaoh falls in battle, the army has the right by acclamation to appoint a regent in the field.'

Asmor took a pace forward and turned to face the ranks of heavily armed guards. He removed his helmet. His face was dark and hard. He pointed his drawn sword to the sky and shouted, 'Lord Naja! Hail to Lord Naja!'

There was a stunned silence before the legion erupted in a roar, 'Hail to Lord Naja, Regent of Egypt!'

THE JOURNEY FROM GALLALA took three days of hard riding. Naja was exhausted, yet he allowed himself only an hour to rest, bathe away the dust of the journey and change his apparel. He now wore a white linen skirt, with a pectoral plate of gold and semiprecious stones covering his bare, muscled chest. On his hip he carried the fabulous blue sword that he had taken from Pharaoh's dead body.

His bodyguard formed up around him, and the full legion fell in behind him. With five thousand men at his back the new Regent of Egypt began his march on Thebes.

Colonel Asmor rode as Naja's lance-bearer. He was young for the command of a full legion, but he had proved himself in battle and he was Naja's close companion. He, too, had Hyksosian blood in his veins, and there was nothing he would not do to hasten his patron Lord Naja's ascension to the throne of Egypt.

'What stands before us now, my old comrade?' Lord Naja asked him as they rode.

'The Yellow Flowers have cleared all but one of the princes of the House of Tamose from your path,' Asmor answered, pointing with his lance to the hills across the grey, silt-laden Nile. 'They lie in their tombs in the Valley of the Nobles.'

Three years previously a plague had swept through the two kingdoms. The disease was named for the dreadful yellow lesions that covered the bodies of the stricken. Eight princesses and six princes of the House of Tamose had died. Of all Pharaoh's children, only one girl and Prince Nefer Memnon had survived. There were those who believed that they would have died also, had not the ancient Magus Taita cut their left upper arms and placed in their blood his magical charm against the Yellow Flowers.

Naja frowned. Even in this moment of his triumph he could still give thought to the strange powers possessed by the Magus. He had already lived so long that no one knew his age; some said a hundred years and others two hundred. Yet he still walked and ran and drove a chariot like a man in his prime. Surely the gods loved him, and had bestowed upon him the secret of life eternal.

Once he was Pharaoh, that secret would be the only thing that Naja lacked. Could he wring it out of Taita the Warlock? First, he must be captured and brought in along with Prince Nefer, but he must not be harmed. He was far too valuable. The chariots Naja had sent to scout the eastern deserts would bring them back.

The gates of Thebes were thrown open as soon as the sentries recognised the blue standard, and the citizens ran out to meet them. But the welcoming cries soon gave way to wild ululations of mourning when they heard the shouts of the leading charioteers: 'Pharaoh is dead! He has been slain by the Hyksos.'

The wailing crowds followed the chariot that carried the royal corpse to the funerary temple. The rest of the usually swarming city was almost deserted, and Naja galloped his chariot team swiftly through the narrow, crooked streets to the river palace. He knew that every member of the council would hurry to the assembly chamber as soon as they heard the dreadful news. At the entrance to the palace gardens, Asmor and fifty men of the bodyguard formed up around Naja. They marched in close order through the inner courtyard, past the ponds of the water garden filled with hyacinth and fish from the river.

The arrival of the armed men took the council unawares. The doors to the chamber were unguarded, and only a few members were assembled. Naja paused in the doorway and looked them over. Menset and Talla were old and past their once formidable powers; Cinka had always been weak and vacillating.

'Noble lords!' Naja greeted them as he strode into the chamber. 'Pharaoh is dead. He was cut down by a Hyksosian arrow while storming the enemy stronghold above El Wadun.'

The council members gawked at him in silence. Instantly Naja realised his opportunity. 'I am the regent of the royal Prince Nefer.' he thundered. 'I was acclaimed by my legions in the field. My noble lords, is there any man among you who would question this?' He looked at each in turn and they dropped their eyes: there was no man to give them direction and the Phat Guards stood shoulder to shoulder around the wall of the chamber.

'My lord Menset'—Naja singled out the president of the council—'does the council ratify the appointment of Lord Naja as the Regent of Egypt?'

Menset raised his eyes and looked around at his fellow members, but not one would catch his eye. 'The president and all the councillors of this assembly acknowledge the new Regent of Egypt,' he whispered at last.

'I accept the duty and heavy responsibility you have placed upon me.' Naja mounted the dais to the throne. 'As my first official pronouncement in my capacity of Regent in Council I wish to describe to you the gallant death of the divine Pharaoh Tamose.' He paused significantly, then for the next hour he related in detail his version of the fatal campaign and the attack on the heights of El Wadun. 'His last words to me as I carried him down the hill were, "Care for my only remaining son. Guard my son Nefer until he is man enough to wear the double crown. Take my daughter under your wings, and see that no harm befalls her."'

It took Lord Naja some moments to bring his grief under control. Then he went on firmly, 'I will not fail the god who was my friend and my pharaoh. Already I have sent my chariots into the wilderness to search for Prince Nefer and bring him back to Thebes. As soon as he arrives we will set him on the throne, and place the scourge and the sceptre in his hands.'

There was the first murmur of approval among the councillors, and Naja continued, 'Now, send for the princess. Have her brought to the chamber immediately.'

When she came hesitantly through the main doors, Heseret smiled shyly around this formidable gathering. She had inherited in full measure the celebrated beauty of her grandmother, Queen Lostris. Her skin was milky, her limbs were smooth and shapely, and there were intriguing lights in her huge dark green eyes.

'Come forward, my pretty darling.' Naja rose from the throne, went down to meet her, and placed his hands on her shoulder. His voice and his expression were tragic. 'You must be brave now, and remember that you are a princess of the royal house, because I have bitter news for you. Pharaoh, your father, is dead.' For a minute Heseret did not seem to understand, then she let out the high keening wail of mourning.

Gently Naja put his arms around her and led her to sit at the foot of the throne. 'The distress of the royal princess is plain for all to see,' he told the assembly. 'The trust and the duty that Pharaoh placed upon me is equally plain. As I have taken Prince Nefer Memnon into my care, now I take Princess Heseret under my protection.'

CHAPTER TWO

Nefer sat in the shadow of the cliff that towered above Gebel Nagara. He had not moved since the sun had first shown its upper rim above the mountains across the valley. At first the effort of remaining still had made his skin itch as though insects were crawling upon it. But he knew Taita was watching him, so he had forced his wayward body into a state of exalted awareness, his every sense tuned to the wilderness about him. He could smell the water that rose from its secret spring in the cleft in the cliff. It came up a slow drop at a time and dripped into a basin in the rock. Much life was supported by this trickle of water: butterfly and beetle, serpent and lizard, the speckled pigeons that nested on high ledges, all drank here. It was because of this precious pool that Taita had brought him to this place to wait for his godbird.

They had begun to make a net on the day of their arrival at Gebel Nagara. Taita had bought the silk in Thebes. It was stronger than thongs of leather but almost invisible to the eye.

When the net was ready Taita had insisted that the boy catch the decoys himself. So, in the baking daylight out on the valley floor, Nefer and Taita had studied the route up the cliff to the ledge where the pigeons roosted. When darkness fell Taita had sat beside a small fire by the entrance to a cave at the base of the cliff, and Nefer had started the precarious climb. He seized two birds while they were still disorientated by the darkness, and brought them down in the leather saddlebag slung on his back.

They selected a spot close to the base of the cliff, but exposed enough to make the birds clearly visible from the sky, and tethered the pigeons by the leg with horsehair thread and a wooden peg driven into the hard earth. Then they spread the gossamer net above them, supported on stalks of dried elephant grass, which would snap under the stoop of the godbird.

When all was set up to Taita's satisfaction, they began the long wait. Soon the pigeons became accustomed to captivity, and pecked greedily at the millet that Nefer scattered for them. Then they sunned and dusted themselves contentedly under the silken net. One hot, sun-riven day succeeded the next, and still they waited.

In the cool of the evening they brought the pigeons into the cave, and then they hunted for food. They grilled gazelle steaks over the fire. The cave had been Taita's retreat during all the years after the death of Queen Lostris when he had lived here as a hermit. It was his place of power.

They had been at Gebel Nagara for many days before Nefer began to understand that they had not come here to find the godbird alone. Taita was teaching him control over his body and being, teaching him to look inward, to listen to the silence and hear whispers to which others were deaf. Even the long hours of waiting beside the decoys were a lesson.

On the twentieth morning of their stay, Nefer took up his position over the decoys. As always, he was deeply aware of the presence of Taita, whose eyes were closed and who seemed to be dozing in the sunlight. His skin was crisscrossed with innumerable fine wrinkles and dappled with age spots. It looked as delicate as the finest papyrus parchment. His face was hairless, no trace of beard or eyebrows; only fine lashes, colourless as glass, surrounded his eyes. Nefer reached out to touch the old man's arm as he slept. Nefer had heard his father say that it was because Taita was a eunuch, gelded after puberty, that his face was beardless and little marked by the passage of time, but he was certain that there were more reasons for the persistence of his strength and life force.

Suddenly Taita's eyes opened, focused and aware. Nefer knew that he had not been asleep at all, but that all his powers had been concentrated on bringing in the godbird to the decoys.

Chastened, he composed himself, and brought his mind and body under control again as Taita had taught him. It was like passing through a secret doorway. Suddenly Nefer was blessed with a marvellous sense that he, too, hung above the world and saw everything happening below him. He saw Taita and himself sitting beside the well of Gebel Nagara, and the desert stretching away around them. He saw cities and kingdoms, the machinations of evil men, and the striving of the just and good. In that moment he was aware of his destiny with an intensity that almost overwhelmed his courage.

In that same moment he knew that his godbird would come on this day, for he was ready to receive it at last, aware with every fibre of his being.

The royal falcon was such a rare creature that few men had ever seen it in the wild. Possession of the bird was proof that Pharaoh had the divine approval of the god Horus to reign in Egypt.

And now the bird was here. His very own bird. He heard its cry, a faint lament, almost lost in the immensity of sky and desert. Seconds later the falcon called again, directly overhead, its voice shriller and more savage.

Now the pigeons were wild with terror, leaping against the threads that secured them to the pegs, while high overhead Nefer heard the falcon begin its stoop on them, the wind singing over its wings in a rising note. He looked up and saw the bird drop against the aching blue of the desert sky. It was a thing of divine beauty. Its wings were folded back, and its head was thrust forward. The strength and power of the creature made Nefer gasp aloud. He wanted to possess it with a longing he had never imagined possible.

He braced himself for the moment of impact. Beside him he felt Taita do the same. The falcon dropped like a thrown javelin, and tore into the pigeons with both sets of talons.

Then Nefer heard an explosive hiss of air. Something huge and glittering black whipped out from behind the net and slammed into the falcon. He saw the thick, glittering coils of a gigantic black cobra. The snake's head was raised, its hood marked with a bold pattern of black and white. Its fathomless black eyes held Nefer in a mesmeric stare. He tried to scream, but no sound came from his throat. Each scale was polished like a jewel, each coil, wrapped around the falcon, was as thick as Nefer's arm, and slowly they revolved upon themselves.

Without thought, Nefer hurled his leather bag away from him.

The cobra's fangs hooked into the leather and the bag and the snake fell away together, the sinuous body still coiling and whipping furiously. It bounced away over the rocks until Nefer lost sight of it among the grey boulders.

'Oh, Taita. It was horrible. It killed my godbird.'

'Gently, lad. Drink.' He offered the water-skin. 'Thanks be to the great god who protected you,' Taita murmured. 'With this cobra apparition, Horus has sent you a portent of terrible dangers. That was no natural serpent.'

He turned and walked back to the entrance of the cave. Nefer followed him slowly, his heart leaden with disappointment. In the gloom of the cave Taita seated himself on the stone ledge below the back wall, and leaned forward to build up the smoky fire of thorn branches until it burst into flames.

They were both silent a long while. At last Taita sighed, and said softly, almost sadly, 'I must work the Mazes of Ammon Ra.'

Nefer watched in awe as Taita went through the ritual of preparing the Mazes. First he crushed herbs with a pestle in a mortar, and poured boiling water over them. The steam that rose was so pungent it made Nefer's eyes water.

While the mixture cooled, Taita brought the tanned leather bag that contained the Mazes from its hiding place at the back of the cave. The Mazes comprised ten ivory discs, each carved with one of the ten symbols of power. Taita rubbed the discs gently between his fingers as he began to chant the incantation to Ammon Ra, and between each verse he blew on them to endow them with his life force. When they had taken on the warmth of his own body he passed them to Nefer.

'Hold them and breathe upon them,' he urged, and while Nefer obeyed these instructions, Taita began to sway as he retreated into the secret places in his mind. He was already in the trance when Nefer stacked the Mazes in front of him, then offered up the infusion to him. Taita drank it to the last drop, and in the firelight his face turned white as chalk. He subsided onto the floor of the cave, and started to twitch and groan, and the sweat streamed down his face. His eyes opened and rolled back in their sockets until only the whites glared blindly into the dark shadows of the cave.

Nefer knew there was nothing he could do for the old man now.

Taita had journeyed far into the shadowy places where Nefer could not reach him. Hardly able to bear the terrible suffering that the Mazes inflicted upon the Magus, Nefer lay down beside him, and after a while he fell into a sleep that was haunted by nightmares.

When he awoke, dawn was glimmering at the entrance to the cave. Taita was sitting at the fire, still looking pale and sick. 'What did you see, Tata,' the boy asked.

'It was obscured,' Taita told him, and Nefer knew that the omen had been unpropitious.

'Explain it to me, Tata,' Nefer insisted.

There was deep anguish in his voice, so Taita softened his answer. 'There are mysteries here. I saw their shadows in my vision. This is a thing beyond the natural order.'

Taita paused and looked to the sky, as if in deep thought. 'First we must fly from the great dangers that beset us. The cobra has returned from the shadows from which it sprang.'

Nefer shivered with superstitious awe, then scrambled up onto the back of his colt.

Taita led the way. By the time the sun was above the horizon they had left Gebel Nagara far behind them.

Nefer knew well that when Taita was in this mood it was wasted effort to speak to him, but he urged his horse alongside and pointed out respectfully, 'Tata, this is not the way to Thebes.'

'We are not going back there.'

Nefer was puzzled. 'Why not?'

Taita turned his head and looked at the boy with such pity that he was silenced. 'I will explain when we are in a safe place.'

Avoiding the crests of hills, where they might be silhouetted on the skyline, Taita wove a path through the gorges and valleys. Always he headed east, away from Egypt and the Nile, towards the sea.

The sun was setting before he reined in his mare and spoke. 'The main caravan road lies just beyond the next line of hills. We must cross it, but enemies may be watching for us there.'

They left the horses tethered in a hidden wadi, then climbed cautiously to the crest of the hills and found a vantage point behind a bank of purple shale from which they could look down onto the caravan road below.

'We will lie here until dark,' Taita explained. He swept another look along the road below them, and immediately ducked his head. 'Someone coming!' he warned.

Nefer flattened himself behind the shale bank and they watched the column of dust coming swiftly down the caravan road from the west. By this time the valley was in deep shadow and the sky was filled with all the glorious shades of the sunset.

'They are moving fast. Those are not merchants, they are fighting chariots,' Nefer said. 'Yes, I can see them now.' His bright young eyes picked out the shape of the leading chariot. 'They are not Hyksos,' he went on. 'They are ours. A cohort of the Phat Guards! We are safe, Tata!'

Taita reached up a bony hand and hauled him down violently. 'Those are the minions of the cobra. Hurry! They must not catch us.'

He dragged the boy off the ridge and started down the slope, jumping from rock to rock, his silver mane of hair streaming out behind him. He reached the horses first, and was on the mare's back in a single leap.

'What is happening, Tata?' Nefer panted.

'Mount! No time to talk.'

As they galloped out of the wadi, Nefer shot a longing look back over his shoulder, and saw the leading charioteer. 'That is Hilto, Tata. I know his face so well. He is a good man.'

Hilto was a famous warrior, who wore the Gold of Valour, but Taita told Nefer sternly, 'Don't be deceived. Trust nobody.'

Obediently Nefer rode on into the wilderness of broken rock. The faint sounds behind them dwindled and were snuffed out by the eternal silence of the desert. Before they had gone much further darkness forced them to dismount and walk through the difficult places where the twisting path narrowed.

At last they had to stop to water and rest the horses. They sat close together and, with his dagger, Taita sliced a loaf of millet bread, and they munched it as they talked softly.

'Tell me of your vision, Tata. What did you truly see when you worked the Mazes of Ammon Ra?'

'I told you. They were obscured.'

'I know that is not true.' Nefer shook his head. 'You said that to protect me.' He shivered from the chill of the night and a sense of dread. 'You saw something of terrible portent. That is why we are fleeing now. You must tell me all your vision. I must understand what is happening to us.'

'Yes, you are right,' Taita agreed at last. 'It is time for you to know.'

He put out one thin arm and drew Nefer close under his shawl. He seemed to be collecting his thoughts, and then at last he spoke.

'In my vision I saw a great tree growing on the banks of Mother Nile. It was a mighty tree and its blooms were blue as hyacinth and over it hung the double crown of the Upper and Lower Kingdoms. In its shade were all the multitudes of Egypt, men and women, children and greybeards, merchants and farmers, priests and warriors. The tree gave them all protection, and they prospered mightily and were content.'

'That was a good vision.' Eagerly Nefer translated it. 'The tree must have been Pharaoh, my father. The colour of the House of Tamose is blue, and my father wears the double crown. But then what did you see, Tata?'

'I saw a serpent in the muddy waters of the river, swimming towards where the tree stood. It was a great cobra. And it crawled from the waters of the Nile and climbed into the tree, twisting itself around the tree, supporting it and giving it strength.'

'That I do not understand,' Nefer whispered.

'Then the cobra reared up above the uppermost branches of the tree, struck down and buried its fangs in the trunk.'

'Sweet Horus.' Nefer shuddered. 'What did you see then, Tata?'

'I saw the tree wither. I saw the cobra still reared triumphantly on high, but now it wore on its evil brow the double crown. The tree began to throw out green shoots. As they appeared the serpent struck at them, and they, too, were poisoned. But one grew in secret beneath the surface of the earth, until it was strong. Then it burst out like a mighty vine and locked itself in conflict with the cobra. Although the cobra attacked it with all its strength and venom, still it survived.'

'What was the end of the conflict, Tata? Which of them triumphed? Which one wore the double crown at the end?'

'I did not see the end of the conflict. It was obscured in the dust of war.'

Nefer was silent. Then he began to shake and Taita realised he was weeping. At last Nefer spoke, with a dreadful certainty. 'Pharaoh is dead. My father is dead. The poisoned tree was Pharaoh. It was the same message at the cave. The dead falcon was Pharaoh. My father is dead, killed by the cobra.'

Taita could not answer. All he could do was tighten his grip around Nefer's shoulders, and try to comfort him.

'And I am the green shoot of the tree,' Nefer went on. 'You saw this. You know that the cobra is waiting to destroy me as he did my father. That is why you would not let the soldiers take me back to Thebes. You know that the cobra waits for me there.'

'You are right, Nefer. We cannot return to Thebes until you are strong enough to defend yourself. We must fly from Egypt. There are lands and mighty kings to the east. It is my purpose to go to them and seek an ally.'

'But who is the cobra? Did you not see his face in the vision?'

'We know that he stands close to your father's throne, for in the vision he was entwined with the tree and gave it support.' He paused, and then went on, 'Naja is the name of the cobra.'

Nefer stared at him. 'Naja!' he whispered. 'Naja! Now I understand why we cannot return to Thebes.'

Despite his grief for his father, Nefer slept at last, but Taita roused him in the darkness before dawn. They mounted again and rode eastwards until the ground fell away behind them and Nefer smelt the salt of the sea on the wind.

'At the port of Seged we will find a ship to take us across to the land of the Hurrians,' Taita told him. 'King Sargon of Babylon is bound in treaty to your father against the Hyksos.'

Ahead of them the sun came up in a furnace glow, and when they topped the next rise they saw the sea below them. Taita turned to look back and stiffened as he made out not one but four separate plumes of yellow dust rising on the plain behind them.

'Hilto, again,' he exclaimed. 'Now he has thrown out a ring of chariots in an extended line to sweep for our tracks. He did not need a necromancer to tell him we would be heading east for the coast.'

Swiftly he looked in every direction for cover. Across the open plain he picked out an insignificant fold of ground that might offer concealment. 'Dismount!' he ordered Nefer. 'We must keep as low as possible and raise no dust.'

When they reached the hidden ground, Taita coaxed the horses to lie flat on their sides. Then he and Nefer lay beside them and watched the encircling columns of dust sweep across the plain.

'They won't be able to pick out our tracks on the stony ground, will they?' Nefer asked.

Taita grunted. He was watching the approach of the nearest chariot. In the dancing mirage it seemed insubstantial, wavering and distorted as an image seen through water. But it came on until they could make out the men on the footplate more clearly. They were leaning over, examining the earth as they passed over it. Suddenly Taita muttered unhappily. 'They have a Nubian scout with them.' It was said that these scouts could follow the track left by a swallow flying through the air.

The tall black man was made even taller by the headdress of herons' feathers he wore. Five hundred cubits from where they lay concealed, the Nubian brought the chariot to a peremptory halt and jumped down. He had lost the tracks where they turned onto stony ground. Bent almost double, he circled out over the bare earth. After a few moments, the Nubian straightened with a fresh air of purpose, and gazed straight in their direction.

'He has found the twist in our tracks,' Nefer said, and they watched the chariot pull in behind the Nubian as he started towards them over the rocky ground.

The boy watched in trepidation as the chariot and its outrider came on steadily. The charioteer was standing high on the footplate and Nefer recognised him as Hilto.

When he finally saw Taita and Nefer, Hilto leapt out of the chariot and went down on one knee.

'Prince Nefer! We have searched for you these thirty days. Thank great Horus and Osiris, we have found you at last.' He cried out, in a voice pitched to giving commands on the battlefield, 'Pharaoh Tamose is dead! Hail, Pharaoh Nefer Seti. May you live for ever.'

Seti was the prince's divine name, given to him at birth but not used until this moment.

'Pharaoh! We have come to bear you to the Holy City.'

'What if I should choose not to go with you, Colonel Hilto?' Nefer asked.

Hilto looked distressed. 'With all love and loyalty, Pharaoh, it is the strictest order of the Regent of Egypt that you be brought to

Thebes. I must obey that order, even at the risk of your displeasure.'

Nefer glanced sideways at Taita, and spoke from the side of his mouth. 'What must I do?'

'We must go with them.'

THEY BEGAN THE RETURN to Thebes with an escort of fifty fighting chariots led by Hilto. Under strict orders the column rode first to the oasis of Boss. Fast horsemen had been sent ahead to Thebes and Lord Naja, the Regent of Egypt, had come out from the city to the oasis to meet the young Pharaoh Nefer Seti.

On the fifth day the squadron of chariots, dusty and battered from months in the wilderness, trotted into the oasis. Nefer stood between Hilto and Taita on the footplate of the leading chariot. His clothing was ragged and his thick locks were matted.

Hilto drove the chariot down the long alley formed by a full regiment of Phat Guards, who cheered Nefer spontaneously. They had loved his father, and now they loved him.

In the centre of the oasis there was an assembly of multicoloured tents. In front of the royal tent Lord Naja, surrounded by courtiers, nobles and priests, waited to receive the king. He was mighty in the power and grace of regency, glistening and beautiful in gold and precious stones, redolent of sweet unguents and fragrant lotions.

On his left hand stood Heseret, the princess of the royal House of Tamose. Her face was pearly white with make-up, eyes huge and dark with kohl, and her skirts were so heavy with pearls and gold thread that she stood as stiffly as a carved doll.

As Hilto brought the chariot to a halt in front of him, Lord Naja stepped forward and led Nefer by the hand to the dais of the council, carved from precious black woods and inlaid with mother-of-pearl. He placed him upon it, then went down on his knees and kissed Nefer's feet. 'As your regent I salute you, Pharaoh.'

He stood up and lifted Nefer to his feet, stripped away the torn kilt to reveal the pharaonic cartouche on the smooth skin of his inner thigh. Taita had tattooed the design, and it was a miniature masterpiece that would for ever endorse Nefer's claim to the double crown. Naja turned the boy slowly so that everyone in the audience could see it clearly.

'Hail, Pharaoh Seti, god and son of the gods. Behold thy sign.

Look upon this mark, all the nations of the earth, and tremble. Bow down before the might of Pharaoh.'

A great shout went up from the soldiers and courtiers packed around the dais. 'Hail, Pharaoh! May he live for ever.'

Naja led the princess forward, and she knelt before her brother to take her oath of allegiance. Then, one by one, the mighty lords of Egypt came forward to take the loyal oath. The ceremony ended when Lord Naja clapped his hands. 'Pharaoh has come on a long journey. He must rest before leading the procession into the city.'

He took Nefer's hand and led him into the spacious royal tent where the master of the wardrobe, the perfumers and hairdressers, the keeper of the royal jewels, the valets, manicurists, masseurs and the maids of the bath were waiting to receive him.

Taita had determined to stay at the boy's side where he could protect him. He tried unobtrusively to include himself among this entourage, but almost immediately a sergeant-at-arms confronted him. 'Greetings, Lord Taita. The Regent of Egypt has sent for you.'

Lord Naja's tent was even larger and more luxuriously appointed than Pharaoh's. He sat on a throne of carved ebony decorated in gold and silver, and the sandy floor was covered with woollen rugs, woven in wonderful colours. Incense burned in silver pots suspended on chains from the ridgepole of the tent, and there were open glass vases filled with perfume on the low table in front of the throne.

At the entrance to the tent, Taita knelt to make obeisance. There was a hum of speculation as he rose to his feet. The foreign ambassadors stared at him curiously, and the warriors and priests nodded and leaned close together as they told each other, 'It is the Magus, the holy Taita, adept of the Mazes.'

Lord Naja looked up from the papyrus he was scanning and smiled. He was truly a handsome man, with sculpted features and sensitive lips. His nose was straight and narrow, and his eyes were the colour of golden agate, lively and intelligent.

Swiftly Taita surveyed the ranks of men who now sat closest to the throne. Many familiar faces were missing, and many others had emerged from obscurity into the sunshine of the regent's goodwill. Not least of these was Asmor of the Phat Guards.

'Come forward, Lord Taita.' Naja's voice was pleasant and low.

Taita moved towards the throne and the ranks of courtiers opened to let him pass. The regent smiled down at him. 'Know you that you stand high in our favour. You have given Prince Nefer invaluable instruction and training. Now that the prince has become Pharaoh Seti, he will stand in even greater need of your guiding hand.'

'May he live for ever,' Taita responded.

Lord Naja gestured. 'Take your seat here, in the shadow of my throne. Even I will have much need of your experience and wisdom when it comes to ordering the affairs of Pharaoh.'

'The royal regent does me more honour than I deserve.' Taita turned a gentle face to Lord Naja. It was prudent never to let your hidden enemy recognise your animosity. He took the seat that was offered him and listened as the business of the regency proceeded.

'We move on now to an important royal matter,' Lord Naja said. 'I come to the consideration of the well-being and status of Princess Heseret. I have consulted with the members of the council. All are agreed that, for her own good, I should take Princess Heseret in marriage. As my wife, she will come under my protection. The ceremony will take place on the day of the next full moon after the burial of Pharaoh Tamose, and the coronation of his heir, Prince Nefer Seti.'

Taita remained unmoving, his face blank, but he felt chilled to his bones. He knew that Lord Naja was intent on making himself a member of the royal House of Tamose, and thus the next in line of succession. There remained only twelve days of the required seventy for the royal embalming of the dead pharaoh. Immediately after the interment of Tamose, the coronation of his successor and the wedding of his surviving daughter would take place. Then the cobra would strike again. Taita felt the certainty of it. He was roused from his preoccupation when the regent declared the levee closed, and retired through the tent flap behind the throne. Taita rose with the others to leave the tent.

Colonel Asmor stepped forward to stop him with a smile and a courteous bow. 'Lord Naja asks you not to leave. He invites you to a private audience.'

There was no point refusing the summons, and so Taita allowed Asmor to lead him to the back of the tent and through to a smaller, single-roomed tent, a place of secret council. At a command from

Asmor, the guards posted at the entrance stood aside and the colonel ushered Taita into the shaded interior.

Naja looked up from the bronze bowl in which he was washing his hands. 'You are welcome, Magus.' He waved to the pile of cushions in the centre of the rug-covered floor. While Taita seated himself, Naja nodded to Asmor, who went to take up position at the tent opening, his sickle sword drawn. There were only the three of them in the tent, and their conversation would not be overheard.

Naja had discarded his jewellery and insignia of office. He was affable and friendly, and indicated the tray of sweetmeats that stood between them. 'Please refresh yourself.'

Taita's instinct was to decline, but he knew that to refuse would advertise his hostility, and alert Naja to his deadly opposition. Instead, he inclined his head in thanks.

'You are a person of inestimable value,' Naja told him. 'You have faithfully served three pharaohs and all have relied on your advice without question.'

'You overestimate my worth, my lord Regent. I am an old man and feeble.'

Naja smiled. 'Old? Yes, you are old. I have heard it said that you are more than two hundred years old.' Taita inclined his head, neither confirming nor denying it. 'But feeble, no! All men know that your wisdom is boundless. Even the secrets of eternal life are yours.'

The flattery was blatant and Taita searched behind it for the hidden reason, tuned his mind to catch the other man's thoughts. They were fleeting but he captured one entire, and suddenly understood what Naja wanted from him. The secret of eternal life. The knowledge gave him power, and the way ahead opened before him like the gates of a captured city.

'My lord, two hundred years is not life eternal.' Taita spread his hands deprecatingly, and dropped his eyes.

'We will speak of these deep matters another time.' There was a triumphant light in Naja's yellow eyes. 'But now there is something else I would ask of you. It would be a way for you to prove that my good opinion of you is fully justified. Taita, beloved of kings and gods, I wish you to work the Mazes of Ammon Ra for me.'

He twists and turns like an eel, Taita thought. And I once believed him to be a dull clod of a soldier. He has been able to hide his ambition from all of us. Not only the double crown of Egypt and eternal life! He wishes also to have the future revealed to him, Taita marvelled. He nodded humbly and replied, 'My lord Naja, I have never worked the Mazes for anyone who was not a queen or a pharaoh, or one who was not destined to sit upon the throne of Egypt.'

'It may well be that one such person asks you now,' said Lord Naja, with deep significance in his tone.

Great Horus has delivered him to me. I have him in my hands, Taita thought, and said, 'I bow to the wishes of Pharaoh's regent.'

'Will you work the Mazes for me this very day?'

'No man should enter the Mazes lightly,' Taita demurred. 'It will take time to prepare for the journey into the future.'

'How long?' Naja's disappointment was evident.

Taita clasped his forehead in a pantomime of deep thought. Let him sniff the bait for a while, he thought. It will make him more eager to swallow the hook. At last he looked up. 'On the first day of the festival of the Bull of Apis.'

THE NEXT MORNING, when he emerged from the great tent for his ceremonial journey to Thebes, Pharaoh Seti was transformed.

His dark curls had been shampooed and combed until they shone with russet highlights. On top of them he wore a circlet of gold depicting Nekhbet, the vulture goddess, and Naja, the cobra. On his chin was the false beard of kingship. His false fingernails were of beaten gold, and there were gold sandals on his feet. On his chest was one of the most precious of the crown jewels of Egypt: the pectoral medallion of Tamose, a jewelled portrait of the god Horus the falcon. He walked with a stately tread for one so young, carrying the scourge and the sceptre crossed over his heart, and Lord Naja walked a pace behind him, splendid with jewels and awesome with authority.

Next came the princess, with the golden feathers of the goddess Isis on her head, and from throat to ankles she was encased in a long dress, the linen so fine and transparent that the sunlight struck through it. Heseret's body was moulded into voluptuous curves, her breasts rosy-tipped through the diaphanous folds.

Pharaoh mounted the processional carriage and took his seat on the elevated throne. Lord Naja stood at his right hand, and the princess sat at his feet.

Companies of priests from the fifty temples of Thebes fell in ahead, strumming the lyre, beating the drum, sounding the horn, chanting praises and supplications to the gods.

Then Asmor's bodyguard took up their positions in the procession, and after them came Hilto's squadron of chariots, all freshly burnished and decked with pennants and flowers. The horses were curried until their hides glowed, and ribbons were plaited into their manes. The bullocks that followed in the traces of the royal carriage were all of unblemished white. Their widespread horns and even their hoofs were covered with gold leaf.

A thousand warriors of the Phat Guards fell in behind them and burst into the anthem of praise. The populace of Thebes had opened the main gates of the city in welcome and were lining the tops of the walls. From a mile outside it they had covered the dusty surface of the road with palm fronds, straw and flowers.

The procession passed through the gates, with the crowds dancing with joy, filling the narrow streets so that the pace of the royal carriage was that of a giant tortoise. It was late afternoon before they reached the docks at the riverside where the royal barge waited to ferry Pharaoh's party across to the Palace of Memnon. Once they had gone on board, two hundred rowers in massed ranks plied their paddles. When they reached the west bank another royal carriage bore Nefer through the crowds to the funerary temple of his father, Pharaoh Tamose. He rode up the causeway, lit on both sides by bonfires, and the uproar was deafening as Pharaoh dismounted and climbed the stairway into the Hall of Sorrow, that holy place where Tamose's mummy lay on its embalming slab of black diorite.

Lord Naja took up his position on the far side of the diorite slab, facing Nefer, and the high priest stood at the head of the dead king. When all was in readiness two priests drew aside the linen sheet that covered the corpse, and Nefer recoiled involuntarily as he looked down on his father.

For all the weeks after his death, while Nefer and Taita had been in the desert, the embalmers had been at work on the king's body. Now as desiccated as firewood, it had been bound up. The linen bandages were laid on it in an intricate design, as incantations to the gods were chanted by choirs of priests. Under them were placed precious talismans and amulets, and each layer was painted with resins that dried to a metallic hardness. Only the head was left uncovered, upon which four of the most skilful artists of the guild of embalmers, using wax and cosmetics, had restored the king's features to lifelike beauty.

They had replaced the eyes with perfect replicas of rock crystal and obsidian that seemed endowed with life and intelligence, so that now Nefer gazed into them with awe, expecting to see his father's pupils widen in recognition. The lips were shaped and rouged so that at any moment they might smile, and his painted skin looked silken and warm, as though bright blood still ran beneath it. His hair had been washed and set in the familiar dark ringlets that Nefer remembered so well.

The high priest came to Nefer's side and placed a golden spoon in his hand. Nefer had been coached in the ritual, but his hand trembled as he placed the spoon on his father's lips and recited, 'I open thy lips that thou might have the power of speech once more.' He touched his father's nose with the spoon. 'I open thy nostrils that thou might breathe once more.' He touched each eye. 'I open thine eyes that thou might behold the glory of this world once more, and the glory of the world to come.'

When at last it was done, the embalmers wrapped the head and painted it with aromatic resins. Then they laid a golden mask over the blind face, and once more it glowed with splendid life.

For the rest of that night Nefer stayed beside the golden sarcophagus, praying and burning incense, entreating the gods to take his father and seat him in the midst of the pantheon.

THAT NIGHT TAITA went out and prayed to Horus for guidance. At dawn he returned to the palace, and had barely time to bathe and change his raiment before he hurried to the royal bedchamber. At the door his way was barred by the two guards, who crossed their spears across the entrance.

Taita was astonished. This had never happened before. He glared at the sergeant of the guard, who dropped his eyes. 'I mean no offence, mighty Magus. It is on the specific orders of the commander of the bodyguard, Colonel Asmor. No person not approved by the regent is allowed in the royal presence.'

Taita strode down the terrace to where Naja was at breakfast with his particular favourites and toadies. 'My lord Naja, you are fully aware that I was appointed by Pharaoh's own father as his tutor and mentor. I was given the right of access at any time.'

'That was many years ago, good Magus,' Naja replied smoothly, as he accepted a peeled grape from a slave. 'Pharaoh Seti is a child no more. In future he looks to me, his regent, for guidance.' Naja stood up from the breakfast board. His bodyguard closed in around him so that Taita was forced to fall back.

The old man watched as Naja's entourage set off towards the council chamber, then turned aside and sat down on the coping of one of the fish pools to ponder this development.

Naja had isolated Nefer. He was a prisoner in his own palace. Once again Taita considered the idea of flight from Egypt, to spirit Nefer away across the desert to the protection of a foreign power until he had grown strong enough to return to claim his birthright. However, he was certain that Naja not only barred the door to the royal quarters but that every escape route from Thebes and Egypt would have already been closed.

There seemed no easy solution, and, after an hour of deep thought, Taita rose to his feet. The guards at the door to the council chamber stood aside for him, and Taita went down the aisle and took his accustomed seat on the front bench.

Wearing the light crown of Upper Egypt, Nefer was seated on the dais beside his regent. The council was considering the latest reports from the northern front, where the Hyksosian King Apepi had recaptured Abnub after a siege that had lasted the previous three years. Taita found the council was bitterly divided in every consideration of the crisis, and he felt more strongly than ever that this war was a running abscess in Egypt's body. Exasperated, he rose quietly and left the council chamber. There was nothing further he could accomplish here, for they were still wrangling over who should be given command of the northern armies to replace the dead Pharaoh.

Next he went to the women's quarters of the palace. Because he was a eunuch he could pass through the gates, which were barred to other men. It was three days since the princess had learned that she was so soon to become a bride, and Taita knew he should have visited her before. She would be confused, sorely in need of his comfort and advice.

When he entered the courtyard, Heseret, who had been strumming her lyre, looked up at him with a sad little smile. 'Darling Taita, I am so glad you have come.'

'I am sorry to have kept you waiting, moon of all my nights.' She smiled faintly at the pet name. 'What service do you wish of me?'

'You must go to Lord Naja, and present him with my sincere apologies, but I cannot marry him.'

She was so much like her grandmother had been at the same age. Lostris, too, had saddled him with an impossible task. Heseret now turned her enormous green eyes on him. 'You see, I have already promised Meren that I will be his wife.'

Meren was a boon companion of Prince Nefer. Taita had noticed him looking at Heseret with calf's eyes, but had never suspected that she returned his feelings.

'Heseret, I have explained to you many times that you are not like other girls. You are a princess royal. Your marriage cannot be undertaken in the light fancy of youth. It is of political consequence.'

'You don't understand, Taita,' Heseret said softly, but with the sweet obstinacy he dreaded. 'I love Meren, I have loved him since I was little. I want to marry *him*, not Lord Naja.'

'I cannot overrule the decree of the Regent of Egypt,' he tried to explain, but she shook her head and smiled at him.

'You are so wise, Taita. You will think of something. You always do,' she told him, and he felt as though his heart would break.

'LORD TAITA, I REFUSE to discuss your access to Pharaoh or my impending marriage to the royal princess. In both these matters my mind is set.' To emphasise that he had closed the subject, Naja returned his full attention to the scroll spread on the writing table in front of him. Enough time passed for a flock of wild geese to rise from the swampland on the east bank and pass over the palace gardens where they sat. At last Taita brought his eyes down from the sky, and rose to leave. As he bowed to the regent and began to back away, Naja looked up at him. 'I have not given you leave to go.'

'My lord, I thought you had no further need of me.'

'On the contrary, I have the most urgent need.' He glared at Taita and gestured for him to sit again. 'You are testing my good temper and favour. I know that you were wont to work the Mazes for Pharaoh Tamose whenever he called upon you to do so. Why do you procrastinate with me? As regent I will brook no further delay. I command you to work the Mazes of Ammon Ra on my behalf.'

Taita bowed his head. For weeks past he had been prepared for this ultimatum, and had delayed only because he was convinced that Lord Naja would make no move against Nefer until he had been given the sanction of the Mazes.

'The full of the moon is the most propitious period for the Mazes,' Taita told him. 'I have already made preparations with the priests at the temple of Osiris at Busiris. I will conduct the mystery in the inner sanctum of the temple. This holy place will magnify the force of our deliberations.' Taita's voice was heavy with arcane meaning. 'Only you and I will be present in the sanctuary. No other mortal must overhear what the gods have to tell you.'

Naja was an Osiris man, and Taita had known that he would be impressed by the place he had chosen.

'So let it be,' Naja agreed.

THE JOURNEY TO BUSIRIS in the royal barge took two days. They landed on the yellow beach under the walls of the temple, and the priests were waiting to welcome the regent with psalms and offerings of gum arabic and myrrh. Afterwards, at Taita's suggestion, they withdrew and left him to make his preparations for the evening. He would put on an impressive show for Lord Naja, but had no intention of subjecting himself to the harrowing ordeal of the authentic ritual.

After sunset the high priest entertained the regent at a banquet and Lord Naja consumed a flagon of rich and heady wine. Then, to the beat of gong and drum, the priests chanted an epic poem of the struggle between good and evil. Finally, as the silver beam of the full moon moved across the flags of the nave towards the closed door of the sanctuary, the high priest gave a signal and the other priests rose and moved out in procession, leaving Lord Naja and Taita alone.

When the chanting of the departing priests had dwindled into a heavy silence, Taita took the regent by the hand and led him down the nave to the sanctuary, which was lit by four braziers, one in each corner. There was a low stool in the centre of the tiled floor. Taita gestured for him to be seated, and placed a hand on his shoulder. 'No matter what you see and what you hear, do not move. Do not speak. As you value your life, do nothing. Say nothing.'

Taita left him sitting and, with stately tread, approached the gigantic statue of the god. He raised a golden chalice high and called on Osiris to bless the contents, then brought it back to Naja and urged him to drink. The honey-viscous liquid tasted of crushed almonds, rose petals and mushrooms. Taita made a mystical pass back and forth before Naja's face, and in the blink of an eye the Mazes of Ammon Ra filled his cupped hands. He invited Naja to cover them with his own hands, while he recited an invocation. 'Greatness in light and fire, furious in divine majesty, approach and harken to our pleas.'

Naja squirmed on his stool as the Mazes grew hot to the touch, and it was with relief that he passed them back to Taita. The old man carried them across the sanctuary and placed them at the feet of the statue of Osiris. The Magus knelt there, bowed over them. For a while there was no sound within the chamber.

Then, abruptly, a terrible shriek rang out. Naja moaned softly and covered his head with his shawl. Again there was silence, until suddenly the flames of the braziers flared as high as the roof, and turned from yellow to fierce shades of green and violet, crimson and blue. Great clouds of smoke boiled from them and filled the chamber. Naja choked and coughed. He felt as though he were suffocating, and his senses reeled.

Taita turned slowly to face him, and Naja shuddered in horror, for the Magus was transformed. His face glowed with green light and his eyes were blind orbs that flashed silver rays in the light of the braziers. He glided towards where Naja sat, and from his gaping mouth issued a terrible chorus of screams and moans, hisses and grunts, retching and insane laughter.

Lord Naja tried to rise, but the sounds and the smoke seemed to fill his skull, and blackness overwhelmed him. His legs gave way and he slumped forward off the stool onto the tiles in a dead faint.

WHEN THE REGENT of Egypt regained consciousness, the sun was high, sparkling on the waters of the river. He found himself lying on a silken mattress on the deck of the royal barge under its yellow awning.

He looked around him blearily, and saw the sails of the escort galleys. The sunlight was dazzling, and he closed his eyes again. He had a consuming thirst, and there was a pounding in his skull as though all the demons of his vision were trapped within it.

Taita came to his side, raised his head and gave him a cool draught of some miraculous brew that soon eased the pounding in his head. When he had recovered enough to speak again, he whispered, 'Tell it all to me, Taita. I remember nothing. What did the Mazes reveal?' Clearly the effects of the essence of the magical mushroom, which Taita had administered to him the night before, had not yet worn off.

Before he would reply Taita sent all the crew and slaves out of earshot. Then he knelt beside the mattress. 'We have almost reached Sebennytos, my lord. We will be back at Thebes before nightfall.'

'What happened, Taita?' He shook Taita's arm. 'Tell it to me! Tell it all to me!'

'Do you not remember how the roof of the temple opened like the petals of the lotus, and we were borne upwards on the backs of two winged lions?'

Naja shook his head, and then nodded uncertainly. 'Yes, I remember the lions, but after that it is all shadowy and vague.'

'These mysteries numb the mind and dim eyes unaccustomed to them. Even I, an adept of the seventh and final degree, was amazed by what we endured,' Taita explained kindly. 'But do not despair, for the gods have commanded me to explain them to you.'

'Speak, good Magus, and spare no detail.'

'On the backs of the flying lions we crossed high above the dark ocean and over all the kingdoms of earth and heaven spread below us. We came at last to the citadel in which the gods dwell, and there it was that great Osiris rose up in all his terrible glory, lifted you off the back of winged lion and placed you beside him on the throne of fire and gold.'

Naja's expression became proud and triumphant. 'Was he not deifying me, Taita? Surely there can be no other meaning?'

'If there had been any doubt it was immediately dispelled, for Osiris took up the double crown of Upper and Lower Egypt, placed it upon your head and spoke "Hail, Brother Divine! Hail, Pharaoh who shall be."'

Naja stared at Taita with glittering eyes as the old man went on, 'With the crown upon your brow, your holiness was manifest. I knelt before you and worshipped you.'

Naja's made no effort to hide his emotions. He was in transport. Taita seized the moment. 'Then Osiris spoke again: "In these wondrous things, your guide shall be the Magus Taita, for he is the Master of the Mazes. Follow his instruction faithfully, and all the rewards I have promised will be yours."'

He watched Naja's reaction, but the regent seemed to accept this without resistance.

'What else, Taita? What more did the great god have to say to me?'

'Nothing more to you, my lord, but now he spoke directly to me. These are his exact words, each one branded in fire upon my heart. "Taita, Master of the Mazes, henceforth you have no other love, loyalty or duty. You are the servant of my divine brother, Naja. Your only concern is to help him fulfil his destiny. You will not cease until you see the double crown of Upper and Lower Egypt placed upon his head."'

'"No other loyalty or love",' Naja repeated softly, the familiar light of cunning growing stronger in his yellow eyes. 'And did you then accept the charge that great Osiris placed upon you, Magus? Say fair and true, are you my man now, or would you deny the word of the great father?'

'How could I deny the great god?' Taita asked simply. He lowered his head and pressed his forehead to the planking of the deck. 'I accept the charge that the gods have placed upon me. I am your man, Divine Majesty. I belong to you.'

Naja raised him up and stared into his eyes, searching for any trace of deceit or guile. Taita looked back at him serenely. The wish is father to the deed, Taita thought. He will allow himself to believe, because he longs for it to be so.

He watched the doubts clear in those yellow eyes and Naja embraced him. 'I believe you. When I wear the double crown you will have rewards beyond your imagination.'

CHAPTER THREE

Over the days that followed, Naja kept Taita close to his side, and the old man used this new position of trust to change some of the regent's intentions. He slaughtered a sheep and examined its entrails. From these he determined that the god would sanction no marriage of Naja to the princess until at least the next inundation of the Nile waters or the flooding would certainly fail. The life of Egypt depended upon the inundations of the great river, so with this prophecy Taita delayed the danger to Nefer, and the agony of the princess.

Naja protested and argued, but he found it impossible to resist Taita's predictions. He was made more amenable by the news from the northern war front. On Naja's orders, and against Taita's counsel, the Egyptians had launched a desperate counterattack to try to retake Abnub. They had failed, losing three hundred chariots and almost a regiment of foot in the fighting around the city. Now Apepi seemed poised to come storming on to Thebes. It was no time for a wedding.

'The only way in which you can stave off an annihilating defeat at the hands of Apepi is to negotiate a truce,' Taita advised the regent.

'This I believe also, Magus,' Naja agreed eagerly, excited by this unexpected support. He had tried without success to convince the individual members of the council to agree to a truce with the Hyksos, but none had supported him. Even the loyal Asmor had risked his wrath by vowing to fall on his own sword rather than surrender to Apepi.

Peace with the Hyksos was the cornerstone of Naja's vision of the two kingdoms reunited and a single pharaoh ruling both. Only a pharaoh who was part Egyptian and part Hyksosian could hope to achieve that, and he knew that this was what the gods had promised him through the Mazes.

He went on earnestly, 'I should have known that you, Taita, were the one person who would not let yourself be blinded by prejudice. After sixty years in the Nile valley, the Hyksos are becoming more

Egyptian than Asian. Their savage blood has been softened and sweetened by ours. I know there are many among them who agree with these sentiments. It would take little for them to join us. Then we can bring peace and unity to the two kingdoms.'

The regent's response to his tentative suggestion was so enthusiastic that Taita was taken aback. Then the veils began to part, and he was reminded of a suspicion he had once heard expressed but had rejected.

'Who are these Hyksos sympathisers?' he asked. 'Are they highly placed? Close to Apepi?'

'Noblemen, indeed. One sits on Apepi's war council.'

It was enough for Taita. That faint rumour of Hyksosian connections in Naja's background must have had substance, and if it was true the rest fell neatly into place. 'Would it be possible to meet these noblemen and speak to them?' Taita asked carefully.

'Yes,' Naja confirmed. 'We could reach them within days.'

For Taita the implications of that simple statement were enormous. The Regent of Egypt had covert allies in the ranks of the traditional enemy. This was the loving friend who was at Pharaoh's side when he was struck down, the only witness to Pharaoh's death. This creature of boundless ambition and cruel purpose admitted to being an intimate of Hyksosian noblemen, and it was a Hyksosian arrow that killed Pharaoh. How deep did the plot run?

He let nothing of this show on his face, but nodded thoughtfully. 'First we must determine if this treaty is feasible. Apepi might believe his military position is unassailable and might decide to prosecute this war to the bitter end.'

'I do not think that will happen. One of our allies on the other side is a man called Trok, paramount chief of the Clan of the Leopards. You must go to him secretly, Taita. I will give you a talisman that will prove you come from me. You are the best emissary for our cause.'

Taita sat a while longer in thought. He tried to see if he could wring any further advantage to Nefer and the princess from the situation, but at this stage he could find none. Whatever happened, Nefer would still be in mortal danger.

'It is my duty, a duty placed upon me by the gods, to help you in every way. I will undertake this mission,' Taita said. 'What is the safest way for me to pass through the Hyksosian lines?'

Naja had foreseen this query. 'You must use the old chariot road through the dunes and down the wadi at El Wadun. My friends on the other side keep the road under surveillance. I will send my own lance-bearer and a squadron of the Blues to take you through,' he promised. 'But the road is long and hard. You must leave at once. Every day, every hour might make the difference.'

TAITA HAD DRIVEN the chariot all the way from the ruined city of Gallala with only four halts. The troopers in the nine vehicles that followed him were in awe of the Magus's reputation. They knew him as the first Egyptian ever to build a chariot and harness a team to it. The old man's stamina was amazing, and his concentration never wavered. His gentle but firm hands on the reins never tired, as hour after hour he coaxed the horses into giving their best. He had impressed every man in the squadron, not least the one riding beside him in the cockpit.

Gil was Naja's lance-bearer. He had a rugged, sun-darkened face and was lightly built, which was desirable for a charioteer, but he possessed also a wiry strength and cheerful disposition.

With the moon waxing and the weather at its hottest they had driven through the cool of the night. Now, in the dawn, they halted to rest. When he had watered the horses, Gil came to where Taita sat on a boulder overlooking Hyksosian territory and handed him a ceramic water jug. Taita took a long swig. It was the first drink he had taken since their last stop at midnight.

The old devil-rouser is tough as a Bedouin raider, Gil thought, and squatted at a respectful distance to await any order.

'Where is the place at which Pharaoh was struck down?' Taita asked at last.

The two men had spoken briefly once or twice since leaving Thebes, but until now there had not been the opportunity for any long conversation.

Gil shaded his eyes against the glare of the rising sun and pointed down the wadi towards the plains. 'Down there, my lord. Near that distant line of hills.'

'Are any other men here who were with you on that day?'

'Only Samos, but he was waiting with the chariots in the wadi when we were attacked,' Gil replied.

'I want you to take me over the battleground,' Taita told him.

Gil shrugged. 'It was no battle, just a skirmish. First Pharaoh dismounted and we went forward with Lord Naja to scout the camp of Apepi. Then I and the rest of the men were ordered to wait, while Lord Naja went forward beyond an outcrop of boulders.'

'Where was Pharaoh? Did he go forward with Naja?'

'No. Not at first. The king waited with us. Lord Naja heard something up ahead, went to scout and disappeared from our view.'

'I do not understand. At what point were you attacked?'

'We waited. I could see that Pharaoh was becoming impatient. After a while Lord Naja whistled from beyond the rocks. Pharaoh sprang up. "Come on, lads!" he told us, and went up the path.'

'Did you see what happened next?'

'Pharaoh disappeared behind the boulders. Then there was shouting and the sound of fighting. I ran forward but Lord Naja was shouting that Pharaoh had been struck down, and they dragged the king back to where I was standing. I think he was dead even then.'

'How close were the Hyksos? How many? Were they cavalry or infantry? Did you recognise their regiments?' Taita demanded.

For the first time Gil looked uncertain 'My lord, I did not actually set eyes on the enemy. You see, they were behind the rocks.'

Taita frowned at him. 'Did any of the others, apart from Naja, see the enemy?'

'I do not know, honourable Magus. You see, Lord Naja ordered us back down to the chariots. We could see that the king was mortally wounded, probably already dead. We had all lost heart.'

'You must have discussed it later with your companions. Did any of them tell you he had engaged an enemy? That he had hit one of the Hyksos with arrow or lance?'

Gil shook his head. 'I don't remember. No, I don't think so.'

'Apart from the king, were any others wounded?'

'None.'

'Why did you not tell this to the council? Why did you not tell them that you had not seen an enemy?' Taita was angry now.

'Lord Naja told us to answer the questions simply and not to waste the council's time with idle boasting.' Gil hunched his shoulders with embarrassment. 'I suppose none of us wanted to admit that we ran without a fight.'

'Do not feel ashamed, Gil. You carried out your orders,' Taita told him, in a kinder tone. Gil's evidence had been coherent and credible, and he had spoken out like the honest, simple soldier he was. When the Hyksosian arrow taken from the Pharaoh's body by the surgeons was shown to him, he had recognised it as the one that had struck down Pharaoh Tamose. The shaft had been snapped in two. Lord Naja had broken it off to ease the pain of the wound.

Taita, too, had examined the broken, blood-caked arrow, fletched in green and red, that had killed Pharaoh, and had peered closely at the signet etched into the painted shaft. It was a stylised head of a leopard, holding the hieratic letter T in its jaws. Now Taita was on his way to see one of Naja's Hyksos allies, a man named Trok.

THEY WAITED HIDDEN in the wadi until after nightfall. Then, the wheel hubs freshly greased with mutton fat to stop them squealing, the horses' hoofs covered with leather boots, they went on deep into Hyksosian territory, with Gil guiding them.

By now they were down on the alluvial plain of the Nile. Twice they had to turn off the road and wait while parties of armed men, anonymous in the darkness, rode past their hiding place. After midnight they came to an abandoned temple of some forgotten god that had been hollowed out of the side of a low clay hill. The cave was large enough to shelter the entire squadron, vehicles, horses and men. It was immediately apparent that it had been used before for this purpose. Lamps and an oil amphora were hidden behind the ruined altar, and bales of horse fodder were stacked in the sanctum.

As soon as they had removed the horses' harnesses and fed them, the troopers ate their own meal and then settled down on mattresses of dried straw. In the meantime Gil had changed his uniform for the nondescript attire of a peasant. 'I cannot use a horse,' he explained to Taita. 'It would attract too much interest. On foot it will take me half a day to reach the camp at Bubasti. Do not expect me back before tomorrow evening.' He slipped out of the cave and disappeared into the night.

Honest Gil is not such a simple, bluff soldier as he seems, Taita thought, as he settled down to wait for Lord Naja's allies to answer the message that Gil was taking to them.

They came in the short summer dusk, twenty armed men riding hard, Gil leading them on a borrowed steed. They swept up to the entrance of the temple, where they dismounted with a clatter of weapons. The leader was a tall man, wide across the shoulders with a heavy beetling brow and a fleshy hooked nose.

'You are the warlock. Yes?' he said, in a thick accent.

Taita did not think it opportune to let them know he spoke Hyksos, so he replied modestly in Egyptian. 'My name is Taita, a servant of the great god Horus. I call his blessing down upon you. I see you are a man of might, but I do not know your name.'

'My name is Trok, commander of the north in the army of King Apepi. You have a token for me, Warlock?'

Taita showed him a broken shard of blue glazed porcelain, the upper half of a tiny votive statue of the god Seueth.

Trok examined it briefly, then took another fragment of porcelain from the pouch on his sword-belt and fitted the two pieces together. The broken edges matched perfectly, and he grunted with satisfaction. 'Come with me, Warlock.'

Trok strode out into the gathering night with Taita beside him. They climbed the hill and squatted down facing each other. Trok kept his scabbard between his knees and his hand on the hilt of his heavy sickle sword. From habit more than distrust, Taita thought.

'You bring me news of the south,' Trok said.

'My lord, you have heard of the death of Pharaoh Tamose?'

'We know of the death of the Theban pretender.' Trok was careful not to acknowledge the authority of the Egyptian Pharaoh. To the Hyksos, the only ruler of the two kingdoms was Apepi. 'We heard also that a child now pretends to the throne of Upper Egypt.'

'Pharaoh Nefer Seti is only fourteen years of age,' Taita confirmed, equally careful to insist on the title of Pharaoh when he spoke of him. 'Until he attains his majority, Lord Naja acts as his regent.'

Trok leaned forward. 'So, then, you come to us with the authority of the Regent of the South. What message do you bring from Naja?'

'Lord Naja wants me to carry his proposal directly to Apepi.'

Trok took immediate umbrage at this. 'Naja is my cousin,' he said coldly. 'He would wish me to hear every word he has sent.'

Taita showed no surprise, although it was a grave indiscretion on Trok's part. His suspicions as to the regent's connections were confirmed. 'Yes, my lord, this much I know. However, I can tell you nothing more.'

'As you wish, Warlock.' Trok stood up angrily. 'King Apepi is at Bubasti. We will go there immediately.'

In silence they returned to the subterranean temple, where Taita called Gil and the sergeant of the bodyguard to him. 'You have done your work well,' he told them, 'but now you must return to Thebes as secretly as you have come. I will remain here. When you report to the regent tell him that I am on my way to meet Apepi.'

By the dim light of the oil lamps the horses were harnessed to the chariots, and within a short time they were ready to leave. Gil saluted respectfully. 'It has been a great honour to ride with you, my lord.'

Taita embraced him. 'Go well, young Gil. I cast your horoscope last night. You will have a long life, and attain much distinction.'

By this time Lord Trok's troop was also mounted and ready to leave. They gave Taita the horse on which Gil had returned to the temple, then clattered out of the cave and turned west, in the opposite direction to that taken by Gil's column of chariots.

With Taita in the centre of the party, they rode on through the night, heading west towards the main enemy base. As they came closer to the river, Taita saw the fires of the Hyksosian troops encamped around Bubasti. It was a field of flickering light that stretched many miles in both directions along the river bank, a huge agglomeration of men and animals.

There was nothing on earth like the smell of an army encamped. It was a mixture of odours: manure and smoke, leather and mouldy grain, unwashed men, cooking food and fermenting beer, unburied rubbish, and the ammoniacal reek of the latrine pits.

Underlying this stifling blend Taita picked out another sickly taint. He thought he recognised it, but it was only when one of the sufferers staggered in front of his horse, forcing him to rein in sharply, that he saw the rose-coloured blotches on the pale face and he was certain. He knew now why Apepi had failed so far to follow up his victory at Abnub, why he had not yet sent his chariots tearing southwards towards Thebes where the Egyptian army was at his mercy. The plague had struck his troops.

They passed the first of the burial carts, laden with corpses, and the men around Taita used their cloaks to cover their mouths and noses against the stink and the evil humours.

Closer to Bubasti the encampments became more numerous, tents, huts and hovels crowding right up to the walls that surrounded the garrison town. The more fortunate among the plague victims lay under tattered roofs of palm fronds, scant protection from the hot morning sunlight. Others lay out in the trampled mud of the fields, abandoned to thirst and the elements, the dead mixed with the dying.

Although his instincts were those of a healer, Taita would do nothing to succour them. They were condemned by their own multitudes, for what could one man do to help so many?

They entered the fortress and found that conditions were not much better within its walls. Plague victims lay where they had been struck down, and rats and pariah dogs gnawed at their corpses.

Apepi's headquarters was the principal building in Bubasti, a massive mud-brick and thatch palace in the centre of the town. Grooms took their horses at the gates, and Lord Trok led Taita through courtyards and dark shuttered halls to Apepi's private quarters. The walls were hung with magnificent carpets and the furniture was of precious wood, ivory and mother-of-pearl, much of it plundered from the palaces and temples of Egypt.

Trok ushered Taita into a luxuriously furnished antechamber, and left him there. It was a long wait. A sunbeam through the single high window moved sedately along the wall. At intervals Taita heard the distant sound of weeping. Finally there came the tramp of heavy footsteps down the passage outside, and the curtains over the doorway were thrown open. A burly man stood in the doorway. He wore a crimson linen kilt belted with a gold chain, there were heavy sandals on his feet and greaves of polished leather covered his shins. His beard and hair were in disarray. His dark eyes were wild and distracted.

'You are Taita, the physician,' he said.

Taita knew him well: to him Apepi was the invader, the bloody barbarian, mortal enemy of his country. It took all his self-control to keep his voice calm as he replied, 'I am Taita.'

'I have heard of your skills,' said Apepi. 'I have need of them now. Come with me.'

Taita slung his saddlebag over his shoulder and followed him out into the cloister. Ahead the sound of weeping became louder, until Apepi threw aside the heavy curtains that covered another doorway and took Taita's arm to push him through.

Dominating the crowded chamber was a large contingent of priests from the temple of Isis in Avaris, chanting over the brazier in one corner and shaking sistrums—percussion instruments of rods that rattled in metal frames. Twenty others, most of them women, were kneeling on the floor, wailing and keening. Only one was making any attempt to nurse the boy who lay on the couch. She seemed not much older than her patient, probably thirteen or fourteen, a striking-looking girl with a determined, intelligent face, and she was sponging him down with perfumed water from a copper bowl.

Taita switched his attention to the boy. His naked body was also well formed, but wasted by disease. His skin was blotched with the plague and dewed with perspiration. On his chest were the wounds where he had been bled by the priests of Isis. Taita saw that he was in an advanced stage of the disease.

'This is Khyan, my youngest son,' Apepi said. 'The plague will take him, unless you can save him, Magus.'

Khyan groaned and rolled onto his side. At once the healers renewed their chants, and the high priest took up a knife and came towards the bed.

Taita stepped forward, barring the man's way. 'Get out!' he said softly. 'You and your butchers have done enough damage here.'

'I must bleed the fever out of his body,' the man protested.

'Out!' Taita repeated grimly, then to the others who crossed the chamber, 'Out, all of you.'

Eventually the chamber was deserted except for Apepi and the girl at the sickbed. 'Who are you?' he demanded.

'I am Mintaka. This is my brother.' She laid her hand protectively on the boy's sweat-damp curls. 'I will not leave him.'

'Good,' said Taita briskly, 'Then you can be of use to me. When did the boy last drink?'

'Not since this morning.'

'Can't those quacks see that he is dying of thirst as much as of the disease? He has sweated and voided most of the water from his body.' Taita picked up a copper jug from beside the bed. 'Go to the kitchens and fetch water. Make sure it is clean. Fill it from the well, not with river water. Hurry, girl.'

She fled, and returned almost immediately with a brimming jug of clean water. Taita opened his bag, prepared a potion of herbs, and heated it on the brazier. When it had brewed, he showed her how to position her brother's head and to stroke his throat as he dribbled the water into his mouth. Soon Khyan was swallowing freely.

'What can I do to help you?' the king asked.

'My lord, there is nothing for you here. You are better at destroying than at healing.' Taita dismissed him without looking up from his patient. There was a long silence, then the tramp of Apepi's bronze-studded sandals as he left the chamber.

Mintaka was quick and willing. She forced her brother to drink while Taita brewed up another cup of medicine on the brazier. Between them they were able to get this down his throat without losing a drop. She helped smear a soothing ointment on his chest. Then they wrapped Khyan in linen sheets and soaked them with well water to cool his burning body. By next morning the fever had broken and Khyan was resting more comfortably.

'Look, my lord,' Mintaka exclaimed, stroking her brother's cheek, 'the blotches are fading, and his skin feels cooler.'

'You have the healing touch of a nymph of paradise,' Taita told her, 'but do not forget the water jug. It is empty.'

She raced away to the kitchens, and came back with a brimming jug. While she gave it to him, Taita studied her face. In the Hyksosian way, it was a little too broad, and her cheekbones too prominent. Her mouth was large, her lips full, her nose strongly bridged. Not one of these features was perfect in itself, but each was finely balanced with, and matched to, all the others. Hers was a different kind of beauty, he thought, but beauty nonetheless.

By that evening Khyan was able to sit up with a little help from his sister, and to drink from the soup bowl she held to his lips. Two days later his rash had disappeared.

Three or four times a day Apepi visited the chamber. On the fifth day Khyan tottered from the couch and tried to prostrate himself before the king, but Apepi stopped him and lifted him back onto the pillows. Even though his feelings for the boy were clear, the king had little to say and left again almost immediately, but in the doorway he looked back at Taita and ordered him to follow with a curt inclination of his head.

THEY STOOD ALONE on the summit of the highest tower of the palace. From here they had a view upriver over the captured citadel of Abnub, which lay ten miles upstream. Thebes was less than a hundred miles beyond that.

Apepi had ordered the sentries to go down and leave them alone in this lofty place, so that they would not be spied upon or overheard. He stood staring out over the great grey river towards the south, his expression serene.

'At least something they say of you is true, Magus.' Apepi broke the long silence. 'You are a physician of great skill.' He looked down over the encampments of his army.

'My lord,' Taita said softly, 'Pharaoh will have reinforced and regrouped his forces before the plague burns itself out and your men are ready to fight again.'

Apepi shook himself with annoyance, like a lion shaking off flies. 'Nefer Seti is a child. I have defeated him once, I will do it again.'

'What is more crucial to you, there is no plague in his army. Your spies will have told you that Pharaoh has five more legions at Aswan, and another two at Asyut. They are already on the river coming north with the current. They will be here before the new moon.'

Apepi growled softly, but made no response.

Taita went on relentlessly. 'Sixty years of war have bled both kingdoms white. Would you pass on the legacy of bloodshed? Is that what your sons will inherit from you?'

Apepi rounded on him, scowling, 'Do not press me too hard, old man.' After an interval long enough to express his disapproval, Apepi spoke again. 'How long will it take you to arrange a parley with this so-called Regent of the Upper Kingdom, this Naja?'

'If you give me safe conduct through your lines, and a fast galley to carry me, I can be in Thebes in three days. The return with the current will be even swifter.'

'I will send Trok with you to see you safely through. Tell Naja I will meet him at the temple of Hathor on the west bank at Perra beyond Abnub. But tell him not to expect many concessions. I am the victor, and he the vanquished. Go now.'

Taita stood his ground. 'Pharaoh Nefer Seti is almost of an age with your daughter, Mintaka,' he said stubbornly. 'You might wish to bring her with you to Perra.'

'To what purpose?' Apepi stared at him suspiciously.

'An alliance between your dynasty and that of the Tamosian pharaohs might seal a lasting peace in the two kingdoms.'

Apepi stroked his beard to hide his smile. 'You intrigue as cunningly as you mix a potion, Warlock. Now, get you gone before you irk me past forbearance.'

THE TEMPLE OF HATHOR had been excavated out of the rocky hillside above the river hundreds of years previously. The priestesses were a rich, influential sisterhood who had survived and even prospered during the long civil wars between the kingdoms.

Dressed in their yellow robes they were gathered in the courtyard of the temple, between the two massive statues of the goddess. They chanted and rattled the sistrum as the suite of Pharaoh Nefer Seti filed into the courtyard from the eastern wing, while King Apepi's courtiers entered through the western colonnade. Both parties had agreed to eschew the double crown. Apepi wore the red crown of Lower Egypt, while Nefer Seti confined himself to the white crown of Upper Egypt.

The entourages of both rulers packed the spacious courtyard, their ranks facing each other, unsmiling and grim. Only a few paces separated them physically, but the bitterness of sixty years' strife formed a mighty barrier between them.

The hostile silence was shattered by a rolling fanfare of rams' horns and the thunder of bronze gongs. This was the signal for the royal parties to emerge from the two wings of the temple.

Lord Naja and Pharaoh Nefer Seti paced out solemnly and took their places on the high-backed thrones, while the Hyksosian royal family emerged from the opposing wing of the temple. Apepi led them, an impressive, warlike figure in full battle armour. He glared across the courtyard at the boy pharaoh. Eight of his sons followed him—all save Khyan, who had not recovered sufficiently from the plague to make the journey upriver—and his daughter.

None of the Egyptians had laid eyes on Mintaka before, and there was a subdued rustle and murmur through their ranks. They had been unprepared for her beauty. The myth was that all Hyksosian women were as ugly as their menfolk.

Pharaoh Nefer Seti leaned forward slightly, and Taita was so familiar with the boy, so attuned to his mind, that he could read his thoughts with ease. He sensed that Nefer was in a ferment of elation and excitement, and he felt smug at what he had achieved with so little effort. It would have complicated all his plans if Nefer had taken a dislike to the Hyksosian girl.

Lord Naja, the Regent of Upper Egypt, greeted Apepi in measured tones, diplomatically referring to him as King of the Hyksos but avoiding any reference to his claims to Egyptian territory. Mintaka stared at him with fascination. He was such a splendid sight, so different from her own father. He shone with gold and precious stones, and his linen was dazzling in its purity. She could smell his perfume across the distance that separated them. His face was a mask of make-up, his skin almost luminous and his eyes outlined and enhanced with kohl. Yet she thought that his was the beauty of a snake or a poisonous insect. She shivered and turned to the figure on the throne beside the regent.

Pharaoh Nefer Seti was staring at her with such intensity that she caught her breath. His eyes were so green—that was the first thing that struck her. She wanted to look away but could not. Instead she started to blush. Then, suddenly, Pharaoh gave her a warm and conspiratorial smile. Instantly, his face was boyish and appealing, and unaccountably her breath came faster. She dropped her eyes and looked at her hands in her lap, twisting her fingers together until she realised that she was fidgeting and stopped herself.

In the ranks opposite, Taita missed not a single nuance of the surreptitious exchanges between Nefer and Mintaka. He saw more than that. Lord Trok, Naja's cousin, was standing close behind Apepi's throne, his arms folded over his chest. Over one shoulder was slung a heavy bow, over the other an arrow quiver covered with gold leaf. Trok was watching the Hyksosian princess with a dark, brooding gaze. Taita could sense his anger and jealousy. He had not foreseen this. Is Trok's interest in Mintaka romantic or political? he wondered. Does he lust for her, or see her merely as a staircase to power? In either case it is dangerous.

The speeches of greeting were coming to an end and nothing of significance had been said; negotiation of the truce would begin in secret session the next day. Both sides were rising from their thrones and exchanging salutations, and the gongs began to beat and the rams' horns to sound again as they withdrew.

Lord Trok was the last of the Hyksosians to march out between the granite pillars of the gateway. As he did so, the arrows in his quiver rattled softly, and their coloured fletchings caught Taita's eye. The feathers were red and green, and, as he gazed after Trok, something evil stirred in Taita's memory.

Taita returned to the stone cell in the temple annexe that had been allocated to him for the duration of the peace conference. His pleasure at what had transpired between Mintaka and Nefer was forgotten as he considered Trok's relationship to the Hyksosian princess, and the complications that might ensue.

Even during their long ride together, Trok had kept his war quiver firmly stoppered and it had not been possible for Taita to compare one of the arrows it contained to the one found in Pharaoh's body. How many other Hyksosian officers had red and green fletchings he could only guess, but it was probably a great number, though each would have its owner's unique signet. The only way to connect Trok to the death of Pharaoh Tamose, and through him to implicate his cousin Naja, was to study one of his arrows. But how to do this without arousing Trok's suspicions?

His train of thought was interrupted. There were voices in the passage outside the door of his cell. One was young and clear, and he recognised it at once. The others were gruff.

'Lord Asmor has given specific orders—'

'Am I not Pharaoh? Are you not bound to obey me? I wish to visit the Magus. Stand aside.' Nefer's voice was strong and commanding. The uncertain timbre of puberty was gone.

The young falcon is spreading his wings, Taita thought.

Nefer jerked aside the curtain that covered the doorway, and stepped through. Two armed bodyguards followed him helplessly.

Nefer ignored them and faced Taita with his hands on his hips.

'Taita, I am much displeased with you,' Nefer said. 'You have been avoiding me. Whenever I send for you they tell me that you are gone on a secret mission to the Hyksos. Then suddenly you pop up from nowhere, but still you ignore me. You did not even look in my direction during the ceremony. Where have you been?'

'Majesty, there are long ears about.' Taita glanced at the guards.

Immediately Nefer turned upon them wrathfully. 'I have ordered you more than once to be gone. Go this instant.'

They withdrew unhappily. Nefer soon forgot his anger and was grinning delightedly.

'Where have you been, Tata? I have missed you so.'

'I will tell you everything,' Taita assured him, and rapidly, in simple outline, he told Nefer what had happened to him since their last meeting. He explained the relationship between Naja and Trok, and described what he had learned from the lance-bearer, Gil. 'Now you can appreciate the danger you are in,' Taita told Nefer. 'I am certain that Naja had much to do with Pharaoh's murder, and the closer we come to the proof of it, the greater that danger becomes.'

'One day I will avenge my father,' Nefer vowed.

'And I will help you do it,' Taita promised, 'but now we must protect you from Naja's malice.'

'How do you plan to do that, Tata? Can we escape from Egypt as we planned before?'

'No.' Taita shook his head. 'Naja has us too securely imprisoned here. If we tried to run for the frontier again we would have a thousand chariots hot behind us.'

'What can we do, then? You are in danger also.'

'No. I have convinced Naja that he cannot succeed without my help.' He described the false divination ceremony and how Naja believed that Taita could share with him the secret of eternal life.

Nefer grinned at the Magus's cunning. 'So what do you plan?'

'Naja sent me to Apepi to arrange this peace conference.'

'Yes, they told me that when I demanded to see you.'

'Well, once Apepi had agreed to the meeting with Naja, I was able to convince him that they should seal the treaty by a marriage between you and Apepi's daughter. Once you are under the protection of the Hyksosian king, Naja's knife will be blunted.'

'Apepi is going to give me his daughter as a wife?' Nefer stared at him in wonder. 'The one I saw at the ceremony this morning?'

'Yes.' Taita agreed. 'Mintaka is her name.'

'I know her name,' Nefer assured him vehemently. 'She is the most beautiful . . .' Seeing the expression on Taita's face, he subsided. 'I mean, she is quite pleasing.' He grinned ruefully. 'When may I speak to her? She does speak Egyptian, doesn't she?'

'She speaks it as well as you do,' Taita assured him.

'Then when can I meet her? You can arrange it for me.'

Taita had anticipated this request. 'You could invite the princess and her suite to a hunt here in the swamps tomorrow at dawn, and perhaps a picnic afterwards.'

'I will send Asmor to invite her this very afternoon,' Nefer decided, but Taita shook his head.

'He would go to the regent first, and Naja would immediately see the danger. Once he was alerted he would do everything in his power to prevent you coming together.'

'What shall we do, then?' Nefer looked agitated.

'I will go to her myself,' Taita promised, and he did, that same day.

THE DAWN SKY the next morning was the glowing shade of a sword blade fresh from the coals of the forge. In this time before the sunrise there was no breath of air, no sound to break the stillness.

Two hunting skiffs were moored in a small lagoon, hard against the reeds that surrounded the open water. Less than fifty cubits separated them. The royal huntsmen had bent tall papyrus stems to form a screening roof over the hunters.

The surface of the lagoon was still and unruffled. It was just light enough for Nefer to make out the graceful form of Mintaka in the other boat. She had her bow across her lap, and sat as motionless as a statue. Any other girl he could think of, particularly his own sister Heseret, would have been hopping around like a canary on a perch.

Out in the swamp a heron boomed. As though this was a signal, the air was filled suddenly with the sound of wings. Nefer tore his eyes off the dainty figure in the boat across the water, and reached for his throwing sticks, determined to impress Mintaka with his hunting skills.

The first flight of glossy black and white ducks came sweeping in low out of the dawn. They turned in a wide circle then started to drop and line up on the open water. They set their wings and streamed in, losing height swiftly, passing directly over Nefer's skiff. Pharaoh judged his moment neatly, with the stick cocked and ready to throw. He waited for the lead bird to flare out and then let fly. The duck saw the missile coming and dropped a wing to avoid it.

Lost bird, Nefer thought bitterly, and before he could throw the second stick, the flight of ducks had angled across the lagoon, directly towards Mintaka's boat. They were still keeping low, going very fast, their blade-shaped wings whistling through the air.

Nefer had almost discounted the hunter in the other boat—at that height and speed the targets were too difficult for all but the most expert archer—but in quick succession two arrows rose to meet the straggle of birds. The sound of the double impact carried clearly across the lagoon. Then two ducks were falling, killed cleanly in the air at the same time. They plopped onto the water and floated there, motionless. The slave-boy retrievers picked them up easily and swam back to Mintaka's skiff, carrying the carcasses gripped in their teeth.

'Two lucky arrows,' Nefer said.

In the bows of the skiff, Taita added, 'Two unlucky ducks.'

Now the sky was filled with birds, which rose in dark clouds as the first rays of the sun struck the waters. They squawked and honked and quacked and bleated and wailed.

Mintaka's light bow was well suited to the task. It was quick to align and draw without taxing her strength unduly. She was firing sharp metal heads especially forged for her by Grippa, the famous armourer. The needle-points drove through the dense plumage and went straight to the bone. She had realised, without a word being exchanged, that Nefer intended to make a contest of the hunt, and she was proving that her competitive instincts were every bit as fierce as his.

Nefer had been badly rattled by his first failure and by Mintaka's unexpected skill. Many of the birds he brought down were only stunned, and eluded his slave boys by diving under the surface and swimming into the thick papyrus beds. The number of dead birds piled on the floorboards of the skiff grew pitifully slowly. In desperation Nefer discarded his sticks and snatched up his heavy bow, but it was too late. His right arm was exhausted by his efforts with the sticks, and his draw was laboured.

Taita watched Nefer flounder ever deeper into the trap he had set for himself. A little humiliation will do him no real harm, he told himself. For once his sympathy was not with the boy, and he smiled secretly as he watched Nefer miss again and Mintaka take down two birds from the same flight as they passed over her head.

However, he felt pity for his king when one of Mintaka's slaves swam across the lagoon, and hung onto the side of Nefer's skiff. 'Her Royal Highness Princess Mintaka's boat begins to sink under the weight of her bag. Now she is hungry for her breakfast.'

An untimely sally! Taita thought, as Nefer scowled furiously at this impertinence. It was time for him to intervene. 'Pharaoh apologises for his thoughtlessness, but he was enjoying the sport so much that he forgot the passage of time. Please tell your mistress that we shall all go in to breakfast immediately.'

Nefer glowered at him, but put up his bow and made no effort to revoke Taita's decision. The two boats paddled back towards the island in close formation. Not a word was said by the crew of either skiff, but everyone was conscious of the results of the morning's hunt.

'Your majesty,' Mintaka called across to Nefer, 'I must thank you for a truly diverting morning. I cannot remember when last I enjoyed myself so much.'

'You are too kind.' Nefer made a regal gesture of dismissal, turned half away from her, and stared broodingly out at the horizon of reeds and water.

First love is such unmitigated joy, Taita thought with sympathetic irony.

They came in to the landing on the island. The boatmen jumped over the side into the knee-deep ooze and held the first skiff steady while the slaves handed the princess and her maids across the gap onto the firm, dry ground at the top of the bank.

As soon as they were safely ashore the royal skiff came in and the slaves handed Nefer across to join Mintaka on the high bank. He led her to a giant kigelia tree under whose spreading branches a breakfast feast was laid out in the shade. At first Nefer was restrained and cool, but soon his natural high spirits reasserted themselves, and he joined in the banter and the chatter.

Mintaka loved to riddle and she challenged him to an exchange. She made it more difficult for Nefer by couching her clues in the Hyksosian language. 'I have one eye and a sharp nose. I run my victim through and through, but I draw no blood. What am I?'

'That's easy!' Nefer laughed triumphantly. 'You are a sewing needle.' And Mintaka threw up her hands in surrender.

Of course Nefer had brought his bao board and stones. Taita had taught him to love the game, and he had become expert. When he tired of the riddles he inveigled Mintaka into a game. Bao was an Egyptian game, and this time he expected confidently to outmatch her.

Taita smiled because he and Mintaka had whiled away a few hours at bao in the palace of Bubasti when they were nursing her little brother. Within eighteen moves her red stones dominated the west castle and were menacing Nefer's centre.

'Have I done the right thing?' she asked sweetly.

Nefer was saved by a hail from the river and looked up to see a galley flying the regent's pennant coming swiftly down the channel. 'What a pity. Just when the game was getting interesting.'

He had been expecting this visitation all morning. Sooner or later the regent must hear about this outing and send Asmor to bring in his errant charge.

The galley nosed into the bank below, where they sat, and Asmor sprang ashore. He strode up to the picnic party. 'The regent is much displeased by your absence. He bids you return at once to the temple, where matters of state await your attention.'

'And I, Lord Asmor, am much displeased by your ill manners,' Nefer told him. 'I am not a house servant to be addressed in that manner, and neither have you shown respect for the Princess Mintaka.' But there was no escaping that he was being treated like a truant from the classroom.

Still, he put a good face on it and invited Mintaka to sail back with him in the skiff while her maids followed in the second vessel. Taita kept tactfully to the bows as this was their first opportunity to hold a private conversation.

The journey was far too short for Nefer's liking, and as they came into the landing he took her hand. 'I should like to see you again.'

'I should like that well enough,' she replied.

'Soon,' he insisted.

'Soon enough.' She smiled and gently took back her hand. He felt strangely bereft as he watched her walk away towards the temple.

'MY LORD, you were present at the divination of the Mazes. You know of the charge placed upon me by the gods. You know that I am committed to your interest. I had good reason to assist the boy in what was only, after all, a harmless escapade.'

Naja was not so easily placated. He was furious that Nefer had given Asmor the slip and managed to spend the morning out in the swamps with the Hyksosian princess. But Taita diplomatically turned aside each of the regent's accusations, until he was no longer ranting but merely grumbling bitterly. 'However, it must not happen again. Of course I trust your loyalty, Magus.'

'My lord, how goes the negotiation with King Apepi? Is there aught that I can do to help you ensure a successful outcome in this matter?' Adroitly Taita set the hounds on a different scent, and Naja followed them.

'I have that old rogue Apepi at the brink,' he gloated. 'This morning he is about to make more concessions than he realises.' He started towards the door, then looked back over his shoulder. 'Come with me,' he ordered. 'I might have use of your powers before I am done with Apepi.'

Binding Apepi to the treaty was not the easy task that Naja had suggested it would be. The Hyksosian leader was still ranting, shouting and banging his fist on the table long after the watchman on the temple walls had called the midnight hour. At last Naja adjourned the conference and staggered off to bed.

The next day, when they met again at noon, Apepi was no more amenable to reason. Taita used his influences to calm him, but Apepi allowed himself to be wooed only very slowly. So it was only on the fifth day that the scribes began to write down the terms of the treaty.

Up to this time Naja had excluded Pharaoh Nefer Seti from the conclave. But by the morning of the sixth day, when the scribes had completed their work and the fifty tablets of the treaty were ready to be ratified, Naja sent for Pharaoh to take part in the proceedings. Likewise, all Apepi's offspring, including Mintaka, were to be present at the ceremony.

Once again the courtyard of the temple was filled with a glittering congregation as, in stentorian tones, the herald royal began to read out the text of the treaty. Immediately Nefer was absorbed by what it contained, certain that he detected Taita's shadowy influence in many areas of the long document.

At last it was time to affix the seals. To a series of blasts on the rams' horns Nefer pressed his cartouche to the damp clay and Apepi did the same. Then, while Naja watched with an enigmatic expression, the new co-rulers of the two kingdoms embraced. Apepi folded Nefer in his bearlike embrace and men rattled their weapons against their shields, or hammered the butts of their lances on the stone flags. Finally Apepi turned to face the crowded courtyard.

'Citizens of this mighty land, which is once again united, I pledge you my duty and my love. In token of these, I offer the hand of my daughter, Princess Mintaka, in marriage to the Pharaoh Nefer Seti, who shares with me the double crown of the Upper and Lower Kingdoms, and who shall be my son.'

There was a long moment of utter stillness in the courtyard. Then the assembly burst out in enthusiastic cries of approval while the drumming of weapons became deafening.

Pharaoh Nefer Seti had an expression on his face that in any lesser mortal would have been described as an idiotic grin. He was gazing across the courtyard at Mintaka. She was frozen, with one hand covering her mouth, and her eyes were wide with astonishment as she gazed at her father. Slowly a dark blush suffused her face and she turned her eyes to meet Nefer's. The two gazed at each other as if no other person was in the crowded courtyard.

Taita watched from the foot of Pharaoh's throne. He realised that Apepi's timing of the announcement had been masterly. Now there was no possible way in which anybody—Naja, Trok or any other—could stand in the way of the marriage.

Standing close to Naja's throne, Taita was keenly aware of the regent's deep consternation. Naja must have sensed Taita's eyes on him, for he glanced in his direction. For a moment only, Taita looked into his soul, and saw the cobra of his vision, the cobra for which the regent was named. Then Naja veiled his fierce yellow eyes, smiled coolly and nodded in approval, but Taita knew that he was thinking furiously.

The Magus turned his head and sought out the burly figure of Lord Trok in the Hyksosian ranks opposite. Unlike the regent, Trok was making no attempt to disguise his feelings. He was in a black rage. He opened his mouth as if to protest, then closed it. With a huge effort he regained control of himself, smoothed down his beard, then turned abruptly and pushed his way out of the courtyard.

As Trok disappeared between the tall granite pillars, Naja rose and stepped in front of Apepi. 'On this auspicious and joyous day, we rejoice not only in the joining of the two kingdoms, but also in the betrothal of Pharaoh Nefer Seti and the Princess Mintaka. Therefore, be it known that the marriage will take place in this temple on the day that Pharaoh Nefer Seti celebrates his majority, or fulfils one of the conditions to ratify his claim to the crown and rules in his own right without a regent to protect and advise him.'

Apepi frowned and Nefer made a small gesture of dismay, but it was too late. It had been announced in full session so, as regent, Naja spoke with the authority of both crowned heads. Unless Nefer captured his own godbird, thereby ratifying his claim to the throne, Naja had prevented the marriage taking place for a number of years.

That was a masterly stroke, Taita thought bitterly. Naja had averted disaster for himself by his quick thinking. Now, he went even further. 'On an equally happy note, I invite Pharaoh Apepi and Pharaoh Nefer Seti to celebrate my own marriage to Princess Heseret. This joyous ceremony will take place ten days from now, at the temple of Isis in the city of Thebes.'

So, Taita thought grimly, in ten days' time Lord Naja will be a member of the Tamosian royal family, and will stand next in succession to Pharaoh Nefer Seti.

BY THE TERMS of the Treaty of Hathor, Apepi's capital would remain at Avaris and Nefer Seti's at Thebes. Each would govern his former kingdom, but in the name of the duumvirate. Twice every year, at the beginning and the end of the inundation of the Nile, the two kings would hold a combined royal assize at Memphis, where all matters concerning the two kingdoms would be dealt with.

However, before the two pharaohs parted, Apepi and his train would sail upriver in company with Nefer Seti's fleet to Thebes. There they would attend Lord Naja's wedding.

The embarkation of both trains from the wharf below the temple was a chaotic affair that took up most of the morning. Taita mingled with the throng of boatmen and dockers, slaves and important passengers. Occasionally a man would look up from what he was doing, recognise him and ask for his blessing, or a woman would bring him a sick child to tend. However, he was able to work his way gradually along the beach, casually looking out for the chariots and equipment of Lord Trok's regiment. He recognised them by their green and red pennants, and as he approached he made out the unmistakable figure of Trok among his men. Taita edged closer and watched him pause to talk to his lance-bearer, then take the path up to the temple.

As soon as Trok had disappeared, Taita approached the lance-bearer. The trooper was stripped to breech-clout and sandals, and as he stooped over one of the chests of Trok's equipment Taita saw the distinctive circular rash of the ringworm on his naked back. 'Come here, soldier,' Taita called him across. 'How long have you had the itch on your back?'

Instinctively the fellow twisted up one arm between his shoulder blades, and scratched himself vigorously. 'Cursed thing has been bothering me ever since we captured Abnub. I think it's a gift from one of those dirty Egyptian whores—' He broke off guiltily. 'Forgive me, Warlock, we are allies and fellow countrymen now.'

'That is why I will attend to your affliction, soldier. Go up to the temple, ask at the kitchens for a jar of lard and bring it to me. I will mix an ointment for you.' Taita sat down on the pile of Trok's luggage, and the lance-bearer hurried away down the beach.

Taita's seat was a stack of wooden chests. The top one bore the seal of Grippa, the Avaris fletcher who made arrows for all the high-ranking Hyksosian officers. Taita untied the cord that secured the lid. A layer of dry straw protected the arrows. He picked one out and turned it in his fingers.

The carved signet leapt out at him, the stylised head of the leopard with the hieratic letter T held in its snarling jaws. The arrow was identical to the one found in Pharaoh's body. It was the last thread in the fabric of treason. Naja and Trok were linked in the bloody plot.

Taita slipped the incriminating arrow under the folds of his kilt and closed the lid of the chest. Deftly he retied the cord, and waited for the lance-bearer to return.

The old soldier was grateful for Taita's ministrations, then pleaded for a further favour: 'A friend of mine has the pox, Magus. What should he do?' It always amused Taita that no man ever contracted the pox himself but always had a friend suffering from it.

THE FEAST TO CELEBRATE the marriage of Lord Naja to Princess Heseret was the most lavish ever recorded. To the common citizens of Thebes, Lord Naja gave five hundred head of prime oxen, and to each of the four thousand invited guests a commemorative carved jewel with the guest's own name engraved upon it between the names of the regent and his bride.

The bride came to meet her groom on one of the state carriages drawn by sacred white oxen. The road was strewn with palm fronds and flowers, and a chariot drove ahead of the wedding coach throwing rings of silver and copper to the crowds that lined the way.

When she reached the temple she was met by her brother. Heseret was as lovely as a nymph of paradise in her snowy robes and glittering jewellery. Months ago she had come to terms with the fate the gods had apportioned her and her girlish interest in Meren had begun to fade. She came to realise that he was an impecunious boy, a common soldier without favour or prospects. Lord Naja's social rank almost matched hers, and his fortune far exceeded her own. He was also a magnificent-looking man.

Now she kept a chaste demeanour as Nefer led her down the temple to the sanctuary where Lord Naja was waiting. He wore a plumed headdress of ostrich feathers and his perfume was a blend of essences from a land beyond the Indus. The aroma stirred her, and she took the hand the Naja offered her without hesitation.

Watching from the roof of the western enclosure, Taita shuddered with a sense of foreboding. Now Naja is of the blood royal, I am the only shield Nefer has, and I am one man and old. Will my powers be enough to turn away the cobra?

LORD NAJA AND HIS NEW WIFE rode back in splendour to the palace gates. There they dismounted and went in procession through the gardens to the banquet hall. Most of the guests had arrived ahead of them, and the commotion as the wedding party entered was deafening. The pair moved through the throng and inspected the gifts stacked in the centre of the banquet hall. Apepi had sent a chariot covered in gold leaf, so brilliant that even in the dimly lit hall it was difficult to look at directly. From Babylon King Sargon had sent a hundred sandalwood chests, filled with jewellery, precious stones or golden vessels. Pharaoh Nefer Seti, at the suggestion of Lord Naja, had deeded to his new brother-in-law three lakhs of pure gold. The regent had become almost as rich as his pharaoh.

When the connubial pair took their seats at the head of the wedding board, the palace cooks laid a feast before them, and to entertain them there were musicians and jugglers, acrobats and huge brown bears.

By nightfall most of the guests were so drunk that few could stand when Lord Naja and his bride retired. Naja led Heseret by the hand to his sumptuous bedroom, which overlooked the river. There Heseret's handmaidens took her behind a screen of bamboo to remove her wedding dress and jewellery.

Lord Naja went out onto the terrace and inhaled deeply the cool river air. A slave brought him a bowl of spiced wine, and he sipped appreciatively. It was the first wine he had allowed himself all evening. He returned to the chamber as two more slaves staggered in, bearing between them a cauldron of hot water, in which floated lotus petals. Naja set aside the wine bowl and went to bathe. One of the slaves dried and braided his hair, while the other brought him a clean white robe. He dismissed them and lay upon the marriage bed, stretching out his long, elegant limbs.

From the far end of the chamber came the rustle of clothing and feminine whispers. He propped himself up on one elbow and looked across at the bamboo screen. The gaps in it were just large enough to afford him tantalising glimpses of pale, smooth skin. Power and political aspiration were the main reasons for this marriage, but Naja had a voluptuous nature. For years he had watched Heseret surreptitiously, and his interest had increased at each stage in her journey towards womanhood. Now, at last, two of the handmaidens led her out from behind the screen, then slipped away quietly, leaving her standing alone in the middle of the floor.

Her silken night-robe fell to her ankles. It was creamy in colour and so fine that it seemed to float around her like river mist, stirring with every breath she took. There was an oil lamp on a tripod in the corner behind her, and the soft yellow light shone through the silk, highlighting the curves of her hips and shoulders. Her skin was flawless and her green eyes hinted at a sly, lascivious streak in her.

'You are beautiful.' His voice caught.

Now a hint of a smile lifted the corners of her lips. 'I am glad that my lord regent finds me so.'

He rose from the bed and went to her. Slowly he lifted her face.

'You also are beautiful,' she whispered, and it was true. In this moment she realised that he was the most beautiful creature she had ever known.

He kissed her and his mouth startled her. His tongue was as flickeringly quick as a snake's, but it did not revolt her. She closed her eyes and touched it with her own. She was so lost in his kiss that when his hand closed over her breast she was unprepared. Her eyes flew open and she gasped. She tried to pull away but he held her, and now he caressed her with a skilful touch that stilled her fears.

With a single movement he swept off her silken robe and let it fall to the floor. She had not the slightest inclination to resist.

Twice during that enchanted night she cried out in a frenzy of pleasure, and when the dawn suffused the chamber with its rose and silver light she lay still in his arms. She felt as though the life force had been drawn out of her, and there was a soft ache deep in her belly that she savoured.

When she opened her eyes he was watching her, and he smiled gently. 'What a splendid queen you would make,' he said softly. This he meant sincerely, sensing that he had found in her someone whose desires and instincts were in perfect harmony with his own.

'And what a splendid pharaoh you would make.' She smiled back, reached up and touched his cheek. 'But that could never happen.' She stopped smiling abruptly and asked softly, seriously, 'Could it?'

CHAPTER FOUR

King Apepi's entourage remained in Thebes for almost a month after the wedding. They were the guests of Pharaoh Nefer Seti and of his regent, and were entertained in royal fashion. Taita encouraged this delay. He felt certain that Naja would take no action against Nefer while Apepi and his daughter were in Thebes.

The royal visitors spent their days hunting, and during these days Mintaka was often at Nefer's side. She rode in his chariot and handed him the lance when they drove up alongside a galloping oryx. She carried her own falcon on her arm as they quartered the reed beds for heron. At the hunting picnics in the desert, she sat beside Nefer and prepared little treats for him.

Every evening there were banquets in the palace and there also she sat at his side. She made him laugh with her wry wit and she was a marvellous mimic: she imitated Heseret to perfection, simpering and rolling her eyes, and speaking of 'My husband, the Regent of Egypt' in the portentous tones Heseret now employed.

As Nefer's chariot sped through the streets of Thebes with Mintaka on the footplate as his lance-bearer, men paused from their labours to shout greetings and good wishes. Their love was so apparent that it cast a glow upon all those around them. Even Naja smiled benignly upon them, although he fiercely resented the attention of the populace being diverted from his own nuptials, and he saw to it that Nefer and Mintaka could never be completely alone.

Their chance came, however, when a royal huntsman came in from the hills above the village of Dabba one day to report that a lion had raided the cattle pens during the night. It had killed eight of the terrified beasts. In the dawn a horde of villagers, brandishing torches, blowing horns, beating drums and screaming wildly, had driven it off.

'When did this happen?' asked Naja.

'Three nights ago, Your Grace.' The man was prostrate before the throne. 'I came upriver as soon as I could, but the current runs strongly and the winds were fluky.'

'What has happened to the beast?' King Apepi interrupted eagerly.

'It has gone back into the hills, but I have sent two of my best Nubian trackers to follow it.'

'I will have the chariots loaded onto the boats at once,' Apepi decided. 'With the state of the river we can be at Dabba early tomorrow morning.'

Naja hesitated. He was not so addicted to the hunt that he wished to neglect the numerous affairs of state that awaited his attention. He had looked forward to the departure of Apepi, whose boisterous, uncouth presence in Thebes had long since palled. And he had other plans afoot. 'Majesty, you are expected to sail back to Avaris tomorrow.'

'You are right, Regent. However, most of our baggage is already loaded and the fleet lies ready to depart. Moreover, Dabba lies on my way homewards. I can afford a day or two in the hunt.'

'Your Majesty,' Nefer intervened, 'we will join in the hunt with the greatest of pleasure.' He saw an opportunity for magnificent sport, and before Naja could prevent him he turned to the huntsman, who still lay with his forehead pressed to the floor. 'Well done, my good fellow. The chamberlain will give you a gold ring for your trouble. Return to Dabba at once in the fastest felucca in our fleet. Make ready for our arrival.'

Nefer's only cause for regret was that Taita would not be with him during his first lion hunt. The old man had disappeared into the wilderness on another of his periodic and mysterious forays.

IN THE EARLY MORNING of the next day the hunting party disembarked on the river bank below the village of Dabba. All the horses and chariots were off-loaded and the lance-bearers sharpened the spear blades, restrung the hunting bows and checked the arrows. While the horses were watered, the hunters ate a hearty breakfast that the villagers had provided. The mood was ebullient.

'Sound the mount-up,' Nefer ordered, and the rams' horns blared as the hunters scattered to the waiting chariots. Mintaka walked at Nefer's side. In these informal circumstances all royal dignity was forgotten, and they were simply boy and girl on an exciting outing.

Led by the royal huntsman, who rode bareback astride a tough little pony, the column climbed into the bare, stony hills. They went at the trot, saving the horses, letting them blow after every steep gradient. Within the hour they found one of the Nubian trackers waiting for them on a hilltop, and the huntsman trotted back to report to the royal party, 'The Nubians have cast the hills but without finding the spoor again. From where we last saw him, he may have gone to the small oasis at the head of the valley, but there are Bedouin encamped there. They might have scared off the beast. There is also a water seep below those hills.' He pointed at a low line of purple peaks on the horizon.

'You have not the least idea where he is, have you?' Lord Naja complained. 'We should call off the hunt.'

'No!' Nefer cut in. 'How can we give up?'

'We must go on,' Apepi agreed, 'but there is much ground to cover.' He paused, then reached a decision. 'We must split up and search each area separately.' He looked at Naja. 'My Lord Regent, take your squadron to the Bedouin encampment. I will ride to the seep below the hills.' He turned to Trok. 'Take three chariots down the valley.' Then he looked at Nefer. 'Pharaoh, you cast in the opposite direction, north towards Achmim.'

Nefer realised he was being given the least promising ground to cover, but he had no complaint. This new plan meant that for the first time he and Mintaka would be away from the direct surveillance of his guardians. He waited for someone to point this out, but they were all so wrapped up in the hunt that no one seemed to realise the significance of this move. Except Naja.

He looked hard at Nefer, weighing the advisability of countermanding Apepi's orders, but in the end he must have realised that this would be unwise, and concluded that Nefer was guarded by the desert as effectively as he would have been by Asmor: there was no place to run to. If he took Mintaka on some wild adventure he would soon have the armies of both kingdoms upon him.

Apepi went on to nominate an assembly point, and to give his final orders. At last the rams' horns sounded the mount-up and the advance, and the columns drove out of the valley. On the level ground they split into their separate squadrons and headed out in diverging directions.

There were two other chariots in Nefer's squadron, commanded by Colonel Hilto, the old soldier who had discovered him and Taita when they had tried to escape from Egypt. He had served under Nefer's father and was loyal unto death. Nefer knew he could trust him without reservation.

Nefer led them fast, wanting to make the most of the remaining daylight, and within an hour the vast green vista of the river plain opened beneath them. He reined in to admire it.

'Colonel Hilto, if the lion is here it will probably be lying up somewhere on the slope of the hills down below us.' He indicated the area with a sweep of his arm. 'I want to extend in line abreast. The left flank must be on the edge of the plain and our right up here on the crest of the hills. We will sweep northwards.' He made a wide gesture, but Hilto looked dubious.

'That is a broad front, Your Majesty. It's almost half a league to the valley bottom. At times we will be out of sight of each other.'

Nefer cut in with a sharp tone and cold expression: 'Do you presume to argue with your pharaoh?'

'Never, Majesty!' Hilto was shocked at the accusation.

'Then do your duty, fellow.'

Hilto saluted and hurried back to his own chariot, shouting orders to his men. As the squadron wheeled out down the slope, Mintaka nudged Nefer and smiled. 'Do your duty, fellow!' She mimicked his haughty tone then laughed. 'Please never look at me like that or use that tone to me, Your Majesty. I am sure I would die of fright.'

She lifted her face to him and her lips were parted slightly. He could smell her sweet breath, and the temptation to reach down for those lips was almost irresistible. 'We have only a little time,' he replied instead. 'We must make the most of it, and find a place where we can be alone.'

He swung the chariot down towards a small grove of thorn trees, almost hidden by a fold in the ground, where a narrow ravine had been cut into the hillside by wind and weather. There must have been subterranean water, for the thorn trees were robust. Their thick foliage provided shade and privacy in this hot midday. Nefer drove down the bank and into the shade. He jumped down and went to fill the bucket from the water-skin to water the horses. Mintaka, aware of a fullness in her bladder, picked her way deeper into the grove of thorn trees.

THE LION WATCHED HER with yellow eyes, flattening its ears against its skull and pressing its body closer to the stony earth. The previous night it had missed an oryx, and hunger was a dull, insistent pain in its gut. It lifted its head, and slashed its tail back and forth, the prelude to the charge.

As Mintaka stood and started back towards Nefer, she heard the rhythmic swish and thud of the tail, stopped and looked up, puzzled. She looked straight into the yellow gaze of the beast. She screamed, a high-pitched sound that struck Nefer to the heart. He whirled round and in an instant took in the situation: the girl, the crouching beast facing her, and his bow and quiver ten paces away, in the rack on the chariot's dashboard.

At that moment the lion growled. It was a terrible sound that seemed to vibrate in Mintaka's bones and make the ground tremble.

Then its mane rose like a dark aura around its head and it launched itself into its charge, coming straight at her.

'Come! Here I am! Come to me!' Nefer yelled wildly, and it swung its huge head towards him. His arm was shaking as he reached down and drew his dagger from the sheath on his belt.

It was a flimsy weapon against this furious beast. The thin bronze blade was not long enough to stab through to the heart, but he had heard the royal huntsman tell tales of miraculous escapes from just such a deadly predicament. The lion hurled itself towards him and, as it launched into the death spring, Nefer fell backwards, not even attempting to resist the beast's weight and impetus. He lay between its forepaws, and the lion opened its jaws to full stretch and thrust its head down to crush Nefer's skull with its terrible fangs.

Nefer steeled himself and thrust his hand, holding the dagger with the blade aligned upright, deep into the open jaws. The lion bit down instinctively, driving the bronze point up through the roof of its mouth. Nefer snatched away his hand before the fangs could crush the bones of his wrist, but the lion's jaws were fixed open by the dagger held between them, and it could not bite down. It ripped at him with both its forepaws, claws fully extended. He writhed beneath the heavy body, evading some of the claw strokes, but felt the bony hooks tearing into his flesh.

Mintaka's own fear was now forgotten. She raced towards the

chariot, the screams and roars behind her goading her on. Ahead of her the terrified horses reared and threw their heads. They would have bolted long ago had not Nefer secured the locking brake on one wheel so they could only turn in a tight right-handed circle. Mintaka ran in under their flying hoofs, jumped up onto the footplate and brought them under control. She knocked off the brake and drove them straight at the lion and its victim. She then snatched the long lance from its rack and, guiding the horses with the reins in her left hand, leaned far out over the side panel and raised the lance high. As they ran past the crouched lion, the back of its neck was exposed. The exact juncture of spine and skull was covered by the dense black bush of its mane, but she guessed at the spot and thrust down with all the strength of her fear and her love for Nefer.

Her lance hand had the impetus of the flying chariot behind it. To her amazement the blade slid in readily, full length through the taut hide, deep into the back of the animal's neck to sever the spinal column. As the chariot raced past, the lance was plucked from her grip. But the lion collapsed in a loose, inert heap on top of Nefer. It did not twitch again, killed on the instant.

She wheeled the crazed horses back to where Nefer lay beneath the huge carcass, and jumped down from the footplate. It was obvious how badly Nefer was hurt. She could see that the enormous weight of the dead beast was crushing the wind from his lungs. Seizing the long tufted tail she heaved with all her strength. Slowly the hindquarters began to swing, then the whole carcass flopped over and he was free.

Mintaka knelt beside him and helped him into a sitting position, but he swayed drunkenly and reached out to her for support.

'You are desperately wounded,' she cried. 'There is so much blood.'

'Not all of it is mine,' he blurted, but from his right thigh rose a crimson fountain where the claws had ripped open a blood vessel. Taita had instructed him long and earnestly in the treatment of wounds, and he thrust his thumb down into the torn flesh and pressed until the jet of blood shrivelled.

'Get the water-skin,' he said, and Mintaka did so and held it for him while he drank thirstily. Then she washed the blood and filth from his face, relieved to find it unmarked. However, when she inspected his other injuries she saw how grievous they were.

'My bedroll is in the chariot.' His voice was weaker. When she brought it to him he asked her to undo the bundle, where she found a needle and silk thread. He showed her how to tie off the spurting blood vessel. Her hands were bloody to the wrists, as with nimble fingers she pulled a thread round the open artery then closed the deeper rents in his flesh. She used strips torn from his tattered kilt to bind up the wounds. It was rough, rudimentary surgery, but sufficient to stem the worst of the bleeding.

'That is all we can do now. I must help you into the chariot and get you to where a surgeon can do the rest. Oh, if only Taita were here.'

Nefer was staring longingly at the carcass of the lion. 'My first lion,' he whispered ruefully. 'Unless we skin it, the trophy will spoil. The hair will slip and slough off.'

In the heat of her terrible concern for him, she lost her temper. 'That is the most stupid piece of man's nonsense I have ever heard. Would you risk your life for a stinking bit of fur?' Angrily she helped him to his feet. He leaned on her with all his weight as he hobbled to the chariot and collapsed weakly onto the footplate. Mintaka used the sheepskin from the bedroll to make him as comfortable as she could, then climbed up and stood over him with the reins in her hands.

'Which way?' she asked.

'The rest of the squadron will be far up the valley by now,' he told her. 'The other hunters are scattered across the desert. We could search for them all day without finding them.'

'We must return to where the fleet is lying at Dabba. There is a surgeon with the ships.' She had reached the only feasible conclusion, and he nodded. She urged the horses into a walk, and they left the grove and climbed to the high ground, heading south once again.

Even though Mintaka kept the horses down to a trot, the collision with every stone or hump was transmitted through the rigid chassis into Nefer's torn body. He winced and sweated, trying to hide his pain from her, but as the hours wore on it became unbearable. He groaned aloud at a particularly nasty impact, and she reined the pair to a halt.

'You are going to be all right, my darling,' she told him, with a confidence she did not feel. She sponged his face, kissed the top of his dusty, blood-caked head, and took up the reins again.

An hour later she gave the last of the water to Nefer and the horses, not drinking herself. Then she stood as high as she could on the dashboard of the chariot and looked about her. At her feet Nefer stirred and moaned, and she looked down with a brave face and smiled. 'Not much further now, my heart. We should see the river over the next crest.'

She rearranged the sheepskin under his head, then stood up and gathered the reins. Suddenly she realised how exhausted she was: every muscle in her body ached and her eyes were sore from the sun's glare and the dust. She forced herself and the team onwards.

Soon the horses were showing signs of distress. They had stopped sweating and the salt rime had dried white across their backs. She tried to urge them into a trot but they could not respond, and at last despair overtook her. She sank down, helpless and lost, and whispered to Nefer as he lay, now unconscious, 'I am sorry, my darling. I have failed you.' She stroked the matted hair from his face. Then she looked up at the low hilltop to the east and blinked. She shook her head to clear her vision, then looked again, but still she could not be sure that what she was seeing was illusion or reality.

On the crest of the hills above them, a gaunt figure stood on the skyline, leaning on his long staff. His silver hair shone like a cloud and the hot, light breeze of the desert flapped his skirts against his heron-thin legs. He was staring down at them.

Beside her, Nefer opened his eyes. 'Taita is near,' he murmured. 'I feel him close.'

'Yes. Taita is here.' Her voice was faint. 'But how did he know where to find us?'

'He knows. Taita knows,' Nefer replied, closed his eyes and slumped back into unconsciousness.

TAITA DROVE DOWN the escarpment towards the river. The horses responded to his touch, moving with an easy motion that cosseted the wounded boy on the footplate. Taita seemed to have known with some deep instinct just what medicines and dressings Nefer would need, and he had carried these with him. After he had redressed the wounds, he led the horses to a hidden water seep nearby to revive them. Then he took Mintaka up on the footplate and turned the horses' heads unerringly in the direction of Dabba.

A red and angry sunset was fading over the Nile like a dying bush fire as they approached the spot where the fleet was still anchored in the stream. Apepi and Naja rode out to meet them. Lord Naja was agitated, and Apepi bellowed at his daughter as soon as they were in range, 'Where have you been, you stupid child? Half the army is out looking for you.'

Lord Naja's agitation abated when he saw Nefer bandaged and unconscious in the chariot cockpit. Barely conscious, the boy was carried gently aboard one of the galleys.

'I want Pharaoh taken up to Thebes with all possible speed,' Taita told Naja, 'even if it means a night journey.'

'You can order the galley to sail at once,' Naja said, in front of the company, but then took Taita's arm and led him a short way along the river bank to where they could not be overheard. 'Bear in mind, Magus, the charge laid on you by the gods. If Pharaoh were to die from his wounds no person in either kingdom would take it as unnatural.' He said no more but gazed into Taita's face.

'The will of the gods will prevail against all else,' Taita agreed.

Naja read in his reply what he wanted to hear. 'We are in accord, Taita. I place my trust in you. Go in peace. I will follow you to Thebes after Apepi has been taken care of.' This last remark struck Taita as odd, but he was too distracted to ponder it.

When he hurried back on board the galley, Taita found Mintaka kneeling beside the litter in tears.

She looked up at him piteously. 'My father is taking me back to Avaris in the morning, but I should be with Nefer. I am his betrothed. He needs me.' She seized his hand. 'Oh, Magus! Will you not go to my father and ask him to let me go back to Thebes to help you to take care of Nefer? My father will listen to you.'

But when Taita attempted to persuade Apepi to let her go back to Thebes with Nefer, the king snorted with laughter. 'Place my lamb in Naja's pen?' He shook his head with amusement. 'I trust Naja as I would a scorpion. Who knows what tricks he would try if I gave him that coin to bargain with? No, Warlock, Mintaka comes back under my wing to Avaris until her wedding day.'

Sadly Mintaka went to take her leave of Nefer. He was on the edge of consciousness, weak from loss of blood, but when she kissed him he opened his eyes. She took the golden locket that hung at her throat. 'This contains a lock of my hair. It is my soul, and I give it to you.' She placed it in his hand and he folded his fingers tightly round it.

So Mintaka stood alone on the bank of the Nile, watching forlornly as the galley bearing Nefer and Taita breasted the current, heading upstream towards Thebes.

THE NEXT MORNING there was a final meeting between Apepi and the regent, Lord Naja, on board the Hyksosian royal barge. All Apepi's nine sons were present, and Mintaka was seated beside her father. Then, with protestations of mutual trust and devotion to the peace, the two fleets diverged, one to return to Thebes, the other to Avaris, and garlands and wreaths of palm fronds were tossed from one vessel towards the other, bestrewing the surface of the wide river.

That evening King Apepi's fleet anchored at Balasfura, opposite the temple of Hapi, where Trok and the officers under his command arranged a banquet and entertainment. On the river bank pavilions were hung with vivid red, yellow and green curtains to receive the royal family. Whole oxen were grilled over pits of glowing ash, and amphorae of the choicest wines cooled in the river waters. Slaves staggered up the bank under the weight of them as one after the other they were drained and Apepi bellowed for fresh jars to be brought.

The king's mood lightened with each bowl he lowered, and soon he encouraged his sons to join him in singing the ribald marching songs of his army. Some were so scurrilous that Mintaka pleaded exhaustion and retired with her maids to the barge.

Mintaka lay on her mattress and listened to the sounds of revelry. She tried to compose herself to sleep, but Nefer was in the forefront of her mind. The sense of loss that she had held at bay all day, and her concern for Nefer's injuries, flooded back, and though she tried to prevent them, her tears welled up.

At last she sank into a black, dreamless sleep, from which she woke with difficulty, roused by drunken laughter and heavy footfalls from the deck over her head. It seemed that her father and her brothers were being carried on board. She had sipped only a little of the wine, but she felt herself drugged and her head ached. Almost immediately she succumbed to sleep again.

The next time she woke she believed that she was in a nightmare, for she could hear screams and she was choking on clouds of thick smoke. Before she was fully conscious she found herself bundled out of her bed, swaddled in a blanket and carried on deck. She struggled, but she was as helpless as an infant in a powerful grip.

On deck the moonless night was lit by leaping flames. They were roaring out of the forward hatch of the royal barge, climbing the masts and rigging in a hellish torrent. She had never seen a wooden hull burn before and the ferocity of the flames appalled her.

She could not stare at them for long, for she found herself carried swiftly across the deck and down the side into a waiting felucca. As it pushed off into the stream she fought to free herself, but the arms that pinioned her were remorseless. She managed to twist her head and see the face of the man who held her.

'Trok!' She was angered by his presumption, at the way he was ignoring her cries. 'Let me go! I command you!'

He did not respond. He held her easily but he was watching the burning galley with a calm, detached expression.

'Go back!' she shrieked. 'My family! Go back and fetch them!'

His only response was to snap an order to the oarsmen. 'Hold the stroke!' They shipped their paddles and the felucca rocked on the current. The crew watched the burning hulk with fascination. There were agonising screams from those trapped below the decks.

Suddenly the main hatch on the burning deck was thrown open, and a figure emerged. Lord Trok's arms tightened around Mintaka. 'It cannot be!' he grated.

Through the smoke and flames, Apepi staggered towards the side of the barge. He carried his youngest son, Khyan, in his arms, and his mouth was wide open, gasping for air.

'The monster is hard to kill.' Trok's anger was tinged with fear.

Even in her own distress Mintaka read the meaning of his words. 'You, Trok!' she whispered. 'You have done this to them!'

Trok ignored the accusation.

Apepi was no longer moving forward, but he stood with legs astraddle and lifted Khyan high above his head. Perhaps he was attempting to throw the boy over the ship's side into the river to escape the flames, but suddenly the deck under Apepi's feet burst open. He and his son dropped through, and in a tall fountain of flame, sparks and smoke were gone.

'It's over.' Trok's voice was dispassionate. He released Mintaka so suddenly that she fell into the bilges of the felucca. He looked at his horrified crew. 'Row to my galley,' he ordered.

'You did this to my family,' Mintaka repeated, as she lay at his feet. 'You will pay for it. I swear to you. I will make you pay.'

But she felt numbed. Her father was gone, that monumental figure in her life whom she had hated a little and loved a great deal. Her family was gone, all of her brothers, even Khyan. She had watched him burn and she knew that the horror of it would stay with her all her days.

The felucca drew alongside Lord Trok's galley and she made no protest as he carried her on board, then down to the main cabin. 'Your slave girls are safe. I will send them to you,' he said, and went out. She heard the locking bar placed across the door, then the sound of him climbing the companion ladder.

She hid her face in pillows that smelt of Trok's stale sweat and wept until her tears were exhausted. Then she slept.

THE BURNING HULL of Apepi's royal barge drifted up onto the river bank opposite the temple of Hapi. In the dawn the smoke rose high into the still air, tainted by the stench of burnt flesh. When Mintaka awoke the smell sickened her. The smoke seemed to act like a beacon, for the sun had hardly risen above the eastern hills before the fleet of Lord Naja came sweeping round the bend of the river.

The slave girls brought the news to Mintaka. 'Lord Naja has come in full array,' they told her excitedly. 'Yesterday he left us to return to Thebes. Is it not strange that he could reach here so soon when he should be twenty leagues upriver?'

'Surpassing strange,' Mintaka agreed grimly.

Her baggage had all gone up in flames in the royal barge, but her maids borrowed clothing from the other noble ladies in the fleet, and they dressed her in a simple linen shift, gold girdle and sandals.

Before noon an armed escort came aboard the galley, and she followed them on deck. Her eyes went to the blackened timbers of the royal barge that lay on the far bank, burnt down to the water line. It was her family's funeral pyre. With an effort she held back further tears, went down into the waiting felucca, and was taken to the bank where Lord Naja was waiting with all his company assembled.

She remained aloof and pale when he embraced her. 'This is a bitter time for all of us, Princess,' he said. 'Your father was a mighty warrior and statesman. In view of the recent treaty between the two kingdoms, he leaves a dangerous gap. For the good of all, this must be filled immediately.'

He took her hand and led her to the pavilion that had last evening been the scene of feasting and festivity, but where now were assembled in solemn conclave most of the nobility of both kingdoms.

She saw Trok in the forefront of this throng, and behind him in packed ranks all his officers, grim, cold-eyed and menacing. They stared at her, unsmiling, and she was bitterly aware that she was the last of the Apepi line, abandoned and unprotected.

She wondered to whom she could appeal, and whose loyalty she still commanded. She searched for friendly, familiar faces in the multitude. They were all there, her father's councillors and advisers, his generals and comrades of the battlefield. But their eyes slid away from her face. None smiled at her. She had never felt so alone.

Naja led her to a cushioned stool at one side of the pavilion. When she sat down, Naja and his staff formed a screen round her, hiding her from view. She was certain that this had been deliberately arranged.

Lord Naja opened the conclave with a lamentation for the death of King Apepi and his sons. Then he continued, 'In the tragic circumstances of his death, King Apepi leaves no male heir to the Crown.' Smoothly he passed over any mention of Mintaka. 'As a matter of urgency I have consulted the senior councillors of both kingdoms. Their choice for the new pharaoh has been unanimous. With one voice they have asked Lord Trok of Memphis to pick up the reins of power, to take the double crown upon himself and steer the nation forward.'

In the uproar that followed, strong hands took Mintaka and spirited her away through the cheering press. She struggled ineffectually, her voice unheard in the storm of cheering. On the river bank she twisted in the arms of her captors and glanced back. Over the heads of the crowd she glimpsed Lord Naja raising the double crown over the head of the new Pharaoh.

Then she was hustled down the bank to the waiting felucca, and back to her locked and guarded cabin on board Lord Trok's galley.

DURING THE VOYAGE downriver from Balasfura, Mintaka had the freedom of the deck while they were under way, but at anchor or at moorings she was locked in her cabin.

One morning Trok insisted that she join him for a lavish breakfast on the foredeck. There were twenty other guests, and Trok seated himself next to Mintaka. She pointedly ignored him and directed all her charm and wit to the officers of his army.

At the end of the meal Trok clapped his hands for attention, and was rewarded with an obsequious silence. 'Your Royal Highness,' he addressed her gravely, 'your divine father of illustrious memory must have had some premonition of the fate that awaited him. Before his tragic death he spoke to me. He placed you under my protection. I accepted this as a sacred charge. You need never appeal to any other for protection.' He placed his right hand upon her bowed head, and in the other hand he raised a scroll of parchment.

'This is my royal proclamation setting aside the betrothal of the Princess Mintaka of the House of Apepi to Pharaoh Nefer Seti of the House of Tamose. Furthermore, it contains a proclamation of the marriage of the Princess Mintaka to Pharaoh Trok Uruk. The proclamation has been ratified by the cartouche of Lord Naja, accepting and confirming it in the name of Pharaoh Nefer Seti.' He handed the scroll to his chamberlain with a terse instruction. 'Have one hundred copies made of this proclamation and cause them to be publicly displayed in every city in Egypt.'

Then, with both hands, he lifted Mintaka to her feet. 'You and I will be husband and wife before the rise of the Moon of Osiris.'

THREE DAYS LATER Pharaoh Trok Uruk arrived at Avaris, his military capital in the Lower Kingdom. The populace was delirious with joy at the news of the Treaty of Hathor, and at the promise of peace and prosperity in the years ahead. However, there was some dismay when one of the first acts of the new pharaoh was to put in hand another massive draft of men for the army. It soon became clear that he was intent on doubling the size of his infantry regiments and building two thousand more fighting chariots.

The question was asked, but not to Trok's face, where he expected to find an enemy now that Egypt was united and at peace. The loss of working men from fields and pastures to the army resulted in a shortage of food, and the expenditure on chariots and equipment necessitated an increase in taxation. There were mutters now that Apepi had not been as bad a ruler as they had believed him to be.

The muttering grew louder when Trok ordered work to commence on the extensive enlargements and refurbishment of the palace in Avaris into which he intended to move with his bride. The architects estimated these works would cost over two lakhs of gold.

A revolt started in the delta, where a regiment of foot, unpaid for over a year, murdered their officers and marched on Avaris. Trok met them with three hundred chariots near the village of Manashi and cut them to pieces with his first charge. He then impaled five hundred mutineers on stakes. Like a macabre forest, they decorated both sides of the road for half a league beyond the village.

A few hundred mutineers escaped the massacre and disappeared into the desert. Trok did not bother to pursue them, for this petty matter had delayed his wedding. He hurried back to Avaris, using up three pairs of horses in his furious impatience.

There his wedding with Princess Mintaka Apepi was carried out in the ancient Hyksosian tradition. First the high priest bound Mintaka to him with a halter rope, and then, at the culmination of the ceremony, Trok cut the throat of his favourite warhorse, a beautiful chestnut stallion, as a sign that he placed a higher value on his bride than on this other precious possession. As the animal fell, the company shouted their acclamation and lifted the couple into the flower-bedecked chariot.

Trok drove back to the palace with one arm firmly round his bride. The army lined the way, showering gifts of amulets and good-luck charms into the cockpit. Others held up bowls of wine to Trok as he drove past, and he gulped them down.

By the time they reached the palace, Trok was sweating and dusty from the ride, reckless with wine, and wild-eyed with lust.

He carried Mintaka through the crowd into their new apartments, and the guards at the door turned back the wedding guests with drawn swords. However, they did not disperse but surrounded the palace, chanting encouragement to the bridegroom and ribald advice to the bride.

In the bedchamber Trok threw Mintaka onto the white sheepskin that covered the mattress, and used both hands to struggle with his sword-belt, trying to loosen the clasp. Mintaka leapt up and raced to the terrace door but locking bars on the outside had been put in place. Desperately she tried to beat open the panels, but the doors were thick and did not even tremble to her onslaught.

Behind her, Trok had at last rid himself of the sword-belt and came lumbering unsteadily after her. 'Fight as much as you wish,' he slurred. 'It sets me on fire when you kick and scream.'

He placed one arm round her waist, and threw her down again, this time pinning her with one huge muscular arm across her chest. His face was inches from hers. His beard prickled her cheeks, and his breath smelt of sour wine. She twisted her face away. He laughed and hooked one finger in the neck of her shift and ripped the silk to below her waist.

He straddled her, sitting across her lower body with all his weight so that she could not struggle, and tore off his tunic. Under it he was naked, and although her vision was distorted by terror, she had an impression of wide shoulders and bulging muscle, limbs thick and thewy as the branches of a cedar of Lebanon.

Still pinning her under him, he twisted round until his belly pressed against hers. He tried to force a knee between her thighs, but she kept them locked together, hooking one of her legs over the other. She fought not only for her modesty, but as if for her very life. Every muscle in her lower body was frozen in a rigor of fear and revulsion, hard and as impenetrable as a granite statue.

Suddenly he swung a heavy blow, flat-handed, across her face. It jarred her clenched jaws, crushing her lips. She felt blood flood into her mouth and darkness fill her head and knew she could not last out much longer.

'Hathor, help me!' She closed her eyes and prayed. 'Sweet goddess, do not let it happen!'

She heard him groan above her, and her eyes flew open. She saw him arch his back and he moaned as though in pain. Mintaka did not understand what was happening. For a moment she thought the goddess must have heard her plea and struck him through the heart with a divine dart. Then she felt hot liquid spray onto her stomach. She tried to twist away to avoid it, but he was too heavy and strong.

At last, he groaned and collapsed on top of her. Then he roused himself and looked down at her. 'You have shamed me, you little slut. You have made me spill my seed in vain.'

Before she knew what he was about, he had grabbed her by the back of her neck and forced her face into the white sheepskin.

'Never fear, I shall use the blood from your nose if I can't have it from your honeypot.' He rolled her aside and inspected the crimson stain from her bleeding face on the pure white wool with grim satisfaction. Then he jumped to his feet, strode to the shutters and kicked them open with a crash. He disappeared out into the bright daylight.

His sword-belt lay where he had dropped it. Quietly Mintaka slipped from the bed and drew the burnished bronze blade from its scabbard. She crept to the door that led onto the terrace and flattened herself against the jamb.

Out on the balcony, Trok was acknowledging the applause of the crowd and flapping the stained sheepskin for all to see. Mintaka tightened her grip on the haft of the sword and gathered herself.

'Farewell, my friends,' Trok shouted. 'I am going back for another bite at that sweet fig.'

She heard his bare feet swish on the tiles as he returned and then his shadow fell across the entrance. She drew back the heavy sword with both hands, and held the point at belly height.

As he stepped into the chamber she braced herself and then with all her strength thrust at him. But Trok possessed a feral instinct for danger and twisted away from the sharp bronze point. It flew the width of a finger past his hairy stomach, without drawing a drop of blood. Then he clamped both her wrists in one of his huge paws and squeezed until she had to let the weapon drop.

He was laughing as he dragged her across the room, but it was an ugly sound. He threw her face down onto the rumpled, sweat-sour bed, and picked up the sword scabbard from where it lay. 'This lesson in obedience is for your own good. A little pain now will save us both a great deal of unhappiness and suffering later.'

The scabbard was of polished leather, bound with gold and studded with metal rosettes. He swung it down across the back of her naked legs. It left a welt with the pattern of rosettes in brighter scarlet.

He lifted the scabbard again. She tried to roll away from him but the next blow caught her across her raised right arm, and the next across her shoulder. Then he knocked her off the bed and when she rolled herself into a ball he lashed her across her back. He spoke to her while he kept the blows falling. 'You will never lift a hand to me again! Next time I come to you, you will behave as a loving wife, or I will have four of my men hold you down while I mount you!'

She clenched her jaws as the blows rained down upon her until mercifully he stepped away, breathing heavily, and pulled on his dust-streaked tunic. He stalked to the door of the chamber. There he paused and looked back at her.

'Remember one thing, wife. Either I break my mares,' he said, 'or, by Seueth, they die under me.' He turned and was gone.

IT WAS LONG after the waning of the Moon of Isis before Mintaka's bruises faded to greenish-yellow stains on her smooth, creamy skin.

Since their calamitous wedding day Trok had left her alone. Most of that time he was campaigning in the south. Even when he returned for brief periods to Avaris he avoided her. Perhaps he was repelled by her unsightly injuries or shamed by his failure to consummate their marriage. Mintaka did not ponder the reason too deeply, but she rejoiced in being free of his brutish attentions.

There had been further serious rebellion in the south of the kingdom, and Mintaka knew that Trok had returned triumphantly to Avaris three days ago, but she had still not seen him. She thanked the goddess for that, but it was premature. The summons came from him on the fourth day. Mintaka was to attend an extraordinary session of the state council. His message warned her that should she choose to ignore his summons he would send his bodyguards to drag her to the conclave. She had no option.

This was the first occasion on which Mintaka had appeared in public since her wedding. With her make-up carefully applied she was as lovely as ever as she took her seat on the queen's throne, below that of Pharaoh, in the lavishly redecorated assembly hall of the palace.

Trok acknowledged the herald, then called upon him to rise and state his news to the council. When he rose to his feet Mintaka saw that he was in the grip of deep emotion. 'Sacred Majesty, I bring tragic tidings from Thebes.' He paused and spread his arms in a gesture of despair. 'Last month, on the eve of the festival of Hapi, the young Pharaoh Nefer Seti, whom we all loved, and in whom we placed so much trust and hope, died of the grievous wounds that he received while hunting.' There was a concerted sigh of despair.

The herald spoke again: 'The Regent of the Upper Kingdom, Lord Naja, who is next in succession, has been raised to the throne in the place of the departed Pharaoh. He purifies the land in his name, he endures unto eternity in his name of Naja, the fear of him through all the world is great in his name of Pharaoh Naja Kiafan.'

The cries of mourning for the dead Pharaoh and the clamour of acclamation for his successor filled the hall.

In the uproar, Mintaka stared at the herald. Trok was watching her and she knew he was revelling in her pain. She listened to the rest of the proceedings, but her thoughts were with Nefer. In her mind a picture of him appeared as though he still lived. She wondered what point he had reached on his dread journey through the netherworld, and she prayed for his safety. She prayed for him to reach the green hills of paradise, and that she should soon be reunited with him there. I shall follow you soon, my heart, she promised him.

TAITA HAD BROUGHT Nefer back to Thebes from Dabba still in a deep sleep. As soon as the galley carrying them moored at the stone jetty below the palace, Taita had him carried ashore on a curtained litter. It would have been unwise to allow Pharaoh's critical condition to become widely known.

Once Nefer was safe in his royal quarters at the palace, Taita was able to work on him in seclusion. His first concern was to examine again the boy's terrible lacerations and assess if there had been any morbid changes.

He unwrapped the bandages, probed the openings gently, and was greatly relieved to find no taint of contamination. He syringed the deepest wounds with a mixture of vinegar and oriental spices. Then he stitched them closed with catgut and bandaged them.

He was rewarded when at last Nefer recovered consciousness and smiled at him. 'Taita, I knew you were with me.'

The following day he sat up and ate a meal of millet bread and chickpea soup. Then he looked around him. 'Where is Mintaka?'

When Taita explained her absence, Nefer's disappointment was almost palpable. Taita tried to console him by telling him that he would soon be well enough to visit Avaris.

The next day the terrible news of the tragedy at Balasfura reached Thebes from the Lower Kingdom. Nefer tried to convince Taita that he was strong enough to make the long journey to be with Mintaka in her bereavement. Gently Taita dissuaded him, but promised that as soon as Nefer was strong enough he would use all his influence to convince Lord Naja to allow him to go. With this goal to strive towards, Nefer rallied strongly. Taita could see him subduing the evil humours in his blood by sheer strength of will.

Lord Naja returned from the north, and within hours Heseret came to visit Nefer for the first time since his mauling by the lion. She brought him gifts of sweetmeats and a pot of wild honey in the comb, excusing herself for having neglected him.

'My dear husband, the Regent of the Upper Kingdom, has been away all these weeks,' she explained, 'and I have pined so much for his return that I was afraid that my unhappiness might affect you badly, my poor darling.' She stayed an hour, sang to him, and related some of the scandalous doings of the court. At last she excused herself: 'My husband does not like me to leave his side for long. We are so much in love, Nefer. He is a wonderful man. You must learn to trust him completely, as I do.'

She rose to her feet and then, as though in an afterthought, she remarked lightly, 'You must have been relieved to hear that Pharaoh Trok Uruk and my dear husband, the Regent of Upper Egypt, have agreed to cancel your betrothal to that little Hyksosian barbarian, Mintaka. I was so sorry for you when I heard that such a disgraceful marriage had been thrust upon you. My husband was against it from the beginning, as I was.'

After she had gone Nefer sank back weakly on the pillow and

closed his eyes. When Taita came to him a little later he was puzzled by the way in which he had relapsed. He stayed with him through that night, exerting all his powers to ward off the shadows of evil that surrounded the young Pharaoh.

At dawn he was startled to hear Lord Naja's commanding voice ordering the guards at the door to stand aside. The regent strode into the chamber and, without greeting Taita, stooped over Nefer's still form and peered into his face. After a long moment he straightened up and signed to Taita to follow him onto the terrace.

'You wished to speak to me, my lord?' Taita asked.

Naja turned to him. His expression was grim. 'You have disappointed me, old man,' he said, and Taita bowed his head but made no reply. 'I had hoped that my way forwards would be cleared by now of impediment.' He stared hard at Taita. 'Yet it seems that, far from allowing this, you have done all in your power to prevent it.'

'This has been pretence. I have merely made a show of caring for my patient. As you can see for yourself, Pharaoh hangs over the great abyss.' Taita made a gesture towards the sick chamber where Nefer lay. 'Surely you can sense the shades drawing in around him. My lord, we have almost obtained our object. Within days the way ahead will be cleared for you.'

Naja was not convinced. 'I am reaching the limit of my patience,' he warned, and strode from the terrace. He passed through the chamber without another glance at the still form upon the bed.

During that day Nefer's condition fluctuated. Taita sat for a while collecting his thoughts, reviewing the plans he had laid so carefully over the past weeks. He could not do it alone, and would have to rely on others, but he had chosen the best. They were ready to act, and they had been waiting for his word. He could delay no longer.

AT HIS BIDDING the slaves brought kettles of hot water and Taita washed Nefer from head to foot.

When he had finished, he warned the guards not to let anybody pass, and barred all the entrances to the chamber. He prayed for a while and then threw incense on the brazier, and in the blue and aromatic smoke made an ancient, potent incantation to Anubis, the god of death and cemeteries.

Only then did he prepare the elixir of Anubis in a new and

unused vessel. He warmed the mixture on the brazier until it was the temperature of blood, and took it to the bed where Nefer was sleeping quietly. Gently he turned his head to one side and poured the elixir into the eardrum a drop at a time. Carefully he wiped away the excess, taking care that it should not touch his own skin. Then he plugged Nefer's ear with a small ball of wool, pushed deeply into the passage.

He watched Nefer's chest rise and fall to his breathing. Each breath was slower and the intervals between them longer. At last they ceased altogether. He placed two fingers on Nefer's throat beneath his ear, and felt the slow deliberate pulsing of the life force within him. Gradually that also faded away until it was only an occasional flutter that took all his skill and experience to detect.

Gently he closed the boy's eyes and placed an amulet upon the lids in the traditional preparation of the corpse. Next he bound a strip of linen over them, and another under his jaw to keep his mouth from gaping open. At last he went to the door and removed the locking bar.

'Send word to the Regent of the Upper Kingdom. He should come immediately to hear terrible tidings of Pharaoh.'

Lord Naja arrived with surprising alacrity. Princess Heseret was with him, and they were followed by the Assyrian doctor, Noom, and most of the members of the council.

Heseret was weeping ostentatiously and covering her eyes with an embroidered linen shawl. Naja glanced at the bandaged body laid out on the couch, then glanced at Taita with a question in his eyes. In reply Taita nodded slightly. Naja masked the gleam of triumph in his eyes, then clapped his hands.

'Let the good doctor Noom come forward,' Naja ordered. 'Let him confirm the Magus's pronouncement of Pharaoh's death.'

The Assyrian's long locks had been curled with hot tongs and dangled to his shoulders. His beard had also been curled in the fashion of Babylon. His robe swept the floor and was decorated with embroidered magical symbols. He knelt beside the deathbed and began an examination of the corpse. He sniffed at Nefer's lips, then placed his ear against Nefer's chest and listened. Taita had placed much store in the Assyrian's ineptitude.

Then Noom took a long silver pin from the hem of his robe and opened Nefer's limp hand. He pricked the point deeply up under the fingernail and watched for a muscular reaction. At last he stood up slowly, and shook his head. 'Pharaoh is dead,' he announced.

Lord Naja threw back his head and gave the first cry of lamentation, and Heseret, standing behind him, took up the wailing cry.

Taita waited for the mourners to file past the couch, and one by one to leave the chamber. When only Naja and Heseret remained, Taita stepped forward.

'Lord Naja, I beg your indulgence. You are aware that I have been Pharaoh Nefer Seti's tutor and servant since his birth. I owe him respect and duty, even now in death. I beg you to allow me to be the one to convey his corpse to the Hall of Sorrow, and there to make the incision to remove his heart and viscera. I would take that as the greatest honour you could bestow on me.'

Lord Naja thought for a while, then nodded. 'You have earned that honour. I charge you with the duty of conveying Pharaoh's sacred body to the funeral temple for embalming.'

THE OLD WARRIOR, Hilto, came swiftly to Taita's summons. He had been waiting in the guardroom at the palace gates. With him he brought four of his most trusted men. One of these was Meren, the friend and companion of Nefer's childhood. He was now a handsome ensign of the guards, and Taita had asked for him particularly.

Between them they carried the long woven basket that the embalmers used to transport their cadavers to the funerary temple. It was heavier than one might have expected.

Taita let them into the death chamber and whispered to Hilto, 'Swiftly now! Every second is precious.'

He had already wrapped Nefer in a long white winding sheet, with a loose fold of linen covering his face. The pallbearers laid the basket beside the couch and lifted Nefer into it. Taita closed the lid, and nodded. 'To the temple,' he said. 'All is in readiness.'

Taita trusted his leather instrument bag to Meren, and they moved quickly through the passages and courtyards of the palace. The sounds of mourning and lamentation followed them. The guards lowered the points of their weapons and knelt as the dead Pharaoh passed. The women covered their faces and wailed.

In the entrance courtyard a squadron of Hilto's chariots was drawn up with the horses in the traces. The bearers laid the basket on the footplate of the leading chariot and secured it. Taita mounted and took the reins. The rams' horns of the regiment sounded a dirge, and the column moved out through the gates at a walk.

The news of Pharaoh's death had spread throughout the city. Crowds lined the route along the river. Women ran forward and threw sacred lotus blossoms onto the basket.

Taita pushed the horses into a trot, then into a canter, desperate to get the basket into the sanctuary of the funerary temple.

The tall, rose-coloured granite walls and portico of the temple were set upon a low prominence overlooking the river. The priests, hastily assembled, were waiting to greet the column. Their heads were freshly shaven and anointed with oil. Taita drove up the wide causeway and halted the chariot at the foot of the staircase that mounted to the Hall of Sorrow.

Hilto and his warriors lifted the basket and climbed the staircase with it balanced on their shoulders. The priests fell in behind them, singing mournfully. Before the open wooden doors of the Hall of Sorrow the pallbearers paused, and Taita looked back at the priests.

'By the grace and authority of the Regent of Egypt, I, Taita, have been charged with lifting Pharaoh's viscera.' He fixed the high priest with a mesmeric gaze. 'All others will wait without while I perform this sacred charge.'

Taita led the bearers through the doorway and they solemnly laid the basket on the floor beside the black diorite slab in the centre of the Hall of Sorrow. Hilto closed the doors with great dignity in the faces of the assembled priests, then hurried back to Taita's side. Between them they opened the basket and lifted Nefer's body. They laid it on the black slab.

Taita folded back the cloth that covered Nefer's face, gently turned his head to one side and nodded at Meren, who placed the leather bag close to his right hand and opened it. Taita selected the ivory forceps, slipped the points into Nefer's ear and drew out the woollen plug. Through a gold tube he carefully sluiced the dregs of the elixir of Anubis from Nefer's eardrum. He had the antidote ready in another phial. When he opened the stopper it released a sharp odour of camphor and sulphur. Hilto helped him to lift Nefer into a sitting position and Taita administered the entire contents of the phial.

Suddenly Nefer coughed harshly. Taita massaged Nefer's bare back and he coughed again, vomiting yellow bile. While Taita kept working steadily at reviving him, Hilto ordered his men to their knees and made them swear a dreadful oath of secrecy as to all that they were witnessing.

Satisfied at last, Taita rewrapped Nefer in the linen sheet, turned back to the basket, and lifted out the false bottom to reveal another corpse laid in the compartment beneath, also wrapped in a white linen winding sheet.

Under Taita's sharp eye they changed the two bodies. They laid Nefer in the hidden compartment in the bottom of the basket, and Meren squatted beside it to watch him and check his condition. The others laid the strange corpse on the diorite slab.

Taita swept away the winding sheet and revealed the body of a youth of about the same age and bodily shape of Nefer. He had the same thick dark hair. The young thief had been put to death by strangulation that very morning and his body was not yet cold.

The Canopic jars were arranged in the small shrine at the end of the hall. Taita ordered Meren to fetch them and open the stoppers ready for filling. While he was doing this, Taita rolled the corpse over and made a sweeping incision down his left side. There was little time for surgical finesse. He thrust his hand into the opening and drew forth the viscera. Then he cut through the diaphragm to gain access to the chest cavity, reaching deep until he could sever the windpipe above its juncture with the lungs. When all the contents of the interior of the chest and abdomen were unanchored, he brought them out onto the diorite slab in a single mass. Meren blanched, fled to the stone basin in the corner and puked noisily into it.

Bloodied to the elbows, Taita flushed out the contents of the stomach and entrails and packed them into their jars. He filled every jar with the pickling natron salts, and sealed the stoppers. Then he washed his hands and arms in the bronze basins filled with water expressly for that purpose.

Working with controlled haste, Taita stitched the abdominal incision closed. Then he bandaged the head until its features were hidden. When that was done, he and Hilto carried the corpse to the large natron bath and lowered it into the harsh alkali mixture, which would leach the fats out of the body and peel the skin away. It would remain in the bath, with the head covered, for the next sixty days. At the end of that time the priests would remove the bandage and discover the substitution. By then, however, Taita and Nefer would be far away.

It took only a little longer to sluice down the slab and pack Taita's instruments before they were ready to leave. Taita knelt beside the basket in which Nefer lay, and laid a hand on his chest to feel its warmth and check his breathing. It was slow and even. Satisfied, he stood up and gestured for Hilto to cover the hidden compartment. When this was done the bearers lifted the basket and Taita led them to the doors. As they approached Hilto threw them open, and the assembly of priests craned forward. They gave the empty basket only a cursory glance as it was carried out, then rushed into the Hall of Sorrow with almost indecent haste.

Ignored by the crowds that had gathered outside the temple, Taita's men loaded the basket onto the leading chariot and drove it to the guard's barracks near the east gate. There the basket was carried through the back entrance of Hilto's private quarters. Here, everything was in readiness. They lifted Nefer out and Taita went to work to revive him fully. Within hours he was well enough to eat a little millet bread and drink a bowl of warm milk and honey.

At last Taita judged it safe to leave him for a while, and drove through the narrow streets. Ahead of him he heard the sudden din of wild cheering. At the palace he found himself enveloped in a dense crowd of citizens celebrating the ascension of the new pharaoh. 'Eternal life to His Sacred Majesty Pharaoh Naja Kiafan!' they cried with loyal fervour, and passed the wine jugs from hand to hand.

The palace guards recognised Taita, and used the butts of their spears to clear the way for him to pass. Once he was in the grounds he hurried to the great hall, and there he found another press of obsequious humanity, waiting to swear fealty.

Pharaoh Naja Kiafan and his queen were in the private cabinet beyond the doors at the end of the hall, but Taita had to wait only a short while before he was granted access to the royal presence.

Naja was already wearing the double crown, and holding the flail and the crook crossed over his chest. Beside him Queen Heseret was as lovely as Taita had ever known her. When Taita entered, Naja dismissed those around him and soon the three were alone. Then Naja laid aside the scourge and the sceptre and came to embrace Taita.

'Magus, I should never have doubted you,' he said. 'You have earned my gratitude.' He took from his right hand a magnificent ring of gold and ruby, and placed it on Taita's right index finger. 'This is but a small token of my favour.'

Heseret came forward and kissed him. 'Dearest Taita, you have always been faithful to my family. You shall have gold, land and influence beyond anything you have ever coveted.'

After all these years she knew so little of him. 'Your generosity is exceeded only by your beauty,' he said. Then he turned back to Naja. 'I have done what the gods required of me, Your Grace, but it has cost me dear. You know that I loved Nefer. Now I owe you that same love. But I must mourn Nefer, and make my peace with his shade.'

'It would be strange indeed if you did not feel for the dead Pharaoh,' Naja agreed. 'What do you wish of me, Magus? You have only to speak.'

'Your Grace, I ask to go into the desert to be alone for a time.'

'How long?' Naja asked, and Taita could see he was alarmed by the thought of losing the key to eternal life, which he truly believed Taita held in his hands.

'Not too long, Majesty,' Taita assured him.

Naja thought about it for a while. He was never a man for hasty decisions. At last he sighed. 'You may absent yourself until the next inundation of the Nile begins, but then you must return to me.' Swiftly he wrote out a safe pass and sealed it with his cartouche. 'This will allow you to travel at large and avail yourself of whatever food and equipment you may need from my royal storehouses.'

Taita prostrated himself in gratitude, but Naja lifted him to his feet in another act of condescension. 'Go, Magus! But return to us on the appointed day to receive the rewards you so richly deserve.'

Clutching the roll of papyrus Taita backed towards the door making the signs of blessing and benediction.

THEY LEFT THEBES early the next morning while most of the city still slept and the guards at the east gate were yawning and heavy-eyed.

Nefer was laid in the back of the wagon, which was drawn by a team of four horses and loaded with essential supplies and the equipment they might need once they had left the river valley. Hilto was dressed as a wealthy farmer and Meren as his son.

Nefer was laid on a straw mattress in the bed of the wagon, under a screen of tanned leather. He was now fully conscious and able to understand all that Taita had to tell him. When the sergeant of the guard climbed into the wagon to inspect the contents, Nefer peered out at him with his gaunt features spotted with the unmistakable stigmata of the plague that Taita had applied. The sergeant swore with horror and leapt down.

'Get you gone!' he shouted. 'Take that poxy wretch out of the city.'

It took them several days to cross the littoral plain of the river and reach the hills that marked the frontiers of the desert, following the old trade route eastwards towards the Red Sea. Now Nefer was able to climb down from the wagon, and for short periods limp along beside it. Soon he was walking more easily and for longer periods.

They rested for three days at the ancient ruined city of Gallala. They refilled the water-skins at the well and let the horses recover from the rigours of the hard, stony road. When they were fit to resume the journey, they travelled in the cool of the night, and took the path known only to Taita that led to Gebel Nagara. Hilto swept their back-trail and covered all signs of their passage.

They arrived in the cave in the middle of a night lit by bright stars. There was not enough water in the tiny seep to supply so many men and horses, so once the wagon was unloaded Hilto started back, leaving Meren to serve Taita and Nefer. Hilto had resigned from his regiment on the pretext of ill health, so he was free to return with every full moon to bring supplies, medicine and news from Thebes.

The first month at Gebel Nagara passed swiftly. In the clean, dry desert air Nefer's wounds healed fully, and soon he was limping out into the desert to hunt with Meren.

At the end of that month Hilto returned from Thebes with the news that Taita's subterfuge had not yet been discovered. He also brought news of insurrections in the Lower Kingdom, and unrest in the Upper Kingdom also, where Naja, like Trok, had increased taxation and ordered an enlistment of men into the army.

'What other news have you from the Lower Kingdom?' Nefer asked eagerly. 'What news is there of Princess Mintaka?'

Hilto looked puzzled. 'None that I know of. I should think she is in Avaris, but I cannot be certain.'

The following evening, Hilto left Gebel Nagara at the setting of the sun, and struck out into the wilderness.

THE NEXT MOON passed more swiftly than the last, as Nefer grew stronger and more restless. Each day his limp became less noticeable. On his latest visit, Hilto had brought with him a full-weight war-bow. Under Taita's instruction Nefer now practised with it every day, building up the muscles in his back and shoulders. Hilto had also brought them a rack of heavy sickle swords, and Taita would bring them out and lead Nefer and Meren through the entire repertoire of cuts, thrusts and parries.

On other evenings Nefer and Meren stripped naked, oiled their bodies and wrestled, while Taita umpired their bouts and called advice and instruction. Then, late into the night, Taita and Nefer sat by the fire and debated every subject from medicine and politics to war and religion. Often Taita placed hidden traps and illogicalities in these lessons, and more often now, and with greater alacrity, Nefer would uncover and question them.

The month passed so swiftly that it was with a small shock of surprise that Nefer, while running through the desert in pursuit of a gazelle, suddenly noticed on the horizon the distant shape of the wagon returning from the river valley. On the instant, he forgot the gazelle he was chasing and raced to meet Hilto.

'Hilto!' Nefer yelled, still at a distance. 'What news? What news?'

Hilto pretended to misunderstand the question, and as Nefer walked at his side he began a long-winded recital of political events in the kingdoms. 'There has been another rebellion in the north. This time Trok found it harder to put down. He lost four hundred men and half the rebels escaped his wrath.'

Later, around the campfire in the cave, it was agony for Nefer to have to listen to Hilto making a long, detailed report to Taita, the most important part of which was that the substitution of bodies had been discovered when the priests of Anubis had unwrapped the head of the corpse in the Hall of Sorrow. Pharaoh Naja Kiafan had done his best to prevent the news becoming public knowledge, for the foundations of his throne would be undermined if the populace suspected that Nefer was still alive. However, it was impossible to keep such an extraordinary event secret, and rumours were rife in Thebes and the outlying towns and villages.

Added to this, trouble was brewing in the east. The Egyptian pharaohs had sent word to King Sargon of Babylon, that mighty kingdom between the Tigris and Euphrates, demanding that Sargon's annual tribute be increased to twenty lakhs of gold. It was a crippling amount to which Sargon could never agree.

'So, this accounts for the build-up of the armies in both kingdoms,' Taita said, as Hilto paused in his report. 'It is clear at last that the two pharaohs are greedy for the riches of Babylon. They are intent on conquest. They know too that war is a uniting factor. If they march on Mesopotamia the populace will rally behind them in a patriotic frenzy. It is a marvellous way to take the minds of the people off their grievances.'

'Yes.' Hilto nodded. 'You are right.'

'Of course, this is to our advantage,' Taita mused. 'I have been seeking a haven for us. If he is at war with Trok and Naja, then Sargon will welcome us to his side.'

'We are leaving Egypt?' Hilto interjected.

Taita explained, 'Now that Naja and Trok know that Nefer still lives, they will come after us. The road to the east is the only one open to us. It will not be for long, just until we have built up our strength and support throughout the two kingdoms and have made ourselves powerful allies. Then we will return to reclaim Pharaoh Nefer's birthright.'

They stared at him. It was Nefer who broke the silence. 'We can't do that,' he said. 'I cannot leave Egypt. I took an oath on my life and eternal spirit that I would not desert Mintaka.' He turned to Hilto. 'You have been evading my questions, Hilto. What news do you have of the princess?'

Hilto opened and closed his mouth, trying to find the courage to tell him the dire news.

'Speak!' Nefer ordered. 'Have you forgotten your duty?'

'Gracious Majesty, the news will not please you. Six weeks ago the Princess Mintaka was married in Avaris to Pharaoh Trok Uruk.'

Nefer stood as still as if he had been turned into a granite statue. For a long time the only sound in the cave was the crackle of the acacia logs in the fire. Then without another word, Nefer stood up and walked out into the desert night.

When he returned the dawn was a faint red promise in the eastern sky. Hilto and Meren were wrapped in their sheepskins at the back of the cave, but Taita sat in exactly the same position as Nefer had left him. For a moment he thought that the old man was asleep also. Then Taita raised his head and looked at him.

'I need you now, more than ever, old friend,' said Nefer. 'You will not desert me?'

'You need not ask,' Taita said softly.

'I cannot leave her with Trok,' Nefer said.

'No.'

Nefer came back to his seat opposite Taita. He picked up a charred stump of firewood and pushed it deeper into the flames. Then he looked up at Taita again. 'You have tried to teach me to overlook at a distance,' he said. 'I have never acquired the gift. Not until this night. Out there in the darkness, I tried to overlook Mintaka. This time I saw something, Taita, but only dimly.'

'Your love for her has made you sensitive to her aura,' Taita explained. 'What did you see?'

'I saw only shadows, but sensed sorrow and grief and despair so insupportable that it made me wish for death. I knew that these were Mintaka's emotions and not my own.'

Taita stared expressionlessly into the fire, and Nefer went on, 'You must overlook her for me. There is something terribly wrong. Only you can help her now, Taita.'

'Do you have anything of Mintaka's?' the old man asked. 'Any gift or token that she gave you?'

Nefer's hand went to the necklace at his throat. He touched the tiny golden locket that hung in its centre. 'It is my most precious possession. It contains a lock of her hair.'

'Then it is highly potent. It contains her essence. Give it to me, if you wish me to help her.'

Nefer opened the clasp and passed him the amulet.

'Wait here,' Taita said, and stood up. He went out into the dawn and climbed to the crest of the dunes, then squatted in the sand, facing the rising sun. He pressed Mintaka's amulet to his forehead and closed his eyes. It seemed to take on some strange life of its own, pulsing softly in rhythm with his own heartbeats. Taita opened his mind and let the currents of existence enter freely, swirling round him like a great river. His own spirit broke free of his body and he soared aloft. In his mind he called for her, Mintaka! He felt the amulet grow warm then burning hot in his hand.

Slowly the images cleared away, and he heard her sweet voice reply, 'I am here. Who is it that calls?'

'Mintaka, it is Taita,' he replied, but he was aware that something evil had intervened and broken the stream between them. He focused all his powers upon it, trying to disperse the dark clouds. They seemed to coalesce, and took the shape of a rearing cobra. Suddenly he knew this was a direct and mortal threat against Mintaka. He redoubled his efforts to reach her, but so much pain and grief interposed between them that it was an impenetrable barrier.

Then he saw a hand, slim and graceful, reach out towards the sinister scaly head. It was Mintaka's hand and Taita understood. Mintaka, overwhelmed with grief, was about to take the way of the goddess and find peace in her bosom.

He held the serpent in check with all his life force, and prevented it from striking Mintaka's hand as she stroked the back of its hood. 'Mintaka!' He exerted himself to reach her, and was rewarded.

'Taita?' she whispered, and because Mintaka was at last aware of him, Taita's view expanded so that he could see it all clearly.

Mintaka was in a stone-walled bedchamber. She was kneeling in front of a large basket woven from palm fronds. Out of it reared the deadly snake.

'You must not take this road,' Taita ordered her. 'It is not for you. The gods have prepared a different destiny for you. Do you hear me?'

'Yes!' Mintaka turned her head, as though she could see his face.

'Nefer is alive. Nefer lives. Do you hear me?'

'Yes! Oh, yes.'

'Be strong, Mintaka. Nefer and I will come for you.'

So fierce was his concentration that he dug his fingernails deeply into the palms of his hands until the blood welled, but he could hold her no longer. She began to slip away from him, but before she was gone he saw her smile, full of love and renewed hope.

'Be strong!' he urged her. 'Be strong, Mintaka!' The echo of his voice came back to him as though from a great distance.

NEFER WAS WAITING for him at the foot of the dunes. When Taita was only halfway down the boy realised that something momentous had taken place. 'You saw her!' he shouted, and ran forward. 'What has happened to her?'

'She needs us,' Taita said, and laid a hand on Nefer's shoulder. He could never tell him of the despair in which he had found Mintaka, nor of the fate she had prepared for herself. It might drive him to some wild endeavour. 'You were right,' Taita went on. 'All my plans to leave this land and find sanctuary in the east must be set aside. We have to go to Mintaka. I have promised her that.'

'Yes!' Nefer agreed. 'When can we leave for Avaris?'

Taita replied, 'There is great urgency. We will leave at once.'

IT TOOK THEM FIFTEEN DAYS of hard travel to reach the tiny garrison station of Thane, a day's travel south of Avaris. En route, they discussed their plans endlessly, knowing that they were pitted against the might of Pharaoh Trok Uruk. The officers they spoke to at the garrisons and camps they passed estimated that Trok now had twenty-seven fully trained and equipped regiments at his disposal and almost three thousand chariots. To oppose this multitude they had a wagon showing the effects of long, hard service, with a back wheel that had a propensity to fall off at the most inappropriate times. There were only the four of them: Nefer and Meren, Hilto and Taita.

Hilto knew the captain in charge of the encampment at Thane, a grizzled old warrior named Socco. Long ago they had fought, roistered and whored together. After they had reminisced for an hour and shared a pot of sour beer, Hilto handed him the requisition scroll that Naja had given to Taita. Socco held it upside down at arm's length and looked wise.

'See the cartouche of Pharaoh.' Hilto touched the seal.

'If I know you at all, Hilto, you probably drew that pretty picture yourself.' Socco handed back the scroll. 'What do you need, you old rogue?'

They selected fresh horses, then Taita went over the ranks of parked chariots in the garrison pool that had just been sent out from the makers in Avaris. He chose three vehicles, and they harnessed the fresh horses.

When they left Thane, Taita was driving the old wagon, while Meren, Hilto and Nefer each drove a chariot. They did not head directly for Avaris but made a detour to a small oasis on the edge of the desert to the east of the city.

While the others unloaded the wagon, Taita went to barter with the Assyrian master of a caravan that was encamped nearby. He bought an armful of tattered clothing and twenty woollen rugs for an extortionate price. 'That Assyrian ape is a robber,' he muttered, as they loaded the carpets onto the wagon.

That night Taita dyed his silver hair with an extract of mimosa bark, which altered his appearance dramatically. In the darkness of early morning they left Meren in charge of the horses and chariots, got into the dilapidated wagon and, sitting on the pile of carpets, headed west towards Avaris. They were dressed in the castoffs that Taita had procured. Taita wore a long robe and sash, the lower half of his face veiled in the fashion of a citizen of the Chaldeans. With his dyed dark hair he was unrecognisable as the Magus.

When they reached the royal city of the north, Hilto went to tour the taverns of the old quarter where he hoped to gather news from former comrades-in-arms. Taita and Nefer made their way to the palace gates, and spent the morning listening to the chatter of those around them, and gossiping with other idlers.

At last Taita struck up a conversation with a merchant from Babylon, who introduced himself as Nintura. The two shared a pot of coffee and Taita exerted all his wiles to charm Nintura, who had been loitering outside the palace for the last ten days, waiting for his turn to display his wares to Trok's new bride.

'They say that Trok has been cruelly treated by his young wife. She will not allow him into her bed.' Nintura chuckled. 'He is wild for her, and is trying to win her favours with expensive gifts. They say he will refuse her nothing.'

'Where is Trok now?' Taita asked.

'He is campaigning in the south,' Nintura replied. 'He is stamping out the flames of rebellion, but no sooner does he turn his back than they flare up again behind him.'

'Whom should I approach to enter the presence of his queen?'

'The palace vizier. Soleth is his name, the fat, gelded freak.' Nintura had not realised Taita's own condition.

Taita knew Soleth only by reputation and that he was one of the secret brotherhood of eunuchs. 'Where can I find him?' Taita asked.

'It will cost you a gold ring just to enter his presence,' Nintura warned him.

Soleth was sitting beside the lotus pond in his own walled garden when Taita was brought to him. Taita made a dignified salutation as he introduced himself under an assumed name. He followed that with the recognition sign of the brotherhood. Soleth waved to Taita to seat himself on the cushions opposite him, and they swiftly established Taita's credentials and common acquaintances within the brotherhood. Without seeming to do so, Soleth was studying Taita's features. At last he asked softly, 'In your travels you might have met the famous Magus, known through both kingdoms as Taita?'

'I know Taita well,' Taita agreed.

'Perhaps as well as you know yourself?' Soleth asked.

'At least as well as I know myself,' Taita affirmed.

Soleth's chubby face creased in a smile. 'Say no more. What service can I perform for you? You need only ask.'

THAT EVENING NEFER and Hilto were on the carpet load when Taita drove the creaking wagon up to one of the side gates of the palace.

Soleth was not there to greet them but he had sent one of his underlings, an old black slave, to act as a guide. The ancient slave hobbled ahead of them, ushering them past the guards and guiding them through narrow passages to an elaborately carved sandalwood door guarded by two huge eunuchs. There was a whispered exchange then the sentries stood aside and the slave went through into a large airy room, 'Your Majesty,' he quavered, 'There is a merchant with fine silk carpets from Samarkand to wait upon Your Grace.'

'I have seen enough rubbish for one day,' a woman replied, and Nefer thrilled to her familiar, well-beloved tones. 'Send them away.'

The guide looked back at Taita and spread his hands helplessly. Nefer dropped the carpet off his shoulder and strode onto the terrace. Mintaka was sitting on the parapet wall with two of her slave girls at her feet.

'Forgive me, Majesty,' he murmured softly. 'I am but a poor fool from Dabba.'

Mintaka screamed, then covered her mouth with both hands. The black slave drew his dagger, but Mintaka recovered herself at once. 'No, leave him.' She raised her right hand to reinforce the command. 'Leave us. I will speak with the stupid fellow.'

Confused, the slave sheathed his blade and backed away. The curtains over the entrance fell back into place as he withdrew. Mintaka was still staring at Nefer. Her girls knew that something strange was afoot. Then suddenly she flew to Nefer and he ran to meet her, enfolding her in his embrace. They clung to each other, both talking at the same time.

The slave girls recovered from their astonishment and clapped their hands with joy. Taita silenced them with a few prods of his staff, then turned back to Hilto. At his direction the man spread the largest carpet out on the tile.

'Mintaka, listen to me! There will be time for that later. We are going to hide you in the carpet to get you out of the palace. Hurry!'

'Do I have time to fetch my—'

'No,' Taita said. 'You have time for nothing other than to obey me.'

She kissed Nefer once more, then threw herself full length on the carpet. She looked up at her girls, who stood amazed in the doorway. 'Do whatever Taita tells you.'

Nefer helped Hilto roll Mintaka in the patterned red carpet, while Taita instructed the slave girls: 'Stay here in the vestibule. You must not open the door to any demands. Tell anyone who asks that your mistress is laid low by her moon sickness and can see no one. Delay them as long as you are able, but when you are discovered, tell them what they want to know. Do not try to hold out under torture. Now, bar the door behind us when we leave.'

The old slave was waiting in the passage when they carried out the rolled carpet on their shoulders.

'I am sorry. I did my best for you,' he told them, 'but since her marriage Queen Mintaka has become curiously sad and angry.' He beckoned them to follow and led them back through the warren until at last they reached the small side gate.

The wagon stood where they had left it. Gently they loaded the carpet and Nefer scrambled up behind Taita on the wagon box as he urged the horses forward.

Taita whipped up the horse. 'The city gates will soon be closed for the night. When Mintaka's escape is discovered the first thing they will do is seal off the city.'

They galloped down the wide avenue leading to the eastern gate. As they approached they saw that the way was blocked by other wagons and chariots lined up in front of the gate. Their progress was tantalisingly slow.

The sun had already sunk behind the walls and the light was fading, but there were still two vehicles ahead of them when the captain of the guard yelled at his men, 'That is enough! The sun has set. Close the gates!'

There were yells of protest from all the travellers still trying to pass out. One of the smaller wagons drove forward deliberately and tried to block the efforts of the guards to force the gates shut. A small riot broke out, with shouting guards swinging clubs, outraged citizens screaming back at them and frightened horses rearing and whinnying.

'Help me!' Nefer shouted to his companions. Lifting the rolled carpet off the wagon and carrying it between them, they squeezed through the narrow gap between the closing gates, then ran into the encampment below the city walls. There, among the leather tents and shacks, they lowered their burden to the ground and unrolled it. Dishevelled and hot, Mintaka sat up and smiled to see Nefer kneeling in front of her. They reached for each other and embraced.

Taita brought them back to reality. He pulled Mintaka to her feet. 'We have lost the wagon. Ahead of us we have a long journey on foot. Unless we set out now it will be after daylight tomorrow before we reach the oasis where we left Meren with the chariots.'

Mintaka sobered immediately. 'I am ready,' she said.

TROK DROVE THROUGH THE PALACE GATES and reined in his dusty, lathered horses in the courtyard before his own magnificent quarters. Two colonels of his cavalry, both members of the leopard clan and his particular cronies, stumped after him into the banquet hall with weapons and bucklers clattering. The house slaves had laid out a feast to welcome Pharaoh home, but Trok was aware that the manner in which his new wife treated him was weakening his reputation, and he was determined to change that this very night.

'There is more food than even you two oxen can eat,' he told his companions, waving at the groaning board. 'Do your worst, but don't expect me to join you before morning. I have a field to plough and an incorrigible filly to break to my will.'

He strode from the hall and two slaves with burning torches ran ahead of him to light his way. In front of the doors to Mintaka's quarters the eunuch sentries had heard him coming. They crossed their weapons over their fat chests in salute.

'Open up!' Trok ordered.

'Your Majesty.' One of the sentries saluted again nervously. 'The doors are barred by order of Her Majesty Queen Mintaka.'

'By Seueth, I'll have none of that!' Trok kicked open the door and marched into the room beyond. The slave girls were against the far wall in a terrified huddle. 'Where is your mistress?'

'She cannot see you. Her moon has come,' they gabbled.

Trok laughed. 'She has used that excuse too often.' He hammered on the door. 'Open up, you little witch!'

At his next blow the door flew open, torn off its leather hinges, and Trok swaggered through. 'Have you missed me, my little lily?' he called. 'Where are you?' He rampaged through the room and kicked in the doors of her closet. It took him only a minute to make sure that Mintaka was not hiding. He strode to the door and seized one of the slave girls. 'Where is she?'

'She has gone,' cried the girl. 'Men came and took her away in a carpet.'

Trok gave her a brutal kick and shouted at the sentries, 'Find Soleth. Bring the fat slug here immediately.'

Soleth came cringing and wringing his plump hands. 'Divine Pharaoh! Greatest of the gods!' He threw himself at Trok's feet.

Trok kicked him with a full swing of his armoured sandal. 'Who were these men you allowed to enter the *zenana*?'

'On your own orders, gracious Pharaoh, I allowed any vendor of fine merchandise to display it before the Queen.'

'Who was the carpet seller, the last one to enter these quarters?' Trok kicked him again. 'What was his name?'

'I remember now. The carpet merchant from Ur. I forget his name.'

'I will help your memory.' Trok picked up his discarded sword-belt and drew the weapon. 'Now, tell me. Who was the carpet merchant?'

'It was Taita!' Soleth screamed, 'Taita took her away.'

'Taita!' Trok exclaimed with astonishment. 'Taita, the Magus.' There was superstitious dread in his tone. 'Where has he taken her?'

'He did not tell me.'

Trok touched the point of the sword to the eunuch's breast.

Soleth whimpered, 'He did not tell me, but we spoke of the land between the two rivers, the Tigris and the Euphrates. Maybe that is where he intends taking the Queen.'

Trok thought about it. By now Taita would know of the strained relationships between Egypt and the eastern kingdoms. He would know that he might find protection there, if he could run that far. But what was his reason for abducting Mintaka? Had she appealed to him to help her escape from Avaris and her marriage? Certainly, she must have gone with him willingly. The manner in which her slave girls had tried to cover her escape proved that.

He put aside those considerations for the moment. The main concern now was to get the pursuit in hand and recapture her and the warlock before they crossed into territories loyal to Sargon of Babylon. He smiled at Soleth. 'I will deal with you when I return. There are hungry hyenas and vultures to be fed.'

The two colonels, Tolma and Zander, were still in the banquet hall, hogging the food and wine.

'How many chariots can we have manned and running eastward before midnight?' Trok demanded.

Colonel Tolma spat out the wine he was about to swallow and leapt to his feet. 'I can have fifty on the road within two hours,' he blurted.

'I want that to be a hundred,' Trok demanded. 'And another hundred running east before dawn.'

TAITA LED THEM through the night under a moon only days from full. The tip of his staff clicked on the stony path, and his shadow flitted ahead of him like a monstrous black bat. The others had to stretch their legs to keep him in sight.

After midnight Mintaka began to fail. She was limping heavily and falling back steadily. Nefer shortened his stride to stay with her and murmured encouragement.

'It is not far now,' he told her, and took her hand to lead her faster. 'Meren will have the horses ready for us. We will ride the rest of the way to Babylon in royal style.'

She laughed but it was a strained, painful sound.

'What is it that ails you?' he demanded.

'Nothing,' she said.

He forced her to sit on a rock beside the path, and unlaced the straps of her sandals. He pulled one off and slabs of skin and flesh came with it, the blood shining in the moonlight. He gently eased off the other sandal. 'You should have warned me of this earlier.' He turned his back to her and braced himself to receive her weight. 'Put your arms around my neck and jump up!' Then he set off after the others who, by this time, were merely a dark shadow on the moonlit desert ahead.

Before long, however, Taita and Hilto came back to search for them. Taita bound up Mintaka's feet and they took turns at carrying her. They went on faster, but the stars were fading and the dawn light was growing stronger when they finally reached the oasis where Meren waited for them with the horses.

All of them were exhausted, but Taita would not allow them to rest. They watered the horses for the last time and refilled the water-skins. While they were doing this Taita half filled a bucket with water from the well and washed the dye from his hair.

'Why does he wash his hair at a time like this?' Meren wondered.

'Perhaps it restores some of his force that he lost when he dyed it,' Mintaka suggested, and no one questioned this.

When they were ready to leave, Taita took Meren in the leading chariot as his lance-bearer. Nefer followed with Mintaka clinging to the dashboard to take the weight off her feet. Hilto brought up the rearguard in the last chariot.

The Assyrian merchant who had sold them the carpets turned to watch them as they passed, and he called a farewell to Taita. But his interest quickened as he saw the girl in the second chariot. Not even her dusty clothing and dishevelled hair could hide her striking looks. He was still staring after them as they topped the last rise and disappeared into the wilderness, heading east.

THE SUN WAS HOT and halfway up the sky when Trok topped the hills above the oasis at the threshold of the wilderness. Following him were two hundred chariots, and five miles behind came Colonel Zander with another two hundred. Each vehicle carried two armed troopers, and was loaded with water-skins and sheaths of spare arrows.

Below them they saw an Assyrian trader coming up the slope from the well at the head of his caravan. Trok rode forward and reined in his chariot in front of him. When he turned from the trader a few short minutes later, Trok began issuing orders to Colonel Tolma, who followed him closely in the second chariot of the column. 'They are only hours ahead of us,' he exulted. 'Top up the water-skins at the well, and let the horses drink their fill. But swiftly, Tolma. Be ready to leave again before noon. In the meantime send your wizards to me.'

Trok found a patch of shade under a gnarled tamarind near the well. The wizards came in response to his summons and squatted around him, two priests of Seueth in their black robes, and a sorcerer from the east known as Ishtar the Mede. Ishtar had one wall eye and his face was tattooed with whorls and circles.

'The man we are pursuing is an adept of the occult arts,' Trok warned them. 'He will exert all his powers to frustrate us. His name is Taita.'

'I know Taita only by reputation,' said Ishtar, 'but I have long looked for an opportunity to match him.'

'Weave your magic,' Trok ordered them.

The priests of Seueth went aside a short distance, laid out their accoutrements and began to chant softly. Ishtar built a small fire near the well and squatted over it, muttering incantations to Marduk, the must powerful of all the gods of Mesopotamia.

Watching him at work, Trok grunted sceptically, but secretly he was impressed. He walked a short way along the road and glared at the line of eastern hills. He was hot for the pursuit. On the other hand he was enough of a general to realise the need to rest and water the horse after the long night ride.

TAITA SIGNALLED the two vehicles that followed him to halt. They stopped in the shade thrown across the sands by a tall dune shaped like an elegant seashell. The horses were already showing signs of distress. They hung their heads and their chests heaved as they breathed. Carefully he measured out a water ration from the water-skins into the leather buckets and the horses drank eagerly.

When he had finished he led Hilto out of earshot of the others.

'We are being overlooked,' he said flatly. 'There is a baleful influence slowly enveloping us. Do you know who Trok has with him who can work such a potent spell?'

'He has sorcerers with all his regiments, but the most powerful of them is Ishtar the Mede.'

'I know of him.' Taita nodded. 'He works in fire and blood. I shall try to turn his influence back on him.'

They went back to where the chariots waited. Before they mounted again Taita spoke to the others. 'We are entering the most dangerous area of the dune-lands. I know you are all tired and thirsty, drained by the rigours of the journey, but it could be fatal for any of you to become careless. Watch the horses and the ground ahead. Do not allow yourselves to be distracted by any strange sound or sight.'

They went forward again, following the valleys between the high dunes, and the heat seemed to increase with every turn of the chariot wheels. The quality of light changed: distances were rendered confusing and distorted. Nefer slitted his eyes against the shimmering glare of the brazen sky. It seemed close enough to touch with the end of his whip.

As they went on Taita looked to the sky more frequently. His expression was sober.

'I have never seen a sky like this,' Hilto said, when they stopped to water the horses. 'The gods are angry.'

It was Hilto, with his warrior's eyes, who picked out the dust cloud behind them. 'Magus!' he shouted. 'Those are chariots behind us, and many of them.'

Trok was there. Even at distance they could make out his bearlike form at the head of his moving column.

'One last fight!' Hilto loosened his blade in its scabbard.

Taita looked up at the bile-coloured sky as another sultry gust rippled his hair. He did not raise his voice but it carried to all of them, 'This way. Mark well my wheel tracks and follow them faithfully.'

To their astonishment Taita turned his horses off into the sand, heading at a right angle from the track. He went on at a steady trot and they followed him closely.

Looking back, Nefer could see there was not the least chance that, when Trok reached it, he would not find the place where the three chariots had left the track. Unless, of course, Taita could weave a spell of concealment.

They kept on for almost another league until abruptly the land ahead changed character. From the soft sand waves rose a dark island of rock. Its sides were honeycombed and eaten away by the abrasive, sand-laden winds, but the peak was as sharp as the fang of some fabulous monster.

When Nefer and Mintaka saw the rock pile looming ahead they were astonished.

'Did Taita know it was here?' Mintaka asked.

'How could he have known?' Nefer replied.

'You told me once that he knows everything.'

Nefer was silenced. He looked back and saw the dust of the pursuit close behind. 'It matters not at all. We might be able to defend those rocks for a while, but there are hundreds of Trok's men.'

'We must trust Taita,' Mintaka said.

He laughed bitterly. 'It seems the gods have deserted us. Who else is there to trust but Taita.'

They went forward. Behind them they heard the faint cries of the captains urging their troopers, the jingle of loose equipment and the groan and whine of dry wheel hubs.

At last they came up under the hill of black and ochre-coloured rock. The accumulated heat radiated from it like a bonfire.

'Drive the chariots close in against the cliff,' Taita ordered, and they obeyed. 'Now free the horses and bring them this way.' Taita led his own team round the angle of the rock face. Here there was a deep fissure cutting into the rock pile.

'This way.' He led them as far as they could go along the sandy floor of the deep, vertical crack. 'Now make the horses lie down.'

At the urging of their handlers, the horses, trained to perform this trick, lowered themselves to their knees and then, grunting and blowing, they went flat on their sides on the floor of the fissure.

Taita had brought a bedding roll from the chariot. With strips torn from it he blindfolded the horses to keep them quiet and submissive. Then he drove a javelin deep into the loose earth and used it as an anchor to tie down the horses' swathed heads and prevent them from rising again. The others followed his example.

Almost as if he knew of its existence, Taita led them to a shallow overhang in the cliff. The headroom under it was so low that anyone trying to enter would have to go down on hands and knees.

'Use the loose scree from the cliff to wall this in.'

Nefer looked puzzled. 'We cannot defend this place. Once we are inside we could not even stand, let alone swing a sword.'

'There is no time to argue.' Taita glared at him. 'Do as I tell you.'

Nefer glared back at Taita. The others watched with interest: the young bull challenging the older one. Abruptly Nefer capitulated. Only one person could save them now. He stooped and picked up a large rock from the scree pile and staggered with it to the shallow cave. The others joined in the work.

Meanwhile Taita climbed until he reached the peak of the hillock. He stood there gazing back in the direction from which Trok would come, and when their work was finished the little party in the gully at the foot of the hillock watched him, outlined against that dreadful sulphur sky. Nobody spoke, nobody moved, until they heard the faint squeal of chariot wheels.

Slowly Taita raised both arms and pointed them to the sky.

'What is he doing now?' Hilto asked, in an awed tone.

Taita stood as still as if he had been chiselled out of the living rock. His head was thrown back, his hair fluffed out silver on his shoulders. The heavens swirled. The light was transient, fading as the sun was covered more heavily, flaring as the clouds thinned.

Still Taita did not move, his staff aimed at the heavens. The sound of the approaching column became clearer still, and suddenly there was a distant blare of a ram's horn trumpet.

'That is Trok's battle call,' Mintaka said quietly.

TROK SHOUTED AT HIS TRUMPETER, 'Sound the advance!'

'Wait!' said Ishtar the Mede. He was watching Taita's tiny figure on the peak of the rock hill. 'Wait!'

'What is it?' Trok demanded.

'As yet I cannot fathom it,' Ishtar said, without taking his gaze off the warlock, 'but it is pervasive and powerful.'

The column remained halted, every man in it staring at the figure on the peak with awe. Only the sky moved. It formed a whirlpool over the head of the Magus, a great turning wheel of smouldering cloud. Then slowly the centre of the whirlpool opened like the single eye of an awakening monster. From the heavenly eye a shaft of dazzling sunlight burst forth.

'The eye of Horus!' Ishtar breathed. 'He has called up the god.' He made a sign of protection, and at his side Trok was silent and rigid with superstitious dread.

The brilliant shaft of light struck the peak, and lit the figure of the warlock. Around his head it spun a nimbus of silver radiance.

He made a slow circular pass with his long staff, and the Hyksosian charioteers cringed like curs under the whip. The clouds opened wider, and the sky was clear. The sunlight danced on the dunes, and they lifted their hands to protect their eyes.

On the peak, Taita described another circle with his staff, and there was a sound, soft at first, like a lover's sigh, then becoming a soughing, a gentle whistling. It came from the east, and slowly all their heads turned towards it.

Out of that strange, cloudless brilliance, they saw it coming: a solid dun wall of sand that reached from the surface of the earth to the highest heavens.

'Khamsin!' Trok whispered the dread word.

The wall of sand undulated and pulsed like a demon, and its voice became a rising howl.

'Khamsin!' The word was yelled from chariot to chariot. They were no longer warriors hot for war, but small, terrified creatures in the face of this destroyer of men, cities and civilisations, this eater of worlds.

The column of chariots lost its formation as the drivers wheeled their teams and tried to run from it. Men leapt from their cockpits and abandoned their vehicles. Instinctively the horses sensed the menace and reared and screamed, trying to escape by kicking themselves free of the traces.

The khamsin bore down upon them inexorably. Men ran before it in mindless panic. They looked back and saw the great storm rolling and roiling upon itself, twisting curtains of sand, brazen where the sunlight struck them, dun and sombre where their own mountainous heights shaded them.

Taita lowered his staff and, without haste, started down the hillock to where Nefer and Mintaka were standing. They welcomed him with bemused expressions. Mintaka's tone was subdued as she asked, 'You called up the storm?'

'It has long been brewing,' Taita said. 'You have all remarked the heat and the yellow mists.'

'No,' said Nefer. 'It was not in nature. It was you.'

'Go into the shelter now,' said Taita. 'It is almost upon us.'

Mintaka led the way, crawling into the low narrow cave through the opening in the rude wall. The others followed her, crowding into the tiny space. Before he entered, Hilto handed in the water-skins. Then, as the storm hurled down on them in all its terrible majesty, Taita stooped through the opening and sat with his back to the inner wall.

'Close it up,' he said, and Meren and Hilto blocked the entrance with the rocks they had placed at hand.

'Cover your heads,' said Taita, and wound his headcloth over his face. 'Keep your eyes closed, or you will lose your sight. Breathe carefully or you will drown in sand.'

THE STORM WAS OVERWHELMING. Trok and Ishtar were gone with magical swiftness, they and all their men, chariots and horses, gone in the rolling billows of the khamsin. The first front picked up Trok's chariot and rolled it over with the horses screaming.

Trok was thrown free. He fought his way to his feet, but the storm struck him down again. He managed to pull himself up. When he tried to open his eyes he was blinded by sand.

As the khamsin ripped at his face, Trok screamed, 'Save me, Ishtar!'

It seemed impossible that anyone could have heard his cry. Then he felt Ishtar seize his hand and together they stumbled on. It seemed endless, their tormented journey to nowhere. Then abruptly Trok felt the force of the wind diminish. For a minute he thought that the storm had already passed them by, but then a sudden gust almost lifted him off his feet and he crashed into a wall of rock.

He clung to the rock like a child to its mother's breast. How Ishtar had brought them to it he neither knew nor cared. All that mattered was that the cliff above them was breaking the full force of the storm.

FOR TWO DAYS and three nights the wind never relented. During this time Nefer managed to keep back the sand just enough to move his head and his arms, but his lower body was encased solidly.

At times he felt Mintaka sobbing quietly beside him and tried to comfort her. She laid her head on his shoulder and they clung to each other. They were entombed in the roaring darkness, dumb and blinded, half suffocated. Each hot breath they drew had to be strained through cloth and taken only a sip at a time to prevent a rush of talcum-fine sand passing between their lips.

They drank the water that remained in their water-skin. Then the thirst came. Even though they were unable to move their bodies to use up moisture, the hot dry sand and air sucked it out of them. Nefer felt his tongue slowly cleave to the roof of his mouth.

He felt himself drifting into haunted dreams of water, of cool green expanses of the great river, of cascades and bright rivulets. He forced himself up from the darkness, and listened. He heard nothing. There was no sound. The roaring clamour of the khamsin had given way to a profound silence. The silence of a sealed tomb, he thought.

He began to struggle, to try to work his way out of the sand, but the effort soon exhausted him and his throat ached with thirst. He closed his eyes wearily, giving up. Then, even through the folds of his headcloth, he was aware of fresh air and a glimmer of light. He pulled the cloth from his face. When his vision had adjusted he saw that there was a hole to the outside.

It was the middle of the morning. Nefer did not know what morning or for how many days they had been buried. There was still a haze of fine sand like gold dust in the air.

He shook his head in wonder, and looked at Taita. He could see that he was dried out and suffering the same agonies as they were.

'Water,' Nefer whispered, touching his swollen mouth.

'Come,' said Taita.

Nefer took Mintaka's hand and slowly they followed the Magus out into the sands. Thirst and exposure had taken their toll on Taita, and he seemed to be wandering aimlessly with Hilto and Meren through the new valleys of fine sand. Once or twice he lowered himself to his knees and touched the earth with his forehead.

'What is he doing?' Mintaka whispered. 'Is he praying?'

Nefer shook his head as once again Taita knelt and placed his face close to the earth. This time Nefer watched him with more attention, and saw that he was sniffing the air close to the surface of the sand. Then he knew what Taita was doing. 'He is searching for the buried chariots of Trok's division,' he whispered to Mintaka. 'He is sniffing for the scent of putrescence below the sand.'

Taita stood up painfully and nodded at Hilto. 'Dig here,' he ordered.

They all crowded forward and began to scrape away the sand with cupped hands. An arm's span deep they struck something hard, and redoubled their efforts. Soon they exposed the wheel rim of a chariot that was lying on its side. Another few minutes of frantic digging and the stench of the dead horses grew stronger.

Suddenly Nefer reached deeper into the hole and they all heard the gurgle and slosh of water. He swept away more of the loose sand and between them they lifted out bulging water-skin. Taita oopened the stopper and poured it into a leather bucket that had lain beside the waterskin at the bottom of the excavation.

The water was the temperature of blood, but when Taita held the bucket to Mintaka's lips she closed her eyes and drank in a quiet ecstasy.

'Not too much at first,' Taita warned her, and passed it to Nefer. They drank in turn, then Mintaka drank again.

The next time they dug they were lucky: not only was the chariot under less sand, but there were three water-skins.

'Our horses now,' Taita told them, and they looked at each other guiltily. In their desperate preoccupation they had forgotten them.

Carrying the water-skins they trudged back through the sand to the base of the cliff.

The narrow gully in which they had pegged down the horses was well aligned to avoid the full force of the khamsin. They found the first horse almost at once. The beast was alive, but barely. The men lifted it between them. It stood weak and shivering, but drank greedily from the bucket Mintaka held and seemed at once to improve.

In the meantime the men were digging for the other horses. They found three dead of thirst or suffocation, but another two still alive. They also responded immediately they were given water.

The men left Mintaka to care for the three pathetic beasts and went back to search for fodder and more water-skins under the sand.

Suddenly they heard Mintaka screaming.

Nefer raced back to her, a sword in his hand, the others following. Mintaka had been hiding behind a ledge in the cliff.

'What is it?' Nefer demanded, as she slid down the cliff into his arms.

'Trok!' she sobbed. 'Trok is alive. Look!'

Taita stayed with Mintaka while the other three men followed a set of footprints in the sand as if they were tracking a wounded lion. They moved along the base of the cliff until they reached a second rocky fissure. Nefer examined the disturbed sand within it and interpreted the signs.

'Two of them,' he said. 'They were buried by the storm, as we were. They dug themselves out. One waited here.' He picked up a thread of wool that had adhered to the rock, and held it to the light. 'Black.' It was a colour seldom worn by Egyptians. 'Almost certainly the Mede.'

Hilto nodded agreement. 'Ishtar would have the witchcraft to survive the storm. 'It is certain he saved Trok, just as Taita saved us.'

'Here.' Nefer stood and pointed out the sign. 'They went this way.'

They followed the footprints a short way out into the desert. 'They have gone west. Back towards Avaris and the Nile. Will they ever reach it?'

'Not if I catch up with him,' Nefer said grimly, and hefted the javelin he was carrying.

'Majesty.' Hilto was respectful but firm. 'They have a long start. They will be well away from here by now. You dare not follow without water.'

Nefer hesitated. Though he saw the sense in what Hilto said, it galled him sorely to let Trok escape.

In the end he turned aside and ran to the top of the nearest dune. Shading his eyes he looked westward, along the string of footsteps on the pristine, windswept sands, until in the distance, half a league or more away, he made out two tiny figures moving steadily towards the west. He watched them fiercely until they disappeared in the wavering heat mirage.

'There will be another time,' Nefer whispered. 'I will come for you. I swear it.'

THEY FOUND AND UNCOVERED another sixteen of the buried chariots. With such an abundant supply of water and food, horses and men recovered swiftly, and by nightfall on the tenth day they were ready to move.

The khamsin had altered the landscape so greatly that Taita had to navigate by the stars. They kept going steadily through the whole of that night, and the one that followed. Before dawn on the second day they reached an old caravan road.

Here, Nefer had a difficult decision to make. 'If we are to make the long journey to the east, we will need supplies and gold. We should not arrive at the Assyrian court as indigent outcasts. When we go to King Sargon we must arrive in some state to show him the support we still command in Egypt.'

Taita nodded.

'Hilto and Meren must go back to Thebes,' Nefer went on. 'I would go myself but all the world will be searching for Mintaka and me.' He removed one of his royal finger rings and handed it to Hilto. 'This will be your token of recognition. Show it to our friends. You must return bringing us men and gold, chariots and horses. Also you must gather news. We must be informed of every action of the false pharaohs.'

'I will do as you command, Majesty,' Hilto agreed.

'We will wait for you at Gallala,' were Nefer's last words to Hilto. Then they watched him and Meren take the high road and disappear.

Twelve days later, with only a few drops remaining in the water-skins, Taita, Mintaka and Nefer reached the deserted ruins.

CHAPTER FIVE

The weeks became months, and still they waited at Gallala.

Mintaka set up quarters for them among the ruins. As a Hyksosian princess, she had never been called upon to cook a meal, so her efforts were disastrous. As he chewed a charred mouthful Taita remarked, 'If we want to destroy Trok's army the most effective way would be to send you to them as a cook.'

'If you are so talented, then perhaps you might honour us with your great culinary skills.'

'It is either that or starve,' Taita agreed, and took her place at the hearth.

Nefer resumed his old role of hunter, and after his first day out in the desert returned with a plump young gazelle and four marvellously patterned giant bustard eggs that were only slightly addled.

Mintaka sniffed her share of Taita's omelette and pushed it away. 'Is this the same man who complained of my cooking?' She looked across the fire at Nefer. 'You are as guilty as he is. Next time I will go with you to make sure that what you bring back is edible.'

Several more hunting trips followed. Then, one evening when they came into the room in the ancient building that they had restored and made habitable, Mintaka shyly stood in the open doorway with the last light of the day behind her. 'I am sorry we are late back, Taita,' she said. 'We followed the gazelles out into the desert.' Taita was at the hearth stirring the contents of the pot upon the coals. He looked up at her. She had never apologised for their late return before, and Nefer was hovering over her with a soft, dazed expression. The emanation of their love was so strong that it seemed to form a shimmering aura around them.

So what was inevitable has happened at last, he mused. The only wonder is that it took so long. He grunted. 'It is evident that you did not catch up with them. Did they run too fast or were you distracted?' They stood awkwardly, knowing that to him they were transparent.

Taita turned back to the cooking pot. 'At least there is one provider among us. I have been able to snare a brace of wild pigeon. We need not go hungry to bed.'

The days that followed passed for the lovers in a golden haze. The two of them spent their time in talking, making love and forming plans for the future, deciding how they might marry and how many sons and daughters she would bear him.

They were so lost in each other that they forgot the world that lay beyond the lonely desert spaces, until one morning when they left the ruined city before dawn and sat down to watch the magnificent spectacle of the dawn breaking over the blue, secret hills.

'Look!' cried Mintaka suddenly, pointing back towards the west along the old trade route. A strange caravan was coming towards them. There were five ramshackle vehicles leading, followed by a straggling column of humanity.

'There must be a hundred men, at least,' Mintaka exclaimed. 'Who can they be?'

'I don't know,' Nefer admitted grimly, 'but I want you to run back and warn Taita of their approach while I go and spy on them.'

She did not argue, but set off immediately for Gallala, racing down the back slope of the hills, while Nefer restrung his bow and checked the arrows in his quiver.

Suddenly he stood up from behind the rock that had hidden him, and shouted with excitement. 'Meren!' He had at last recognised the tall figure who held the reins of the first chariot. Meren pulled up the horses, then he, too, shouted and waved as he saw Nefer on the skyline. Nefer ran down the slope, and he and Meren embraced, laughing and both speaking at once.

'Where have you been?'

'Where are Mintaka and Taita?'

Then Hilto was hurrying to Nefer, and making loyal salutations. Behind him crowded a host of exhausted and wounded men. Even the men in the wagons and on the litters, who were too far gone to stand, lifted themselves to stare in awe at Nefer.

After Hilto had greeted Nefer he turned back to them, and shouted, 'It is even as I promised you! Here before you stands your true pharaoh, Nefer Seti. Pharaoh is not dead! Pharaoh lives!'

They were silent. They stared at him uncertainly. Most had never laid eyes on their king before. Even the few who had seen him in formal palace processions had done so from a distance. They could not reconcile that remote figure with this strapping young man, his face tanned by the sun and his expression alive and alert.

While they still stared without comprehension, or exchanged dubious glances, another figure seemed to materialise beside Nefer. This one they knew well, both by repute and by sight.

'It is Taita the Warlock,' they breathed with awe.

'I know what you have suffered,' Taita told them, in a voice that carried clearly to every ear. 'I know what price you have paid to resist the tyranny of the assassins and usurpers. I know that you have come here to find if your true king still lives.'

Suddenly Nefer knew who they were: survivors from the rebellion against Naja and Trok. Where Hilto had found them was a mystery, but these men had once been fighting troopers and elite charioteers.

'This is where it begins,' Taita said softly at his side. 'Hilto has brought you the seed of your future legions. Speak to them.'

Nefer picked out a man in the ranks who was older than the others. His expression was intelligent and he had an air of authority. 'Who are you, soldier? What is your rank and your regiment?'

The man lifted his head and squared his gaunt shoulders, 'I am Shabako, Commander of the Mut Regiment.'

A lion of a man! Nefer thought, but said only, 'I greet you, Shabako.' He lifted his kilt and exposed the cartouche tattooed upon his thigh. 'I, Nefer Seti, the true Pharaoh of Upper and Lower Egypt, greet you.'

A sigh went through the scarecrow ranks. As one man they threw themselves to the earth in obeisance.

Mintaka had come with Taita and now Nefer reached out and took her hand. 'I give you the Princess Royal, Mintaka of the House of Apepi. Mintaka, who will be my queen and your sovereign lady.'

They greeted her with a shout of acclamation.

'Hilto and Shabako will command you,' Nefer decreed. 'For the time being Gallala will be our base, until we return victoriously to Thebes.'

They rose to their feet and cheered him, their voices thin in the silence of the desert, but the sound filled Nefer with pride. He climbed up into the leading chariot, took the reins from Meren and led his raggle-taggle army down into his ruined capital city.

LATE INTO THAT FIRST NIGHT, and for many nights that followed, Nefer sat with Shabako and the other officers and listened to their accounts of the rebellion, their defeat by the combined forces of the two pharaohs, and the terrible retribution that they had visited on those rebels who had fallen into their clutches. They also detailed the order of battle of the new Egyptian army, and the total of men, chariots and horses that Naja and Trok had at their disposal.

In the meantime Taita, with Mintaka assisting him, set up an infirmary where they worked during all the daylight hours, setting broken bones, drawing out barbed arrowheads, stitching sword cuts and in one case even trepanning a skull that had received a blow from a hardwood war club.

When the light faded and he could no longer work with the sick, Taita joined Nefer and his commanders as they pored over maps drawn on tanned lambskins, planning and scheming by the light of the oil lamps. Although Nefer was nominally their supreme commander, in reality he was a student of the art of war and these experienced old soldiers were his instructors.

In total there were fewer than a hundred and fifty souls and fifty horses in Gallala, but within the first few days it became evident that the wells of the city could not support even these meagre numbers. Each day they emptied them and each night it took longer for them to refill, and the water became more bitter and brackish.

At last, after they were forced to ration the water, Taita took Nefer and Mintaka and a party of fifty-six men, all carrying shovels and metal-tipped digging staves, up the valley to the foot of the hill.

For two days they dug into the rock, prising out each lump, digging out the earth that lay behind it. When they struck a solid stratum of blue, crystalline rock, they stacked firewood against it, let it burn until the rock glowed, and quenched it with water from the failing wells. In clouds of hissing steam, the rock crackled and burst. They let it cool, prised out great blackened chunks of it, then repeated the arduous process until they had driven a shaft of twenty cubits into the hillside.

On the third morning, the teams of weary, disgruntled men assembled round the mouth of the tunnel to await the Magus. With his usual sense of the dramatic, Taita came up the slope with the first rays of the rising sun behind him, suffusing his silver hair with light. He stood in the entrance to the excavation and began to chant the invocation to Horus. Then he strode down the shaft until he stood before the blue-grey wall of newly exposed rock at the end. Tiny crystals of feldspar were embedded in it and sparkled in the sun.

'*Kydash!*' Taita cried, and struck the wall with his staff. '*Mensaar!*' He struck again. '*Ncube!*' He struck for the third and last time, then stepped back.

Nothing happened, and Taita stood unmoving as the sun climbed higher.

Then the men stirred and whispered as a dark, damp spot appeared in the centre of the rock face. It spread gradually and a single drop of moisture oozed out, sparkling like a tiny gem in the sunlight, and trickled slowly down the wall.

Taita turned and walked out of the shaft. Behind him there was a sharp sound, and a fine crack split the rock from top to bottom. Water dripped to the floor. Then with a roar the entire rock face collapsed, there was a rush of mud and a gushing fountain of crystal-bright water. Knee-deep, it swept the length of the shaft, burst from the mouth and spilled down the hillside, rippling over the rocks.

There were shouts of amazement, praise and disbelief from the dusty ranks. Men threw off their clothing and rushed naked into the stream. Nefer could not long resist the temptation before he, too, shed all dignity and jumped in.

Taita stood on the bank of the stream and looked down on the mayhem with a benign expression. Then he turned to Mintaka. 'Put the thought out of your mind,' he said. 'It would be an outrage to have a princess of Egypt cavorting with a rabble of rough, naked soldiers.' He took her hand and led her away down the hill, but she looked back wistfully at the revels.

'How did you do it, Taita?' she asked. 'How did you make the fountain appear? What kind of magic was it?'

'The magic of common sense and observation. The water has been there for centuries, just waiting for us to dig down to it.'

'But what about the words of power?'

Taita smiled and touched the side of his nose. 'Sometimes a little magic is a tonic for flagging spirits.'

For months thereafter every man was employed in the digging of a channel to lead the sweet flood of water down the hillside into the old wells. When they brimmed over, Taita surveyed the old fields at the lower end of the valley that were now a stony desolation. The outlines of ancient irrigation ditches were still visible, however, and it took small effort to clean out the contour lines and divert the overflowing waters into them, so that within months they had reaped their first millet harvest.

Almost every day more fugitives drifted into the city, having braved the desert crossing to escape the tyranny of the false pharaohs. They came singly or in small parties, weary and almost dying of thirst. The guards posted along the hills intercepted them, and sent them in to Hilto. He made them swear the oath of fealty to Pharaoh Nefer Seti, then issued them with rations and sent them to the training regiments or put them to work in the fields or restoring the city. These waifs were not the only recruits, however. A cohort of deserters from the armies of the false pharaohs marched in smartly with their javelins, shouting the praises of Nefer Seti as soon as they were in sight of the walls. Then a squadron of twenty chariots brought plundered treasure and the momentous news that Naja and Trok were at last marching against King Sargon of Babylon.

The two pharaohs had crossed the desert that linked Egypt with the eastern lands in the full of the moon, using its light and the cool nights to sweep past Ismailiya and on up to Beersheba, gathering the forces of their vassal satraps as they went.

Nefer and Taita had been preparing the defences of Gallala against an imminent attack by the false pharaohs. Their presence in the ancient city should by now have been common knowledge throughout the two kingdoms, and they had expected Naja and Trok to move against them first, before starting on the Mesopotamian adventure. They were amazed to have this reprieve.

'Can we be certain that this is not a diversion?' Nefer asked thoughtfully. 'Is the eastern expedition a pretence? Perhaps their true offensive will be directed against us after they have lulled us into a false sense of security.'

'There is always that possibility. Trok is a bull, but Naja is cunning and devious. It is the type of bluff he might try.'

'We must keep the expeditionary army under observation,' Nefer decided.

The following day Shabako and his most trusted men were sent as scouts and spies to the towns and villages of the Nile valley. They drank in the taverns and questioned the travellers they met on the road. They scouted each fort and garrison, and counted the troops they saw entering, leaving and drilling. When they returned weeks later, the intelligence they brought back was detailed and accurate.

They reported that the false pharaohs had left at least half of their army to counter any threat to their rear. All the border forts were fully manned, and the garrisons seemed alert and vigilant.

'What of the remount divisions?' Nefer asked, when Shabako had come to the end of his long report.

'Trok has taken most of his chariots with him to Mesopotamia. He has left less than two regiments in reserve in Egypt. However, all the army workshops are hard at work building more chariots.'

'Horses?' Nefer demanded.

'They have commandeered every animal in both kingdoms that they could lay their thieving hands on. They have even sent army dealers to Libya to buy what they could find. The remount depots at Thane and Manashi are at full strength. However, most of these animals appear young and untrained. The battle-hardened animals have been taken with the main army to the east.'

'Thane,' Nefer decided. 'It's much closer to the edge of the desert than Manashi.' He recalled that Thane was where Hilto had used his requisition order to obtain fresh horses and chariots from Socco, his old comrade-in-arms, while they were on their way to rescue Mintaka from Avaris.

'Tell me all you can about Thane. Is Socco still in command there?'

'We drank beer in the local brothel with a sergeant of the garrison. He told me that Socco has done such a good job there that Trok has promoted him to the rank of Best of Ten Thousand.'

TEN DAYS LATER, Nefer and Taita sat in the thick green grass and pretended to watch over the herd of goats that grazed around them. Although the land around the garrison of Thane was rich in grazing, it was also flat and featureless. There were no hills from which they could overlook the camp.

The two of them were disguised in the ragged dusty black robes of the Bedouin and were able to blend into the landscape. At intervals they herded the goats a little closer to the garrison, then squatted down again in the characteristic attitude of the Bedouin herdsman.

Not far from where they sat, the herds of remounts were grazing. 'I would think there are upward of two thousand animals here,' Nefer guessed.

'Perhaps not as many as that.' Taita shook his head. 'Closer to fifteen hundred, but still more than we can handle.'

They watched and waited through thc long, lazy afternoon. In the stockades alongside the cavalry lines the handlers were breaking the young animals to the chariot harness. Their shouted commands and the crack of the whips carried faintly to where Nefer and Taita sat.

In the late afternoon the herds of horses were driven in from the fields and stockades to the long horse lines beyond the fort. From a distance they watched them tethered and bedded down for the night.

As the sun was setting Nefer and Taita rounded up their goats and drove them slowly back towards the desert. In the dusk a small detachment of four chariots came bowling down the road from Avaris. At the reins of the leading vehicle stood a burly officer wearing the silver pectoral plate of the Best of Ten Thousand. As he came closer they both recognised him.

'The curse of Seth on it,' Nefer murmured. 'It is Socco, Hilto's old comrade-in-arms. Will he recognise us?'

They bowed their heads, slumped their shoulders, and shuffled along after the goats. Socco swerved off the road and drove directly at them. 'You stinking scum!' he shouted. 'How often must I warn you to keep your filthy, disease-ridden beasts off my grass and away from my horses?' He leaned out and struck Nefer across the shoulders. The whiplash hummed and cracked against his flesh, and red rage blinded Nefer. Before he could drag Socco out of the chariot, though, Taita made a restraining gesture that riveted him where he stood. It seemed to affect Socco, too, for suddenly the bellicose light in his eyes faded. He stammered wordlessly. He was gawking at the cartouche on Nefer's thigh.

'Majesty,' he gasped. 'Forgive me! Strike! Take my worthless life as forfeit for those stupid words of mine. I heard the rumours that you still lived, but I had wept at your funeral and could not believe in such a miracle.'

Nefer smiled with relief. He had not wanted to kill him—he was an attractive old rogue, and Hilto said that he was one of the finest horse-handlers in all the armies of Egypt. Hilto should know. 'Will you swear the loyal oath to me as Pharaoh?' he demanded sternly.

'Gladly, for all the earth fears you in your name of Nefer Seti, beloved of all the gods, and light of this very Egypt. My heart beats only for you and my soul will sing my duty to you until the hour of my death.'

'Then, Socco, I promote you to Master of a Thousand Chariots, for you turn a pretty phrase.'

'Let me kiss your foot, Pharaoh,' Socco pleaded.

'Give me your hand, rather,' Nefer said, seizing his horny fist.

Three days later, when they rode into Gallala, they were driving nigh on four hundred horses, and Socco rode proudly at the right hand of his new pharaoh.

AS QUARTERMASTER GENERAL of the armies of the false pharaohs, Socco had been able to bring with him much of the depot's treasure store. He was also able to give Nefer and his council the exact tally of all the enemy fighting chariots and transport wagons, and where they were deployed. From memory he drew up a list of the numbers of horses and bullocks in depots of the delta, and the latest inventory of weapons stored in the armouries.

'Trok and Naja have taken almost the last serviceable fighting chariot with them on the expedition to the east. There are fewer than fifty left in Egypt, in either the Upper or Lower Kingdom. The military workshops at Avaris, Thebes and Aswan are working day and night, but every chariot they turn out is sent immediately along the road to Beersheba and Mesopotamia.'

'Horses we now have, thanks to you, even though most are young and unbroken, but we cannot fight a campaign without chariots,' said Hilto gloomily. 'Soon Trok must hear of our successes. He will realise that we have become a real threat. As soon as he has captured Babylon, he will divert part of his army to attack us here. If he sent only a hundred chariots, we could not stand against them in our present state.'

When all the others had had their say, Nefer stood to address the council. He did not speak long. 'Socco, you train the horses for me,' he said. 'Taita and I will find the chariots.'

FAR OUT IN THE DESERT, Taita stood on a black rock outcrop. Around him the sand dunes stretched away to the limit of the eye. From the base of the rock a hundred men watched him, puzzled but intrigued. All of them were warriors who had come to Gallala of their own accord, forsaking the false pharaohs to offer their allegiance to Nefer Seti. That allegiance would wear a little thin if they found themselves without chariots, for daily there were fresh rumours that Trok was on the march to seek vengeance for their desertion.

Pharaoh Nefer Seti stood beside the warlock. They were in deep discussion. Occasionally one or the other would point towards the west, where there was nothing to see but sand. They talked through the heat of the day and came down from the pinnacle and walked out into the dunes. Without any apparent purpose the warlock wandered along one of the dune faces. He stopped at intervals and made strange, esoteric gestures with his long staff, then went on again.

At last, in the gathering dusk, the Magus planted his staff in the soft sand and spoke quietly to Pharaoh Nefer Seti. Now, suddenly, orders were shouted and twenty men ran forward carrying the digging tools with which they had been issued. Under the direction of Hilto and Meren, and under the daunting eyes of their king and the Magus, they began to dig. When the hole was shoulder deep the loose sand ran back into it almost as fast as they shovelled it out, and they were forced to redouble their efforts. Finally there came an excited shout from the bottom of the excavation. Nefer strode forward and stood on the lip.

'There is something here, Divine Majesty.' A man was kneeling in the bottom of the hole.

'Let me see.' Nefer jumped down and pushed the man out of the way. A patch of hide was exposed, still covered with hair.

Nefer looked up at Taita. 'It is the body of a horse!' he called.

'What colour?' Taita asked. 'Is it black?'

'How did you know?' Nefer was not really surprised.

Taita answered his question with another. 'Does the halter carry the golden cartouche of Pharaoh Trok Uruk?'

'Dig it open!' Nefer ordered the sweating men around him. 'But gently now. Do no damage.'

They worked with great care, using their bare hands to sweep away the sand. Gradually they exposed the complete head of a black horse that wore on its forehead the cartouche of Trok, embossed on a gold disc, just as Taita had foreseen.

Then they went on to uncover the rest of the carcass, wonderfully preserved by the hot dry sand. The embalmers in Thebes would have difficulty in matching what the desert had achieved. Beside it lay its harness mate. Nefer had last seen these magnificent animals as they drew Trok's chariot forward under the dust clouds of the khamsin.

By this time night had fallen and the workmen lit the oil lamps and went on with the work through the night. The dead horses were unbuckled from the traces and lifted out, and the harness was recovered in a perfect state of preservation. Nefer set his grooms to work oiling the leather and polishing the gold and bronze parts.

Now they worked on the chariot itself, and a gasp went up from the diggers as the dashboard was cleared of sand: it was covered with gold leaf, and gleamed in the lamplight. The javelins and lances were still in their bins on either side of the cockpit, ready to the hand of the charioteer. Trok's great war-bow, too, was still in its rack, and only the bowstring needed to be replaced.

When the entire chariot had been uncovered they passed ropes under the chassis and lifted it out of the excavation.

Now it was morning, and the sun was climbing above the horizon. Nefer and Taita circled the chariot as it gleamed in the light. It was so sleek and graceful that it seemed already in motion.

Nefer stroked the lovely gold work. 'It seems to be a living creature,' he breathed. 'Surely there was never a more magnificent weapon of war ever conceived. Now I need only the blue sword that Naja stole from my father to complete my armoury.'

Over the weeks that followed Taita pinpointed the other buried vehicles and their accoutrements. Teams of workmen dug them out and sent them to the chariot-makers and armourers, who sharpened swords and lances, rebound the shafts and checked each vehicle, balancing and lubricating the wheels to run true and sweetly. Then they sent them on to Gallala, to equip the army that Hilto, Shabako and Socco were training.

Many of the vehicles were so deeply buried under the burning yellow dunes that they were lost for ever, or until the next great storm uncovered them, but in the end they salvaged a hundred and five. Enough to equip five squadrons.

BY THIS TIME a thriving smuggling route existed between Gallala and Egypt, and other caravans came in regularly from the port of Safaga on the eastern sea. Nowadays there were few luxuries that could not be obtained in the city's souks, so Mintaka was able to procure a wagonload of the finest red wine for the welcome banquet she had arranged for the evening that the charioteers returned.

At her orders, the butchers spitted and roasted ten oxen, and fast relays of the new chariots brought up fresh fish and baskets of lobsters from the coast. The banquet was a joyous celebration, and the wine had flowed to great effect when Nefer rose to welcome the guests.

'With the weapons and chariots we now have, we are well able to defend ourselves against Trok and Naja. As you are aware, every day sees fresh recruits to the blue banner. Soon it will be a case not merely of defending ourselves but of avenging the terrible deeds that those two monsters have perpetrated. They are the murderers of King Apepi, who was the father of the noble lady at my side, and they slew my own father, Pharaoh Tamose.'

The guests were silent now and puzzled.

Then Hilto rose to his feet. Nefer had primed him, and placed the question on his lips. 'Divine Majesty, forgive my ignorance but I do not understand. King Apepi died in an accident when his barge caught fire while anchored at Balasfura. Now you lay the guilt for his death on the pretenders. How can that be?'

'There is one among us who was a witness to the true events of that tragic night.' Nefer reached down and drew Mintaka to her feet. The company listened to her with all their attention as she related the story of the murder of her father and brothers. She used simple words and spoke to them as friends and comrades, yet she was able to share with them her own horror and grief.

Now Shabako rose and asked his prepared question: 'But, Divine Pharaoh, you spoke also of the death of your own father, King Tamose of blessed memory. How was he murdered—and by whom?'

'For the answer to this question I must call upon the Magus, Lord Taita, from whom no secret, however grisly, can be hidden.'

Taita faced them and spoke in a whisper that riveted their attention. His every word carried to the ears of even those on the outskirts of the gathering. At the end he held up a broken arrow with crimson and green feathers. 'This is the instrument of Pharaoh Tamose's death. The arrow that bears the signet of Trok and which was loosed by Naja, the man whom Pharaoh trusted as a brother.'

They howled their outrage and their craving for justice to the starlit skies above Gallala. Taita hurled the arrow onto the nearest fire over which one of the oxen was roasting. It would not have borne closer inspection, for it was not the arrow that had killed Pharaoh but one of those he had taken from the buried chariot. He sat down and closed his eyes, as if composing himself to sleep.

CHAPTER SIX

Between the two great rivers the city lay before him like a lotus flower, ready for plucking. Its walls were of burned brick. They were twenty-seven cubits thick and taller than the tallest palm trees of this fertile and well-watered land.

'How far is it to ride around this city?' Trok asked Ishtar the Mede. He knew that Ishtar had lived in Babylon for fifteen years, and had learned much of his magic here in the temple of Marduk.

'Ten leagues, Majesty,' Ishtar told him. 'Half a day's ride.'

Trok stood on the footplate of his chariot and cast a general's eye along the wall. There were watchtowers at every two hundred paces, and at regular intervals the massive walls were heavily buttressed.

Ishtar knew what he was thinking. 'There is a road along the top of the wall, wide enough for two chariots to ride abreast. Within an hour Sargon can move five thousand men along it to any point threatened by a besieging army.'

Trok grunted. 'Any wall can be undermined and sapped. We need only one breach.'

'There is an inner wall, Divine Pharaoh,' Ishtar murmured in a silky tone. 'It is almost as impregnable as the first.'

'If we cannot go through, we will find a way round.' Trok shrugged. 'Are those the gardens of Sargon's palace?' He indicated the terraces that rose in tiers into the sky. They were so skilfully raised upon each other that they seemed to float, free of the bounds of the earth.

Ishtar pointed with one sinewy, blue-tattooed arm. 'There are six terraces built round a vast courtyard. The *zenana* alone has five thousand rooms, one for each of Sargon's wives. His treasure is buried deep below the palace, Majesty, and I tell you straight that in all your army you do not have sufficient wagons to carry away such a treasure.'

'And I tell you straight, Ishtar, that I can always build new wagons.' Trok threw back his head and laughed with animal high spirits.

Once Ishtar had dissuaded him from leading an army into the eastern desert to attack Nefer Seti and to capture Mintaka, his runaway woman, the march to Babylon had been one long triumph, an unbroken string of victories.

They had met Ran, Sargon's eldest son, on the banks of the Bahr al Milh: between the chariots of Trok and Naja they had ground his army to fragments, and had sent Ran's severed head to his father, skewered on a spear. Maddened with grief, Sargon had charged into the trap they had prepared for him. While Naja retreated before him to lure him on, Trok had circled out to the south then come at him from the rear with a thousand chariots. When Sargon turned back to defend his baggage train, they had him in a glittering ring of bronze.

Sargon had managed to break out with fifty chariots, but in his headlong retreat he had left two thousand chariots and eleven thousand men behind him. Now Babylon lay before Trok, little more than a year since he and Naja had marched from Avaris.

'You know the defences, Ishtar. You helped design some of them. How long before the city falls?' Trok demanded impatiently.

'A year,' Ishtar murmured thoughtfully. 'Or two, maybe three.' But there was a sly look on his tattooed face, and his eyes were shifty.

Trok laughed and pushed him away so hard that he almost fell from the footplate of the chariot. 'A year, you say? Two? Three? I have not that amount of time to sit here. I am in a hurry, Ishtar the Mede, and you know what that means, don't you?'

'I know, god without peer. And I am but a man, fallible and poor.'

'Poor?' Trok shouted in his face. 'By Seueth, you slimy charlatan, you have milked me of a lakh of gold already, and what do I have to show for it?'

'You have a city and an empire. After Egypt itself, the richest in the world. I have laid it at your feet.'

'I need the key to that city.' Trok watched his face, happy with what he saw there. He knew Ishtar well. 'Give me the city, Ishtar. Give it to me within three full moons and you shall have two more lakhs of gold from the treasure of Sargon,' he promised.

'If I give it to you before the next full moon?' Ishtar rubbed his hands together like a carpet trader.

Trok's grin left his face at the prospect. He said seriously, 'Then you shall have three lakhs, and a convoy of wagons to carry them away.'

THE ARMY OF THE TWO PHARAOHS went into camp before the legendary Blue Gate, and Trok sent an emissary to Sargon to demand the immediate surrender of the city. In reply, Sargon, defiant behind his walls, sent the messenger's decapitated head back to Trok. The preliminaries having been dealt with, Trok and Naja made a circuit of the walls to allow the Babylonians to view their full might and splendour.

They drove golden chariots, Trok's drawn by six black stallions, Naja's by six white. Heseret rode beside Naja, glittering with jewels. They were preceded by a vanguard of five hundred chariots and followed by a rearguard of another five hundred. The slow, stately circuit of the city took all that day, and at sunset Heseret retired to her tent with all her slave girls, leaving her husband and Trok to pore over a map of the city by lamplight with Ishtar. The map was a work of art, drawn in coloured detail on finely tanned sheepskin.

'How came this map into your possession?' Naja demanded.

'Twelve years ago, by the command of King Sargon, I surveyed the city and drew this map with my own hands,' Ishtar replied. 'No other could have achieved such accuracy and beauty.'

'If he commissioned it, why did you not deliver it to Sargon?'

'I did.' Ishtar nodded. 'I delivered the inferior draft to him, while secretly I kept the fair copy you see before you. I knew that one day someone would pay me more handsomely than Sargon ever did.'

For another hour they studied the map, silent and absorbed. As fighting generals with a professional eye for the salient features of a battlefield, they were able to admire the depth and strength of the walls, the towers and redoubts.

At last Trok stood back from the table. 'There is no weakness that I can divine, magician. You were right the first time. It will take three years of hard work to break through those walls. You will have to do better than this to earn your three lakhs.'

'The water,' whispered Ishtar. 'Look to the water.'

'I have looked to the water.' Naja smiled at him, thin-lipped. 'There are canals supplying every quarter of the city, enough water to grow Sargon's six terraces of gardens for a hundred years.'

'Pharaoh is all-seeing, all-wise.' Ishtar bowed to him. 'But where does the water come from?'

'From two mighty rivers that have not failed in this millennium.'

'But where does the water enter the city? How does it pass through, under or over those walls?' Ishtar insisted, and Naja and Trok exchanged looks of dawning comprehension.

HALF A MILE NORTH of Babylon, outside the city walls, on the east bank of the Euphrates, at a point where the river broadened and ran sluggishly, stood the temple of Ninurta, the lion-headed winged god of the Euphrates. It was built on stone piers that extended out into the river, with multiple images of the god engraved on a frieze on the outer walls.

Trok, with twenty troopers at his back, strode through into the temple courtyard where the purple-robed priests of Ninurta were gathered. He killed the high priest with a single thrust through the old man's throat. Wailing at such sacrilege, the other priests prostrated themselves before him.

Trok sheathed his sword and nodded to the captain, who commanded the guard. 'Kill them all. Make certain no one escapes.'

Then he turned to watch Ishtar, who had entered the courtyard to work a charm to counteract the baleful influence of Ninurta. At four corners he burned bundles of herbs, which emitted thick, greasy smoke. Once Ishtar had completed the purification, he took a bunch of heavy keys from the body of the high priest, then led Trok and his troopers into the holy places of the temple.

Their cleated sandals rang hollowly in the high cavernous hall, and even Trok felt a religious chill as they approached the image of the god on his plinth. The lion's head snarled silently and the wings of stone were spread wide. Ishtar led Trok into the narrow space between the rear wall and the idol's back. Built into the body of Nintura was a grilled gate. Trok tried two of the keys in the lock, and the second turned the ancient mechanism. The gate swung open on creaking hinges.

Trok peered down a descending spiral staircase into darkness, and he heard the sound of running water far below.

'Bring torches!' he ordered, and the captain sent four of his troopers to take down the burning torches from their brackets. With a torch held above his head, Trok started down the narrow steps. He went gingerly, for the stone treads were slippery. The sound of running water grew louder as he went down.

Ishtar followed him closely. 'This temple and the tunnels beneath it were built almost five hundred years ago,' he told Trok.

Now there was the gleam of water below them, and the sound of the torrent running swiftly in the darkness. At last Trok reached the bottom, and by the wavering torchlight he saw that they stood in a wide tunnel with a curved roof, an aqueduct of impressive dimensions. The roof and walls were lined with ceramic tiles, laid in geometric patterns. Both ends of the tunnel shaded off into deep darkness.

'This footpath on which we stand runs the full length of the aqueduct,' Ishtar explained. 'The priests who repair and maintain the tunnel use it to gain access.'

'Where does it start and where does it end?' Trok demanded.

'The far end of the aqueduct emerges in the other temple of Ninurta within the walls of Babylon. Only the priests know of the existence of this tunnel. All others believe that the water is a benevolent gift from the god. After it gushes from the fountain in the temple precinct, the water is lifted by water wheels to the gardens of the palace, or sent by canals to every quarter of the city.'

'I do believe, Ishtar the Mede, that you are close to earning your three lakhs.' Trok laughed with delight. 'It remains only for you to lead us down this rabbit hole, and into the city.'

TROK CHOSE two hundred of his best and most reliable men, all members of his own leopard tribe. He divided them into two groups. Once they had fought their way through the aqueduct into the city, the first group was to secure the Blue Gate and keep it open until Pharaoh Naja Kiafan could lead the main force through it. The second, smaller group was to make its way into the palace and seize Sargon's treasury.

The chosen two hundred were dressed in the uniforms of Sargon's army, taken from the prisoners and the dead men left on the battlefield. They wore only a red sash to distinguish them from the foe. Rough copies of the city map were hastily drawn by army scribes and issued to the captains of both divisions so that they knew the layout of streets and buildings. By evening every man knew exactly what was expected of him once he entered the city.

As soon as it was dark, Naja quietly moved his assault force up into position outside the Blue Gate, ready to dash through into the city as soon as Trok's men threw it open.

In the courtyard of the river temple of Ninurta, Trok mustered his division. While it was still daylight, he and Ishtar led them in single file down the spiral staircase. They marched in silence, every tenth man carrying a torch, giving just sufficient light for the men who followed to make out their footing on the slimy stones. At their left hand the never-ending flow of water rustled darkly by.

Abruptly Ishtar stopped and pointed ahead. The faint glimmer of light was reflected off the shiny ceramic walls. Trok signalled the men following him to halt, then went forward with Ishtar. Over their own garments they wore headdresses and purple robes taken from the bodies of the slaughtered priests.

As they went towards the source of the light, they saw another gate across the tunnel, and the distorted shadows of men thrown on the walls by the light of a torch set in a bracket. On the other side of the grille two robed priests were seated on stools, with a bao board between them, absorbed in their game. They looked up when Ishtar called softly to them.

The fat one stood up. 'Are you from Sinna?' he called.

'Yes!' Ishtar assured him.

'You are late. We have been waiting since nightfall.'

'I am sorry,' Ishtar sounded contrite, 'but you know Sinna.'

The fat priest chuckled, 'Yes, I know Sinna. He taught me my responses thirty years ago.'

His key jangled in the lock of the gate, and then he swung it open. 'You must hurry,' he said. Trok trotted forward with the hood over his face, holding his sword in the fold of his robe. The priest stood back against the wall to let him pass. Trok stopped in front of him, whispered, 'Ninurta will reward you, brother,' and killed him.

With a shout of alarm, the priest's companion leapt to his feet, knocking over the bao board and scattering the stones across the pier. With two long strides Trok reached him and chopped his head half off. Without another sound, the priest fell backwards.

Trok gave a soft whistle and his men moved up into the torchlight with drawn swords. Ishtar led them forward until they reached the foot of another steep stone stairway. They went up it quickly until they came to a heavy curtain blocking their way. Ishtar peeped around its edge and nodded. 'The temple is empty.'

Trok stepped through and looked about him. Below them the image of the god crouched over the mouth of the aqueduct from which the water spurted into a deep pond, then spilled over into the canal that carried it to the city. Although the smell of incense was thick in the air, the great hall of the temple was deserted.

Trok signalled his men to come forward. Ishtar led the smaller band through a side door of the hall into a corridor that connected with the palace of Sargon. Trok led his men out into the narrow lane behind the temple and, working only from his memory of the map, turned at the second lane into the wide avenue that he knew led to the Blue Gate. It was still dark in the sleeping city.

They met a number of cloaked figures on the way, one or two staggering drunk, but the others scurried out of their way and let the column of dark armed warriors pass. They reached the end of the avenue without being challenged, but as the gateway loomed ahead a voice sang out at them from the door of the guardhouse.

'Stand ho!' The centurion of the gate, with five men at his back, stepped out into the torchlight. But they were ill-prepared, without helmets and body armour, their faces still crumpled with sleep.

Trok gave the hand signal for his troops to charge. 'Open the gate and stand aside!' he ran straight at the centurion.

For a moment longer the man stood uncertainly. Then Trok was on him, and dropped him with a single blow. His men swarmed over the other guards before they could defend themselves, but the noise had alerted the sentinels on the parapets above the gate. They sounded the alarm with braying rams' horns, and hurled their javelins down into the attackers.

'Winkle them out of there!' Trok ordered, and half of his men rushed up the ramps on either side of the gateway to reach the parapet. They were at once locked in close and desperate fighting with the guards on the wall. Trok kept half of his men with him.

Ishtar had described the gate room that housed the heavy winches and pulleys that operated the massive gates. After only a few minutes of furious fighting Trok's men had killed or wounded most of the defenders within. The survivors fled out of the postern gate, and Trok led his men to the massive winches. With two men on each spoke of the capstans they began to open the gates.

Outside the walls Naja's men had swarmed forward with crowbars and levers. They forced the heavy gates wider and wider, until at last a squadron of chariots could pass through. Then they stood aside, and Naja led a phalanx of fighting chariots in a brutal charge through the gateway, and swept the avenue from side to side. The army of Egypt poured through behind them. Trok took command of them and led them rampaging through the city towards the palace.

The sack of Babylon had begun.

THE DEFENCE OF THE PALACE was stubborn, led by Sargon himself. However, by that evening Trok had opened a breach in the outer walls of the first terrace. He led a strong contingent through and the defence collapsed. When they burst into Sargon's bedchamber he was kneeling before the image of Marduk, the devouring god of Mesopotamia, with a bloody sword through his breast. Beside him lay the body of his favourite wife, a grey-haired woman who had been with him for thirty years. Before falling on his sword he had given her a merciful death, compared to what she might have expected from Trok's men.

The women from the *zenana* were herded out of the palace. Trok selected twenty, the youngest and prettiest, for his personal entertainment, and the rest were given to his senior officers.

It took another two days to break into the treasury buried deep in the earth below the palace, for many ingenious constructions and devices guarded it. Without the expertise and first-hand knowledge of Ishtar the Mede, it might have taken even longer to penetrate to the chamber.

When the way was clear, Trok and Naja, Heseret following them, descended the stairway and entered the chamber. Ishtar had lit the interior with a hundred oil lamps, and even the two pharaohs were stunned into silence by the splendour of the treasure. Heseret had to shade her eyes against the dazzle of the masses of precious metal. Naja walked forward slowly between the stacks, which were higher than his head, stopping every few paces to stroke the ingots.

Trok picked up a heavy bar in each hand and laughed with delight. 'How much?' he demanded of Ishtar.

'Splendid and Divine Majesty, the scrolls of Sargon's scribes record the total weight of silver at fifty-five lakhs, the gold at thirty-three.' He spread his tattooed hands deprecatingly. 'But who would trust the count of a Babylonian?'

'Sargon is a greater robber than I gave him credit for.' Trok made it sound like a compliment.

'At least there is enough here to pay me the pittance you promised?' Ishtar suggested smoothly.

'I think we should discuss that further.' Trok smiled at him genially. 'I am a kindly and generous man, Ishtar, as you know full well. However, stupid I am not.'

Once he had finished gloating over the contents of the treasury, there was much else to see and marvel at within the city. Trok and Naja toured the palace, climbing to the top terrace with its fountains and gardens. From this height they could look down on both the great rivers and the vista of fields, marshes and papyrus beds outside the city walls.

Next they visited all the temples, for these magnificent buildings were also stuffed with bullion, beautiful furniture, statuary, mosaics and other works of art. The greatest of these temples was that of Marduk the Devourer. Trok found this to be not only a mine of precious metal and jewellery but a place of endless fascination.

He knelt on a pile of leopardskins spread on the stone floor in the inner sanctum of the temple before the altar. The golden image of the god was of a comely youth, three or four times life-sized.

'You told me that Marduk was a terrible god, crueller than any other in the pantheon, more ferocious even than Seueth,' Trok challenged Ishtar, 'yet this is a pretty boy.'

'Divine Pharaoh, be not deceived!' Ishtar warned him. 'This is the face that Marduk shows the world. His true aspect is so hideous that any man who looks upon it is instantly rendered blind and mad.'

Sobered by that thought, Trok remained silent while the priests brought in two kids and offered them to the god. Ishtar slit their throats so skilfully that they made hardly a sound as they bled into the golden divination bowl that he held beneath them and then placed before the altar into the incense braziers. Chanting and mumbling, he threw handfuls of herbs on the flames until the vault filled with fragrant blue smoke. After a while Trok found it difficult to think clearly and his vision became distorted. He closed his eyes and pressed his fingers into the lids. When he opened them again he saw that the sweet smile on the face of the god had become a leer. He tried to look away but found he could not.

'The great god Marduk is pleased,' Ishtar announced, reading the auguries reflected in the surface of the blood-filled bowl. After a long silence he began to rock gently back and forth with the bowl in his lap. He looked up at last. 'Behold Marduk, the great god of Babylon! Speak to us, dreadful one, we entreat you!'

He opened his arms to the golden statue, and the god spoke in the voice of a child, lisping and mellifluous.

'I greet you, my brother Trok,' said this strange voice. 'You wish to know about the fledgling falcon that spreads its wings and sharpens its talons in the desert places.'

Trok was startled not only by the disembodied voice but also by the accuracy of this statement. Indeed, he had intended asking for counsel on his plans to attack and destroy Nefer Seti. He recalled bitterly how Ishtar had dissuaded him from leading another army into the eastern desert to attack Nefer Seti, with predictions of dire consequences, with warnings of disaster and death. Now he spoke as much to himself as to the golden god. 'I must have Nefer Seti. The double crown will sit uneasily on my head until I kill him and throw his body on the flames so that he will never know resurrection.'

In his anger and hatred he sprang to his feet. 'I demand that you deliver the person and the soul of Nefer Seti to me, in justice and retribution. I will not accept another refusal from you and your minion here.' In his fury Trok aimed a kick at Ishtar. His sandal caught the divining bowl and the blood of the kids splattered down the altar.

A hush had fallen over the sanctum. Then there was the sound of breathing, like that of a sleeping child to begin with but then growing harsher and stronger. Now it was the breathing of a wild beast, then of some monster that echoed through the temple.

Then a terrible voice spoke, harsh and unearthly. 'Hear me! Trok Uruk, you mortal man who claims to be Pharaoh, part of the godhead!' The thunder rolled around the dark recess of the sanctum. 'Hear me, blasphemer! If you march against Gallala in defiance of me and my prophet, Ishtar the Mede, I shall destroy you and your army just as I buried your other army in the sands of the desert. This time you shall not escape my wrath.'

Even though he was fearful of the rage of Marduk, Trok still sensed some false note in the force of his fury.

He tried to identify exactly what had given him pause. He realised that the thunderous voice issued from the belly of the statue. He stared and saw that the navel of the god was a dark slit. He took a step towards it and Ishtar cried, 'Beware, Pharaoh! Do not approach him.'

Trok ignored him and took another step forward, seeing a faint gleam in the depths of the aperture, a shadowy movement. Often in battle he had sensed the exact moment when the fates had swung in his favour and he felt it now. He steeled himself and shouted, above the awful sound of the god's breathing, 'I defy you, Marduk the Devourer! Strike me down if you are able.'

Suspicion became certainty as that glimmer showed again in the slit in the god's belly. Trok drew his sword and, with the flat of the blade, knocked Ishtar out of his way. Then he ran forward, ducked down, and peered into the slit. A human eye looked back at him. The pupil widened with astonishment, and Trok gave a mighty shout: 'Come out of there you slime!' He placed his shoulder against the idol and heaved with all his strength. The statue wobbled on its stone base, and Trok heaved again. Slowly the image went down with a crash onto the stone flags.

Ishtar screamed and leapt out of the way. In the silence after the shattering impact there was a scrabbling sound from the interior of the fallen idol. A trap door at the back of the idol flew open and a girl crawled out. Trok seized her by a thick head of curls. 'Mercy, great King Trok,' the girl pleaded, in a honey-sweet voice. 'I was doing the bidding of others.' She was such a lovely child that, for a moment, Trok felt his rage subside. Then he snatched her up by the ankles and dangled her upside-down in one fist, writhing in his grip.

'Who ordered you to this?' Trok demanded.

'Ishtar the Mede,' she wept.

Trok dashed the child against a temple column then let her corpse drop. He turned back to the golden idol and thrust his sword into the opening, rummaging around in the belly of the god. There was another squeal and a grotesque creature shot out, a hunch-backed dwarf, the ugliest man Trok had ever laid eyes upon.

'Forgive me that I tried to deceive you, mighty god and King of Egypt!' Trok slashed at him with the sword, but the creature ducked and dodged roaring with terror. Trok found himself laughing at his antics. The dwarf shot behind the curtains at the back of the chamber and disappeared through a secret doorway.

Trok let him go and turned back to Ishtar, just in time to seize a handful of his hair as he tried to flee from the chamber. He flung him full length on the stone floor.

'You have lied to me.' Trok was no longer laughing. 'You have deliberately misled me and diverted me from my purpose.'

'Please, master,' Ishtar wailed. 'It was for your good alone. How could we go against a warlock who commands the storm to his will?'

'You are afraid of Taita.' Trok stood back to regain his breath. 'The warlock?' he demanded incredulously.

'He overlooks us. He can turn my own spells back upon me! I

cannot prevail against him. I sought only to save you from him, great Pharaoh.'

'You sought only to save your own blue-tattooed skin,' Trok snarled, and rushed in to slam kicks into Ishtar's doubled-up body.

'I beg of you, first of all the gods,' Ishtar cried, covering his head with both arms, 'give me my reward and let me go. Taita has dissipated my powers. I cannot confront him again. I can be of no further use to you.'

Trok stood with one foot drawn back, frozen in the act of delivering another kick. 'Your reward?' he demanded in astonishment. 'Surely you do not believe that I will reward your disloyalty? If you wish to live another day then you will lead me to Gallala, and take your chances in a trial of magical strength with the warlock.'

IT SEEMED THAT ALL EGYPT had heard that Nefer Seti had an army in Gallala. Each day visitors from all over the country arrived. Some were colonels of the regiments that Trok and Naja had left to guard Egypt in their absence. Others were emissaries from the great cities along the Nile—Avaris and Memphis, Thebes and Aswan—and the high priests from the temples in those cities. Sickened and saddened by the tyrannies and excesses of Naja and Trok, and emboldened by their absence in Babylon so far to the east, all had come to swear allegiance to Nefer Seti.

'Egypt is ready to welcome you,' the emissaries told him.

'Our regiments will declare for you as soon as they see your face, and know that the rumours of your survival are true,' the colonels assured him.

Nefer and Taita questioned them keenly. It soon became apparent that Trok and Naja had skimmed the cream of the regiments for their Mesopotamian adventure, and left only the reserve battalions, made up mostly of new recruits, the very young and untried, or the elderly nearing the end of their military lives.

'What of the chariots and horses?' Nefer asked the crucial question. They shook their grey heads and looked grave. 'Trok and Naja stripped the regiments bare. Almost every vehicle went with them. They left hardly enough to patrol the eastern borders to discourage the Bedouin raiders from the desert.'

Taita assessed this information. 'The false pharaohs are fully aware of the threat we pose to their rear. They want to ensure that if the regiments they have left in Egypt rebel against them and declare for the true Pharaoh, Nefer Seti, they will lack cavalry and chariots to be an effective force.'

'You must return to your regiments,' Nefer ordered the officers. 'We are too many in Gallala already, and we are near the limits of our food and water. Do not allow any more vehicles or horses to leave Egypt. Keep your men in training, and equip them with new chariots as they become available. I will come to you very soon, to lead you against the tyrants.'

They left, with renewed assurances of their loyalty, and the little army of Gallala redoubled its efforts to build itself into a force to challenge the might of the false pharaohs. They were inspired by their young commander, for Nefer worked harder than any of them. He rode out with the first squadrons long before dawn, and gradually forged his divisions into a cohesive body. When he rode back into the city, weary and dusty in the evening, he would go to the workshops where he cajoled and argued with the armourers and chariot builders. Then, after he had eaten, he would sit up in the lamplight with Taita, going over the battle plans and the dispositions of their forces. Usually it was after midnight when he stumbled to his bedchamber, where Mintaka took his head onto her bosom and held him until he woke to dawn's first promise.

NEFER LOOKED BACK along the column of chariots. They were at full gallop, four abreast. The platoon commanders were watching for his signal. He looked ahead and saw the line of enemy foot soldiers out in the plain, distorted by the heat mirage so that they seemed to be swimming in a lake of shimmering water where there was no water. He steered for their centre.

As they raced in he saw the enemy formation change. Like a giant hedgehog, it rolled itself into a ball, a tight circle two ranks deep, facing outwards, the outer rank with their long lances levelled, and the second rank with their lances thrust through the gaps, so that they offered a glittering wall of bronze spearheads. Nefer raced straight at the centre of the double row of lances, and then, when they were only two hundred paces away, he gave a hand signal and the formation of chariots opened, wheeling alternately right and left, spreading like wings to envelope the crouching infantrymen. The chariots whirled around them and the arrows from the short recurved cavalry bows flew into them.

Nefer gave the signal to break off the attack and withdraw. As he swept past the infantry circle, he raised his right fist in a salute, and shouted, 'Well done! That was much better.'

He slowed the horses and turned them, trotting back to halt his squadron in front of the ranks of infantry. Taita stepped out of the defensive circle to greet him.

'Any injuries?' Nefer asked. The tips of the arrows they shot into the hedgehog were padded, but they could still inflict damage.

'A few bruises.' Taita shrugged.

'They have done well,' Nefer said, then shouted to the centurion commanding the infantry, 'Let your lads fall out. I want to speak to them. Then we will practise the false retreat.'

There was an outcrop of rock that formed a natural podium, and Nefer climbed to the top of it while all the men—infantry and charioteers—gathered below him.

Taita squatted at the base of the rock and watched and listened. Nefer reminded him strongly of Pharaoh Tamose, his father, at the same age. He had the easy manner, and spoke simply, in language that his men understood.

Nefer reviewed the morning's exercises, giving them the credit they deserved, but ruthlessly picking out every deficiency. 'I think you are almost ready to give Trok and Naja the surprise of their lives,' he ended. 'Now, get something to eat. We have not finished for the day.' They began to disperse.

Nefer jumped down from the rock, and as he did so Taita sprang to his feet and said quietly but urgently, 'Stop, Nefer! Do not move!'

The cobra must have had its nest in the rock pile, but the noise and the trampling of feet and hoofs had disturbed it. It had come slithering out of the crack in the dark rock, and reared up behind Nefer, almost as high as his waist. Its hood was flared open, and its feathery black tongue flickered between the thin, grinning lips. Its eyes were beads of polished onyx, with sparks of light in the black centres, and they were fastened on Nefer's long bare legs, which were within easy striking distance.

The nearest men had heard Taita's warning. They turned back but none dared move. They stared in horror at the mortal predicament of their pharaoh.

The cobra gaped wide, the preliminary to the attack, and the bony fangs came erect in the pale roof of its mouth. Drops of venom sparkled on the needle points.

Suddenly there was a shrill cry from the sky above. They had all been so intent on the cobra that no one had seen the falcon hovering high in the blue above them. Now it stooped towards the earth, and in full flight sank its talons into the flared hood, an inch behind the head. Then it rose on heavily flogging wings, carrying the cobra dangling and twisting below it.

Taita watched the bird as it bore away the snake. It dwindled in size in the distance and at last disappeared into the blue-grey heat-haze that shrouded the horizon. Taita stood a long time staring after it. When he turned his expression was grave.

'It was an omen,' Nefer said, and glanced at him. He saw by Taita's face that this was so.

'Yes,' said Taita. 'It was a warning and a promise.'

'What does it mean?'

'The cobra threatened you. That means great danger. The royal bird flew towards the east with the snake in its talons. It means great danger in the east. But in the end the falcon triumphed.'

They both looked towards the east. 'We will take out a scouting expedition tomorrow at the first light of dawn,' Nefer decided.

IN THE CHILL DARKNESS before the dawn Nefer and Taita waited on the mountaintop. The rest of the scouting party were encamped on the back slope. All told they were twenty men.

Hilto, Shabako and Meren had taken other scouting parties to cover the terrain to the south; between them they could sweep all the eastern approaches to Gallala.

Nefer had brought his party down along the western shores of the Red Sea, looking in on every port and fishing village along the way. Apart from a few trading caravans and wandering bands of Bedouin they had found nothing, no sign of the danger foreshadowed by the omen. Now they were camped above the port of Safaga.

Taita and Nefer had woken in the darkness and left the camp to climb to the lookout peak. They sat close together in companionable silence. Taita looked to the eastern sky, where the morning star hung low on the horizon.

He stood up suddenly and leaned on his staff. Nefer never failed to be amazed by the acuity of those pale old eyes. He knew Taita had seen something.

'What is it, Old Father?'

'The omen was not false,' Taita said simply. 'The danger is here.'

The sea was grey, but as the light strengthened, the surface was speckled with white. Like a vast flock of egrets returning to the roost, a fleet of dhows was heading into the port of Safaga.

'If this is the army of Trok and Naja, why would they come by sea?' Nefer asked quietly.

'It is the shortest route from Mesopotamia. The crossing will save the horses and men for the road through the desert. Without the warning of the snake and the falcon, we would not have expected danger from this direction.' Taita nodded approval. 'It is a cunning move.'

They scrambled back down the mountain to the camp in the gorge below. The troopers were awake and alert. Nefer called in the sentries and gave them their orders. Two would ride back with all speed to Gallala, carrying his orders to Socco, whom he had left in command. Most of the other men he split into pairs and sent south to find the scouting parties and bring them in.

Nefer and Taita watched the men Nefer had dispatched ride away, then they mounted and rode down through the hills to an abandoned watchtower overlooking Safaga.

'The first boats are entering the bay.' Nefer pointed out the largest of them all. At the peak of her stubby mast she flew the snarling leopard-head gonfalon of the House of Trok Uruk. 'There he is.' He pointed to the unmistakable figure in the bows.

'And that is Ishtar beside Trok: the dog and its master.' Taita had a fierce gleam in his pale eyes as they watched the strange pair wade ashore.

'Do you see Naja's standard on any of the ships?' Nefer asked.

Taita shook his head. 'Trok alone leads the expedition. He must have left Naja to hold Babylon and Mesopotamia. He has come to take care of personal business.'

'How do you know that?' Nefer demanded.

'There is an aura around him. It is like a dark red cloud. I can sense it even from here,' Taita said softly. 'All that hatred is focused on one person alone. He comes for Mintaka.'

THE MORNING AFTER HIS LANDING at Safaga, Trok captured two Bedouin leading a string of donkeys down the road to Safaga. His reputation had penetrated even into these desert fastnesses, so the Bedouin were desperate to please. They told Trok of the lush pastures that surrounded Gallala. They also gave him an estimate of the numbers of chariots that Nefer Seti commanded, and Trok realised that he outnumbered his enemies five to one. Most important of all, they told him the route from Safaga to the ancient city and assured him he could reach Gallala in two days and a night of hard riding.

It took him two more days to disembark all his squadrons. On the second evening he was ready to begin the forced march on Gallala. Each of the chariots had two spare teams behind it on lead reins. They would not stop during the night to rest the horses, but would change them as they tired. Any exhausted animals would be turned loose and left behind for the remount herds to bring up.

Trok led the vanguard, and set a killing pace. Once the waterskins were empty there would be no turning back. By midmorning the following day the heat had become fierce, and they had used up most of the spare horses. The Bedouin guides kept assuring Trok that Gallala was not far ahead, but each time they topped a rise the same daunting vista of rock and baked earth shimmered in the heat mirage ahead. Fifty or sixty chariots burned out their last horses, and Trok left them scattered back along the road.

The sun came up on the second day, warm as a kiss, but it was a treacherous kiss. Soon it stung and dazzled their bloodshot eyes. For the first time Trok faced the possibility of dying here on this dreadful road to nowhere.

'One more hill,' he called to his last team of horses, and tried to whip them into a trot, but they stumbled up the easy incline with their heads hanging, and the sweat long ago dried to white salt on their flanks. Just below the crest Trok looked back down the straggling column of his army. Even without counting them he saw that he had lost half of his chariots. Hundreds of dismounted troopers were staggering along behind the column, and there were vultures in the sky following them, dark specks turning in high circles against the blue.

'There is only one way,' he told Ishtar, 'and that is forward.' He cracked the whip over the backs of his team. They went on painfully.

They reached the top of the hill, and Trok gawked in astonishment at the scene in the valley below him. The ruins of the ancient city of Gallala lay before him, ghostly but eternal. As he had been promised, the city was surrounded by fields of cool green, and a network of canals. His horses smelt the water and strained against the reins with renewed strength.

Even in his desperate haste, Trok took time to assess the tactical situation. He saw at once that the city was helpless and undefended. The gates stood wide open and from them poured the panic-stricken populace. Carrying their children and pathetic bundles of possessions they streamed away up the narrow, steep-sided valley to the west. A few foot soldiers mingled with the refugees, but there was no sign of cavalry or of fighting chariots. They were a flock of sheep before the wolf pack, but the wolves were parched and weak with thirst.

'Seueth has delivered them into our hands,' Trok shouted with triumph. 'Before the sun sets this day you will have more women and gold than you can use!'

The men who had followed him over the ridge rode down to the first irrigation ditch and spread out along the length of it, the horses sucking up the blessed liquid. The men threw themselves full length along the bank, plunging their faces under, or filling their helmets and pouring it over their heads and down their throats.

'YOU SHOULD HAVE LET ME POISON the canals,' Nefer said flatly, as they watched from the other side of the valley.

'You know better than that.' Taita shook his silver head. 'That would have been an offence against nature that the gods would never forgive.'

He and Nefer gave their full attention to the unfolding scene in the valley below. Trok's men and horses had drunk until their bellies bulged and now they were mounting. Even though he had lost many chariots on the approach march, Trok still outnumbered Nefer's forces at least three to one.

'We dare not meet him on open ground,' Nefer mused, and looked down upon the mass of refugees escaping up the valley below them. Mintaka, together with all the women and children, the sick and wounded, had been evacuated from Gallala two days before. Nefer had sent them all to Gebel Nagara, where Trok would never find them.

Now Gallala was stripped of everything of value. Nefer gazed down on the refugees with satisfaction. Even from this close it was difficult to tell that they were not women and civilians but disguised foot soldiers, stumbling in their long skirts and shawls. The bundles they carried were not swaddled infants, but their bows and swords. Their lances had been cached among the rocks higher up the valley where the main force was concealed.

The enemy's chariots were coming on across the pastures in tight formations, wave after wave of fighting vehicles. The water had revived them, and before them lay the promise of plunder. They were close enough now for Nefer to be able to pick out Trok's chariot at the front of the moving mass of vehicles, as it wheeled into a position across the mouth of the valley.

'Come, Trok Uruk!' Nefer whispered. 'Order the charge! Ride into history!'

ISHTAR THE MEDE crouched beside Trok in the leading chariot. He was so agitated that he reached up to tug at Trok's beard.

'The smell of the warlock hangs in the air.' His voice was shrill, and saliva frothed on his lips. 'He waits for you, I can feel his presence. Look up, mighty Pharaoh!'

Trok was distracted enough to glance up at the sky. The vultures had dropped lower.

'Yes! Yes!' Ishtar pressed the small advantage. 'They are Taita's chickens. They wait for him to feed them with your flesh.'

Trok looked back up the valley at the prize that lay before him, but the shadows of the vultures flitted over the earth between them and he turned his head to look down at the skinny figure of Ishtar beside him.

The Mede tugged at his armour. 'It is a snare laid for you by the warlock. If you never trust me again, you must trust me now. There is death in the air.'

Trok scratched his beard, and glanced over his shoulder at the ranks of chariots parked wheel to wheel and his troopers leaning forward in cruel anticipation of his order.

'Turn aside, mighty Trok. Seize the city and the water. Nefer Seti and the warlock will perish out there in the desert. That way is certain. The other way is madness.'

ON THE HILLSIDE Nefer narrowed his eyes as he watched his disguised troopers scurrying away up the valley, and he knew that the moment was passing. 'What is holding Trok? Will he not commit to the charge?'

'Look to the head of the valley.' Taita had not opened his eyes.

Nefer glanced up the valley, and stiffened with alarm. His fist tightened on the hilt of his sword. 'It is not possible!' he growled.

Near the top end of the valley, but fully visible from where Trok's chariots were drawn up, was a slab of rock. On top of this, above the stream of fleeing refugees, had appeared a woman, young and slim, with long, dark hair that hung to her waist.

'Mintaka!' Nefer breathed. 'I ordered her to go to Gebel Nagara.'

'We know that she would never have disobeyed you.' Taita smiled ironically. 'Therefore, it seems that she must have misheard you.'

'This is your doing,' Nefer said bitterly. 'You are using her as bait for Trok. You have placed her in mortal danger.'

'Perhaps I can control the khamsin,' Taita said, 'but not even I can control Mintaka. What she does, she does of her own free will.'

BELOW THEM, TROK had turned round and was staring up the long rising valley. He saw the tiny figure standing high on the yellow rock platform, and recognised in an instant the object of all his hatred.

'Mintaka Apepi,' he snarled, 'I have come for you, you adulterous little bitch. I will make you plead for death.'

'It is an illusion, Pharaoh,' Ishtar howled. 'Don't let the warlock deceive you. There is death all around us.'

He tried to leap down from the footplate and run, but Trok seized him and hauled him back. He raised his clenched fist high above his head and shouted, 'Forward! March!'

The chariots on either hand rolled forward together, and the ranks behind followed Trok into the valley, the sun sparkling on the javelin heads. The tail of the fleeing refugees was three hundred paces ahead when Trok gave his next order.

'Forward at the gallop! Charge!'

The horses leapt away, and in a rising thunder of hoofs and wheels they swept up the narrow valley.

'Trok has committed,' Nefer said softly. 'But at what cost? If he takes Mintaka . . .' He could not bring himself to go on.

As the phalanx of chariots swept by below where Nefer stood on the side of the valley, he stepped out from behind the rock that had concealed him. The complete attention of Trok and his troopers was fixed on the victims ahead of their racing chariots. They had no eyes for the tall figure that appeared suddenly high on their flank, but all Nefer's men could see him clearly. They were hidden among the boulders down both slopes of the valley. Nefer raised his sword above his head, and as the last chariot sped past he brought it down sharply.

The wagons were poised on the steep gradient, screened from view with dried grass and so heavily laden with rocks that the axles sagged. At Nefer's signal his wagoners pulled out the wooden chocks that held them, and from both sides of the valley the wagons rolled forward, gathering speed, bounding down to the massed chariots below.

When Ishtar screamed at his side, Trok tore his eyes from Mintaka's figure at the far end of the valley, and he saw the huge vehicles tearing down upon his squadrons. 'Back!' he shouted. 'Break away!' But there was no space to manoeuvre.

The first wagons crashed into the head of the charge. There was the rending of wood, the screams of crushed men and horses, the thunder of wagons overturning and shedding their loads of rock. In an instant the magnificent charge was transformed into a shambles of shattered vehicles and crippled horses.

The wagons had sealed off the valley at both ends. Even the chariots that had not been smashed and capsized were now bottled up, held by walls of stone, and Nefer's archers were on the slopes above them. The first volleys decimated the unprotected charioteers. Within minutes the valley was transformed into a slaughterhouse.

Trok looked around him wildly, seeking some way out of the trap, but behind him the other vehicles were so crowded that there was no room for him to turn or back up. Arrows and javelins were singing around him, clattering against the sides of the chariot, clanging off his helmet and breastplate.

Before Trok could restrain him, Ishtar took advantage of the confusion to spring down from the footplate and scuttle away between the plunging horses. Then Trok looked ahead again, and saw Mintaka still standing on the rock pile just ahead of him, a cold look of revulsion on her lovely face.

He drew his sword, sprang down to the ground and ran forward under the hoofs of his rearing horses. Two of Nefer's men jumped out from behind the rocks to oppose him but he hacked them down, his eyes fastened hungrily on the girl.

Nefer saw Trok break out of the trap, and he ran down the slope and sprang out onto the level ground in front of him.

Trok went on guard as Nefer confronted him and his face twisted into a ferocious grin. 'Come, puppy,' he said. 'Let us test your claim to the double crown.'

Nefer's men had seen him charge down the hillside. They followed his example, left the cover of the rocks and within seconds the valley was choked with struggling, hacking, thrusting men.

Nefer feinted at Trok's hip, aiming at the joint of his armour. When Trok covered, he swung backhanded at his face. Trok was surprised by the change of direction and by the speed of the stroke. Though he jerked his head back the point of Nefer's blade split his cheek open. The wound galvanised him, and Trok roared and rushed at Nefer, his sword seeming to form an impenetrable wall of shining bronze around him. Nefer was forced to fall back before the attack until he felt the stone slab on which Mintaka stood pressing into his back.

He could no longer retreat or manoeuvre, and he was forced to pit himself against all Trok's strength, and trade him blow for blow. In a contest of this nature, there were few men who could stand against Trok, who never seemed to flag. As much as the years of battle training had hardened Nefer they had not prepared him for this. He felt his right arm tiring. He knew that his only chance of surviving was to break away.

He caught the next cut high on his blade and deflected it just sufficiently to make an opening through which he could escape, but as he leapt into it he exposed his left flank. Trok recovered and drove in a low thrust that laid open his thigh. The blood ran down into his sandal and squelched at every pace he took. The last of Nefer's strength was ebbing away, and Trok swept up his blade and locked it with his own, forcing his guard higher. Nefer knew that if he attempted to break away he would expose his chest for the killing thrust.

Gradually Trok forced aside his blade and towered over him, so they came chest to chest, then suddenly he shifted his weight to the left, towards Nefer's wounded leg. Nefer tried to counter, but his leg gave way under him. Trok hooked his foot behind Nefer's heel and threw him over backwards.

The sword flew from Nefer's grip, and as he sprawled on the sun-baked earth, Trok lifted his blade above his head with both hands for the killing stroke. Suddenly his expression changed. He opened his mouth to say something, but a double stream of bright blood trickled from the corners of his mouth and he turned slowly away from Nefer. Trok stared up at Mintaka, who stood on the rock above him. With a detached feeling of disbelief, Nefer saw the shaft of her javelin sticking out of the back of Trok's neck.

Trok toppled forward on his face, and Nefer turned to Mintaka. She flew to him, and clung to him with all her strength. Now that the danger was past, she had lost all her icy control and was sobbing, barely coherent. 'I thought he was going to kill you, my love.'

'He almost did, but for you,' Nefer gasped. 'I owe you my life.'

He became aware that the sounds of battle from further down the valley had changed. With his arm still around her, he turned to look back. Trok's men had seen him cut down, and the fight had gone out of them. They were throwing down their weapons.

With the realisation of victory, Nefer felt the last strength flow out of his battered and bleeding body. He had just enough left to raise his voice, and shout, 'Give them quarter. They are our brother Egyptians. Give them quarter!'

As Nefer slumped down, Taita materialised at his side and helped Mintaka lower him to the ground. While the two of them staunched the bleeding from the deep cut in his thigh, his officers came to report to Nefer. And with joy, he saw that his trusted captains, Hilto and Meren, Shabako and Socco, were among the men who crowded around him, exulting in the victory.

They made a litter of lances and carried him back down the valley to Gallala. Three times before they reached the gates of the city, Nefer signalled for his litter to be lowered and allowed captured centurions and captains to come forward. 'I spare you from the traitor's death you so richly deserve,' he told them sternly, 'but you are all reduced to the rank of sergeant, and must prove once more your duty and loyalty to the House of Tamose.'

They praised him for his mercy, and his own men joined their voices to those of the defeated.

Nefer issued his orders with a frowning mien. 'The corpse of Trok Uruk, the false claimant to the double crown of Egypt, shall be burned without ceremony, here upon the battlefield, so that his soul shall wander through all eternity, seeking but never finding a home. The name of Trok Uruk shall be erased from every monument and building in the land.'

They shouted their approbation at this decree, and Nefer went on. 'All the possessions of Trok Uruk, all his treasure and estates and slaves, shall be forfeited to the state. Send water wagons back along the road to Safaga, and bring in all the horses, chariots and men that Trok Uruk left along the way during his march on Gallala. If they repudiate the false pharaohs and swear allegiance to the House of Tamose, the prisoners shall be pardoned and recruited into our armies.'

By the time Nefer had issued his last decree for that day, his voice was hoarse, he was pale and almost exhausted. As they carried him through the city gates he asked Mintaka quietly, 'Where is Taita? Has anybody seen the Magus?' But Taita had disappeared.

ON THE HILLSIDE above the battlefield, Taita had picked up the tracks that Ishtar had left as he escaped out of the valley. He followed them until they were impossible to discern in the earth on the top of the hills, which was baked hard as mosaic tiles by the sun. Then he stopped and crouched down. He opened his mind and reached out to detect the Mede's aura, the trace he had left as he passed.

The aura was dark and tainted. Taita stood up and went on again after it, striding out on his long legs. Every so often he saw physical confirmation that he was on the right track, a smudged footprint in softer earth or a recently dislodged pebble.

Ishtar had circled round to the south then come back towards Gallala. Taita was alarmed and lengthened his stride. If Ishtar was trying to get close to Nefer again to work some mischief, Taita must intercept him. However, the pursuit led him to one of the chariots Trok had abandoned on his march up from the coast. From the wreck Ishtar had salvaged a water-skin, and had then gone back to the ridge above the city, where he had crept down to the bank of the closest irrigation canal. The imprint of his knees was clear in the wet clay where he had knelt to drink and then to fill the skin he carried. Taita drank himself. Then he rose and followed the traces Ishtar had left as he started back eastwards along the road towards Safaga and the coast.

Night fell and Taita kept on. Sometimes the aura of the Mede faded away completely, but Taita followed the road. At other times it grew stronger, until Taita smelt it, a faint, musty, unpleasant odour. When it was this strong he could fathom the essence of the Mede. He could detect his vengeful nature. He divined that Ishtar was demoralised by the turn that the fates had taken against him, but his powers were still formidable. He constituted a great and real danger. Taita himself was not immune to his baleful spirit.

A LEAGUE AHEAD Ishtar the Mede was hurrying along the track. He was by now fully aware of the pursuit. I must turn aside and conceal my path, he decided. He ran on along the road and found the place where it crossed an intrusion of grey schist, so hard that even the passing of Trok's legions had left no mark upon it.

With his left forefinger he traced out lightly the sacred symbol of Marduk on the rock, spat on it and uttered the three hidden names of the god that would summon him.

'Hide me from my enemies, mighty Marduk. Bring me back safely to your temple in Babylon.'

Then he turned sharply off the road and set out at right angles to it, heading into the northern wilderness. He went swiftly, trying to open the distance between him and the man who pursued him.

TAITA REACHED THE POINT where the ridge of grey schist crossed the road and stopped abruptly. The aura that had been so strong only moments before had disappeared like mist in the warmth of the rising sun. He went on down the road a short way, but found that the trail was dead and cold. Quickly he retraced his steps until he reached the point where he had lost it.

He looked up at the sky, from the starry firmament picked out the single red star low on the horizon, the star of the goddess Lostris, and began to chant the Praise to the Goddess. He had barely completed the first stanza when he felt an angry, alien presence. Another god had been invoked on this spot, and knowing Ishtar he could guess well enough who that was. He started on the second stanza of praise and on the bare rock ahead of him appeared a glow, like that of a furnace.

Marduk is affronted, and shows his anger, he thought. He intoned, 'You are far from your own land, Marduk of the furnace. Few worship you in Egypt. Your powers are dissipated. I invoke the name of the goddess Lostris, and you cannot stand against it.'

He lifted his kilt. 'I quench your fire, Marduk,' he said, and urinated on the rock. It sizzled like a bar of metal from the forge, drenched in the trough. 'In the name of the goddess Lostris, Marduk the Devourer, stand aside and let me pass.'

The rock cooled quickly, and as the steam dispersed he could make out once more the shadowy traces of the Mede. The veil that Ishtar had laid was pierced and torn. Taita stepped through it and set off again after him.

The horizon paled and the light increased to a golden radiance. Taita knew that he was gaining steadily, and he strained his eyes ahead for the first glimpse of his quarry. Instead he came to an abrupt halt. At his feet gaped a terrible abyss, whose sheer sides dropped into darkness far below.

Taita looked across at the far side. It was a thousand paces across, and there were vultures soaring over the bottomless gulf. Taita shook his head with admiration. 'Wonderful, Ishtar!' he murmured. 'Even the vultures. That was a masterful touch. I could not have improved upon it. But such an effort called for a great expenditure of strength. It must have cost you dearly.'

Taita stepped out over the edge of the cliff. Instead of airy space there was firm ground under his feet. The vista of cliffs and vultures wavered and broke up as a mirage does when you walk towards it.

The abyss was gone and in its place was a gentle plain of stony ground. In the middle of this plain, not five hundred paces away, stood Ishtar the Mede. Seeing Taita striding towards him he turned and broke into a shambling run, his black robes swirling around his legs. Taita followed him with his long, indefatigable strides, and Ishtar was only a few hundred paces ahead when he reached the low hills and disappeared into one of the gullies.

When Taita reached the mouth of the gully he saw Ishtar's footprints strung along the sandy floor ahead of him, but they disappeared round the corner where the gully turned sharply to the right. Taita followed him, but as he reached the corner of pale limestone pillars, he heard the thunderous roaring of a wild beast. Standing foursquare in the way, its tail lashing from side to side, was a huge male lion. Its eyes were golden, the pupils implacable black slits.

Taita didn't break his stride. As he walked straight at the slavering animal, the roaring became muted and the outline of its head turned transparent so that he could see the rock walls of the gulley through it. Then, like river mist, the lion faded and was gone.

Taita walked through the space where it had stood and rounded the corner. Ahead of him the gully became narrower and the sides were steeper. It ended abruptly against a wall of rock.

Ishtar stood with his back against the rock, staring at Taita with mad eyes. He raised his right hand and pointed a long bony finger at Taita. 'Back, Warlock!' he screamed. 'I warn you!'

Taita walked towards him and he screamed again, this time in a guttural language. Then he turned and bolted into a narrow opening in the rock wall behind him, which had been screened from Taita by his body. Taita paused before the entrance, and tapped the stony portals with his staff. The rock rang true. This was no illusion, but the rear entrance to a cavern in the limestone cliff.

Taita stepped through after him, and could hear the echoes of Ishtar's footsteps distorted in the tunnel ahead. Taita counted his paces as he went forward into darkness. After a hundred and twenty the tunnel took a sharp bend, and as he stepped round it Taita found himself in a large, high-roofed cavern. From the floor rose sharp-pointed stalagmites, the crystals glimmering. From the high roof hung down matching stalactites, some shaped like spear-heads and other like the shining wings of the gods. In the centre of the roof was an aperture through which a beam of bright sunlight fell to the floor.

Across the cavern Ishtar crouched against the far wall. There was no escape that way. When he saw Taita appear in the mouth of the tunnel he began to blubber, 'Mercy, mighty Magus! There is a bond between us. We are brothers. Spare me.'

So abject were his entreaties that, despite himself, Taita felt his resolve waver. Ishtar picked up the tiny chink in his armour, and exploited it instantly. He flung out one hand with the thumb and forefinger forming a circle, the sign of Marduk, and shouted something in that strange guttural tongue.

From behind him Taita felt an insupportable physical weight bear down upon his shoulder, and something like the invisible tentacles of an octopus envelop his body, trapping his arms to his sides, wrapping around his throat in a strangler's grip. He smelt scorching human flesh, the aura of the Devourer, suffocating him. He could not move.

On the far side of the cavern Ishtar danced and capered, his tattooed face contorted in a grotesque mask. 'Your goddess cannot protect you here deep in the earth, Taita. You can no longer prevail against Marduk the Devourer and Ishtar, his minion,' he shrieked. 'Our contest is over. I have defeated you and all your wiles, Warlock! Now you will die.'

Taita turned his eyes up towards the high, dim roof of the cavern and fixed all his attention on one of the long, gleaming stalactites that hung down from it like a great shimmering dagger. He gathered all his reserves, lifted the staff in his right hand and pointed it upwards. With the last breath in his lungs he shouted, '*Kydash!*', the word of power.

There was a crack like the ice shattering in the depths of a glacier, the stalactite broke from the roof and plunged downwards. Driven by its own immense weight, the point struck Ishtar on the top of his shoulder, transfixed him through chest and belly and pegged him down on the cavern floor.

As Ishtar twitched convulsively in his death throes, Taita felt the weight lifted from his shoulders and the pressure on his throat relax. Marduk retreated and the smell of burnt flesh was gone.

He picked up his staff, turned and walked back along the tunnel into the open air. At the entrance he turned back and with his staff struck the limestone portals of the tunnel, once, twice, three times.

Deep in the earth there was a rumble of collapsing rock, and a gust of air blew from the tunnel mouth as the cavern roof caved in.

'With the stone spike driven through your heart, not even your foul god can free you from your tomb. Lie in it through all eternity, Ishtar the Mede,' Taita said, and he turned and struck out along the road back to Gallala.

WHEN THE MESSENGERS reached Babylon, Pharaoh Naja Kiafan gave them audience on the uppermost terrace garden of the palace of Babylon. Queen Heseret sat beside his throne, wearing the most magnificent jewels that the treasury of King Sargon had yielded.

The messengers were all high officers from the army that Pharaoh Trok had taken westward four months before. They threw themselves at the foot of the throne on which Naja sat in glory and splendour. 'All hail to you, Pharaoh Naja, mightiest of the gods of Egypt,' they greeted him. 'We are bearers of terrible tidings.'

'Speak!' Naja commanded sternly.

'In the desert that surrounds the ancient city of Gallala there took place a mighty battle between the armies of Pharaoh Trok Uruk and those of the usurper Nefer Seti,' said one of the officers. 'By the means of cowardly deceit the army of Pharaoh Trok Uruk was lured to destruction. He is slain. Those of his men who survived have gone over to the enemy, and have rallied to the standard of the false pharaoh Nefer Seti.'

Naja sank back on his throne and stared at him in astonishment. At his side Heseret touched Naja's arm with a bejewelled finger, and when he leaned towards her she whispered in his ear, 'Praise to the gods, and all hail to the one and only Pharaoh of the Upper and Lower Kingdoms, the mighty Naja Kiafan!'

Naja tried to remain expressionless but a tiny smile played for an instant over his handsome features. It took him a moment to suppress it then he rose. His voice was soft but menacing. 'Pharaoh Trok Uruk is dead. We commend his soul to the gods. I declare before you all that there is now only one ruler over both kingdoms, and over all the territories and all the conquered lands and possessions of Egypt. I declare further that ruler to be myself, Pharaoh Naja Kiafan.'

The courtiers and captains who stood around his throne drew their swords and beat them on their shields. 'Exalted be the king-god Naja Kiafan!'

'Send word to all my commanders and the generals of all my armies. We will meet in war council at the noon hour this same day to prepare all our forces for the campaign against Nefer Seti.'

He looked down at Heseret. 'Do you feel no pity for your brother?'

'None!' She shook her head. 'You are my pharaoh and my husband. Whosoever rises against you deserves death.'

'Death he shall have, and the treacherous warlock will share his funeral pyre,' Naja promised her grimly.

THEY SMELT THE RIVER from afar, the perfume of the sweet cool waters on the desert air. The horses lifted their heads and whickered. The infantry quickened their step and gazed ahead, eager for the first glimpse of the Nile's waters.

Nefer and Mintaka rode together in his chariot at the head of the long cavalcade that wound down the caravan road from Gallala. Meren rode at his right hand in the second chariot of the column.

The leading chariots topped the escarpment, and below them stretched the green valley of the Nile. Coming to meet them was the army Trok Uruk had left in Avaris, armed charioteers, generals and captains leading their regiments, legions of foot soldiers following. Behind them came the elders, the priests and the governors of every nome, all dressed in their robes, chains and decorations of office, some in carriages and others in litters borne by slaves, and still others riding astride or on foot. After them came the dense masses of citizenry, laughing and dancing.

The two cavalcades came together and mingled, and elders and generals prostrated themselves before Pharaoh's chariot. Then Nefer led the vast concourse back along the river bank towards the city of Avaris. For a league outside the city the road was lined with the welcoming crowds.

When they reached the city the gates stood wide open and the populace lined the walls. They sang anthems of loyalty, praise and welcome as Nefer, with Mintaka beside him, drove under the arch of the gateway.

Beautiful as a young god and goddess, they drove first to the magnificent temple on the river bank to give thanks to the god and to sacrifice a pair of perfect black bulls before the stone altar. After the religious service Nefer declared a week of holiday, festivity and feasting.

'You are a sly one,' Mintaka told him. 'They loved you before; now they will adore you.'

For how long? Nefer wondered. As soon as the news of our arrival reaches Naja in far-off Babylon, he will be on the march, if he is not already. The common people will love me until he knocks upon the gates.

PHARAOH NAJA KIAFAN left five hundred chariots, two thousand archers and infantry to hold and secure Babylon. Then, with the bulk of his army, he began the march on Egypt. As he went, vassal kings flocked to his standard, so that by the time he stood on the heights of the Khatmia Pass his army had almost trebled in size.

Ahead of him lay a great expanse of desert, with no spring or oasis to sustain his army until he reached Ismailiya. Once again he was reduced to laying down water points along the route ahead, and for months had been at work building up dumps in the desert, burying the filled pots in the sand, then leaving detachments of infantry to guard them while they returned for the next load.

It would take his army ten days and nights to make the crossing. During that time they would be strictly rationed, allowed just enough water to sustain the long night marches, and to eke out the burning days when they lay up to rest, enduring the heat in any scrap of shade afforded by linen tents or shelters made from branches and grass.

'I will ride with you in the vanguard.' Heseret spoke at his elbow, breaking into his train of thought.

He glanced at her. 'We have discussed this before.' He frowned. After years of marriage her charms and beauty had begun to pall, overshadowed by her petulance, jealousy and demanding tempers. 'You will come up with the other women in the baggage train, under the wing of Prenn, the centurion of the rearguard.'

Heseret pouted. Once, that had been appealing but now it was merely irritating.

'You become tiresome, wife.' Naja lifted his upper lip in a smile that was more a snarl.

She gave him a furious glare, then called for her litter with its cushions of silk to take her back down the column, to where Prenn was bringing up the rearguard.

ON TAITA'S ADVICE, Nefer had established a screen of scouts along the edge of the Great Sand Desert. Taita was certain that Naja's main invasion force must come this way. Naja knew the route well, and his army was too large to bring across the Red Sea in boats as Trok had done with his much smaller force.

Very soon it became apparent that Taita had assessed the situation correctly, and Naja was indeed intent on a frontal assault through the Great Sand Desert. A squadron of scouts commanded by Meren watched Naja's water carts carrying their loads of clay jars forward and building up dumps in the arid land. Meren asked to be allowed to attack them but Nefer sent orders to him merely to keep them under observation and note carefully where they placed the water stores.

Then Nefer ordered the last reserves that he had been holding on the river to be brought up. When these were encamped around Ismailiya, he called a war council of all their commanders. Mintaka sat on the council. Her contributions were invaluable: she was Hyksos born, and knew well those officers on Naja's staff who had once been on her own father's staff. As a child she had listened to her father's assessment of each of them, and she had a formidable memory.

'Now, there is one, Centurion Prenn, who commands Naja's rearguard, who is related to me, for he was one of my father's cousins. I know him well. He taught me to ride. I used to call him Uncle Bear.' She smiled at the memory. 'My father said of him that he was loyal as a hound, and once he had sunk his teeth into the throat of an enemy he would hang on to the death.'

All that night they sat in council while Nefer laid out his battle plan. They were to let Naja advance unopposed for the first five days. Then, once he was deeply committed, they would raid and destroy his water stores, both in front and to the rear of his advance. This would trap him in the midst of the sands.

'Taita and I have devised a plan to lead his vehicles into a trap in which we can exploit the small advantage that we have. In front of the town we will throw up a series of low stone walls behind which our archers and infantry can conceal themselves. These works will be just high enough to block the advance of a chariot.' With a charcoal stick Nefer sketched out a design on the sheet of papyrus spread in front of him. 'The walls will be laid out in the design of a fish trap.' He drew an inverted funnel with the apex aimed back towards the fort of Ismailiya.

'How will you lead him into the funnel?' Shabako asked.

'With a charge of our own chariots and the mock retreat you have practised so often,' Nefer explained. 'Our archers and slingers will remain concealed behind the walls until Naja follows us into the funnel. The deeper they penetrate, the more tightly his squadrons will be compressed between the walls. I intend to shut them up in a stockade like cattle, just as we did with Trok.'

They discussed the plan with enthusiasm, offering suggestions and refinements. In the end Nefer put Shabako in charge of building the walls, work that must begin as soon as it was light the next day.

The council broke up at last, the officers hurried away, and only three remained in the room: Nefer, Taita and Mintaka.

Mintaka spoke up again. 'We have already discussed Centurion Prenn,' she said. 'If I could meet him, I am sure I could convince him to throw in his lot with us.'

'What do you mean?' Nefer's voice was harsh. 'Meet him?'

'Dressed as a boy, with a small detachment of good men and fast horses, I could circle around Naja's main army and get through to Prenn in the rear. There would be little risk.'

Nefer's face blanched with anger. 'Madness!' he said quietly. 'Stark raving madness of the kind you exhibited at Gallala when you showed yourself as bait to Trok. I will not hear of it. Can you imagine what Naja would do to you if you fell into his hands?'

'Can you imagine what Naja would do if, in the critical moment of the battle, Prenn and his legions fell upon him from his own rear?' she flashed back at Nefer.

'We will not speak of it again.' Nefer came to his feet and slammed his fists down on the tabletop.

Taita looked on, expressionless. He waited with interest to see how this would be resolved.

'You deliberately disobeyed my orders at Gallala. I cannot trust you not to do the same now. You leave me no alternative.' Nefer shouted to the sentry outside the door to send for Zugga, the head eunuch of the royal harem. Then he turned back to Mintaka. 'I am sending you back to the *zenana* in the Avaris palace. You are to remain there in the care of Zugga.' And Zugga led Mintaka away. At the door she looked back over her shoulder at Nefer, and Taita smiled as he read her expression. Nefer had taken on a more stubborn adversary than both the false pharaohs combined.

TAITA AND NEFER rode out and inspected the stone walls that Shabako had hastily thrown up along the eastern approaches to the oasis of Ismailiya.

'Shabako's efforts will not rank among the great architectural achievements of the age,' Taita gave his opinion, 'but that is all to the good. From the direction in which Naja will come, they appear to be natural features and will excite no suspicion until he enters the funnel and finds his front progressively narrowed.'

Nefer nodded. 'Your plan has the towering virtue of allowing us to choose our own battleground. With the help of Horus, we will turn it into a slaughter-ground.' Then he laid his hand upon Taita's skinny arm. 'Once again I find myself deeply in your debt, Old Father. This is all your work.'

'No.' Taita shook his head. 'It was a gentle nudge I gave to you. The rest of it is yours. You have inherited the military instincts of your father, Pharaoh Tamose. You will achieve the greatness that might have been his, had he not died so cruelly.'

'It is time for me to avenge that death,' Nefer said. 'Let us ensure that we do not let the cobra slither away again.'

MINTAKA SPENT MUCH of the journey back to Avaris huddled in the screened litter. Her first endeavour was to make herself agreeable to Zugga, her guardian and jailer, and impress him with her submissive resignation to his authority. By the time they reached the palace in Avaris four days later, she had him completely gulled. There, in the most convincing manner, she appealed to him to allow her to visit the temple of Hathor to pray for Nefer and his victory in the looming battle. With some misgivings Zugga acquiesced, and she was able to spend almost an hour alone with the high priestess in the sanctuary of the temple. Great was Zugga's relief when she re-emerged.

A few days later when she asked to be allowed to pray again in the temple, and to make sacrifice to the goddess, Zugga was amenable to the request. Once again the high priestess led Mintaka into the sanctum and without misgivings Zugga settled down to await her return.

Two hours later a priestess came to him with a message: 'The princess has pleaded for sanctuary within the temple. The holy mother has granted her plea, and taken her under her protection.'

Zugga was thrown into turmoil. The sanctuary of the temple was inviolate. He could not demand the return of his charge. The only course open to him was to return to Ismailiya and confess his failure, but that was risky. The young pharaoh had not yet revealed his true nature, and his rage might well be fatal.

THE MOMENT THE TEMPLE DOORS closed behind her, Mintaka dropped her pretence of resigned innocence. 'Have you made the arrangements, Holy Mother?' she demanded eagerly.

'Have no fear, daughter. All is in readiness.' The priestess's old eyes sparkled with amusement. Clearly she was enjoying this escapade, a break from the tranquil routine of temple life. She led the way to a cell where the items Mintaka had requested were laid out. Mintaka dressed hastily in rough peasant garments and covered her head with a woollen shawl. Then she followed the high priestess out through a low doorway into the sunshine and onto the jetty where a large dhow was moored. 'The captain has been paid,' the priestess told her.

'You know what to tell Zugga,' Mintaka said.

The old woman smiled again. 'I am sure that Hathor will forgive me such an insignificant falsehood. It is in such a good cause.'

As Mintaka jumped down onto the deck of the dhow, the captain steered out into the mid-flow of the current and turned the bows downstream, heading for the delta. In the late afternoon the dhow moored briefly against the east bank and two armed men came aboard. Immediately the dhow captain hoisted sail again and they pressed on with all speed downriver. The two men came to the cabin and prostrated themselves before Mintaka.

'May all the gods love you, Majesty,' said the bigger of the two, a bearded Hyksos with large nose and strong features. 'We are your servants. We came as soon as we received your summons.'

'Lok!' Mintaka smiled with pleasure to see his well-remembered face, and then turned to the other man. 'And surely this is your son, Lokka.' He seemed as doughty as his father. 'You are both well met. You, Lok, served my father well. Will you and your son do the same for me?'

'With our lives, mistress!' they told her.

'I will have hard employment for you once we go ashore, but until then rest and prepare your weapons.'

The dhow captain selected one of the many mouths of the delta where the current meandered through swamps and lagoons, and steered his craft unerringly until at last the miasma of the swamps was blown away on the clean salt airs of the Mediterranean.

During the rest of that day and the following night they sailed eastwards along the coast. Next morning the dhow edged in towards the beach at El Arish, and as soon as the water was waist-deep the two bodyguards, Lok and Lokka, carried Mintaka ashore then waded back to the boat to fetch the baggage. The small party stood and watched the crew of the dhow set the sail and head back out to sea for the return to Egypt.

It was not quite as easy to find transport as Mintaka had imagined. The quartermasters of Naja's army had been ahead of them seizing wagons and horses, and in the end they had to settle for a string of five decrepit donkeys. On the third day after landing they reached the tail of the army of Pharaoh Naja, this great host filling the main east-to-west road in both directions as far as the eye could see, and fell in with the baggage train.

In her dusty, bedraggled clothing Mintaka excited little notice. Lok and Lokka chaperoned her closely, and discouraged the attentions of any other travellers. The rate of march was of the slowest, so even on the poor donkeys they were moving a little faster than the rest of the cavalcade and drifted forward towards the head.

That evening they kept on travelling after the main army had encamped, and after sunset they came upon a large zareba of poles and thorn bushes just off the road. This had been set up in an easily defended defile of low hills. The entrance was heavily guarded, and there was much marching and countermarching of the sentries around it. Above the gate of the stockade flew a gonfalon that Mintaka recognised at once: the head of a wild boar.

'This is the man we are looking for,' Mintaka whispered to Lok.

'But how do you get in to see him?' he asked doubtfully, eyeing the sentries.

They made their open camp a little further down the road, but within sight of the gates of the regimental headquarters of General Prenn, the commander of the rearguard of the pharaonic army.

From one of the leather saddlebags Mintaka brought out the precious oil lamp that had so far survived the journey, and by its light she wrote a short message on a scrap of papyrus parchment. It was addressed to 'Uncle Bear' and signed 'from your little cricket'.

She washed her face, dressed her hair, and shook out her tunic. Then she approached the gate of the stockade.

'You look like a kind and good man,' Mintaka told the sergeant of the guard. 'Will you deliver a message for me to Centurion Prenn?' She proffered the rolled parchment.

The sergeant took it, and gawked at her. She spoke the Hyksos language in the cultured tones of the aristocracy. Despite her clothes she was clearly a young woman of high rank.

'Forgive me, my lady,' he mumbled. 'I am sorry but I will have to ask you to wait here until I have an instruction from him.'

He came hurrying back within a very short time. 'My lady! I am desolated to have kept you waiting. Please follow me.'

He led her to a pavilion of coloured linen in the centre of the stockade, and there was another short delay as he whispered to the junior officer in charge of the entrance. Then she was led through into the tent. The interior was sparsely furnished and the floor was covered by animal skins, oryx, zebra and leopard. On these a man was sitting cross-legged with maps and scrolls spread about him. He looked up as Mintaka entered. His face was gaunt, his cheeks sunken, and a leather patch covered one eye.

'Uncle Bear!' Mintaka stepped into the lamplight and threw back her head shawl.

The man came to his feet slowly, then suddenly he grinned. 'I did not think it possible!' He embraced her and lifted her off her feet. 'I heard you had deserted us and gone over to the enemy.'

When he put her down again she gasped, 'That's what I have come to speak to you about.'

He heard her out silently, but his expression changed as she described to him in detail the events of that terrible night when her father and all her brothers had died in the burning galley on the river at Balasfura.

When at last she finished speaking Prenn said simply, 'I loved your father, almost as much as I love you, little cricket, but what you are proposing is treason.' He sighed. 'All this I will have to think on. But in the meantime, you can't return whence you came. It is much too risky. You must stay under my care until this affair is resolved.'

When she protested, he overrode her brusquely. 'It is not a request. It is an order.'

'Can I at least send a message to Nefer Seti?' Mintaka pleaded.

'That also is too great a risk. Have patience. It will not be for long. Naja is poised on the heights of the Khatmia. Within days he will begin the march on Ismailiya.' His voice dropped to a growl. 'And I will be forced to a decision.'

CHAPTER SEVEN

From a distance Meren watched the great host of Pharaoh Naja come down the escarpment from the Khatmia Pass into the arid lands. He shadowed the stately progress of the enemy legions across the desert, and when Naja's full army was committed to the crossing, and the leading elements had passed the halfway mark between Khatmia and Ismailiya, Meren circled out in front of the heavily encumbered, slowly moving host, back to where he had left the bulk of his force concealed.

They were fifty chariots manned by crack troops and drawn by some of the finest horses in all Nefer's army. Meren paused only to water, and to change the pennants his chariots flew from the blue to the red of Naja's army. He consoled himself that this was a legitimate ruse of war. Then he drove his squadron furiously ahead of Naja's intended line of march.

The men who had been left to guard the water dumps saw the approaching chariots coming from where they expected their comrades to arrive. When they recognised the colours flying above them they were lulled. Meren gave them no time for second thoughts, but raced in upon them, and cut down any who tried to resist. The survivors were given a choice: death or defection. Most came over to Nefer Seti. A single mallet blow was sufficient for each of the disinterred clay jars, and the precious fluid poured out into the sand. Meren's squadron mounted again and went on to the next dump.

PHARAOH NAJA REINED in his chariot and gazed out over the remains of his water dump. Although the scouts had warned him, he was still appalled by the extent of the destruction.

'Will you give the order to turn back?' asked one of his captains.

Naja turned on him coldly. 'The next coward who suggests such a thing I will have tied behind my chariot and I will drag him into battle.' He wiped the sweat from his forehead and gave new orders. 'Collect all the water-skins from the entire army. From now on the water supply is under my direct control. There is no turning back, no retreat. All the fighting chariots will move to the front of the column. I will take the cavalry ahead and seize the wells at Ismailiya . . .'

HESERET THRUST HER HEAD out of the opening of her tent, and called to the captain of her bodyguard, 'What is the trouble, fellow? This is a royal and sacred enclosure, so what are those rogues doing in my stockade?'

She pointed at the men who were taking the water-skins from one of her personal baggage carts parked alongside her tent. 'What do they think they are up to? How dare they remove our water! I have not yet bathed.'

'It is your divine husband Pharaoh's order, Majesty,' the captain explained. 'All the water is needed for the forward squadrons.'

'Such orders cannot apply to the Queen of Egypt,' Heseret screamed. 'I shall go at once to Prenn. I shall have new orders for you when I return.' Then she turned to the officer of her bodyguard. 'Ready my chariot and an escort of ten men.'

Across the flat and open plain, Prenn's headquarters camp was in clear view of Heseret's tent. It took only minutes for her chariot to carry her there, but the guard at the gate of the stockade barred her way. 'Your Divine Majesty, General Prenn is not here,' he told her. 'He left an hour ago with all his cavalry. He had orders from Pharaoh to join the vanguard.'

'I do not believe that,' Heseret flared at him. 'I know he would not have left without informing me. Stand aside!'

He jumped hurriedly out of her way, and she went straight to the yellow and green striped command tent, stooped through the doorway, and stopped dead in the threshold.

A young woman was sitting on the piles of animal skins in the centre of the floor. She looked up at her startled.

'Who are you?' Heseret demanded. 'Where is the general?' Suddenly Heseret's eyes narrowed. 'You!' she screamed. 'You treacherous, poisonous bitch!' She pointed a quivering finger at the girl. 'Guards!' Heseret shrieked at the top of her voice. 'Guards, here, at once!'

Mintaka came to her senses. She darted across the tent and out through the rear opening.

'Guards!' Heseret yelled again. 'This way!' Her bodyguard burst in through the doorway behind her.

'Stop her!' Heseret shouted. 'Don't let her escape. She is a spy and a traitor.'

Her bodyguard charged after Mintaka, shouting to the guards at the gate, and the sentries drew their swords and ran to cut her off. She fought desperately, kicking, scratching and biting, but the soldiers overwhelmed her at last and dragged her back to the command tent to face Heseret.

The Queen was smiling vindictively. 'Bind her securely. I am sure that my husband, the sole ruler of Egypt, will devise a suitable punishment for her crimes when he returns. Until that time she is to be caged like a wild animal and kept at the door of my tent where I can keep her under my eye.'

One of the carts of Heseret's baggage train carried her stock of livestock in cages, chickens, pigs and young goats for her kitchen. The cage that had contained the suckling pigs was now empty—they had been slaughtered and eaten—and the guards shoved Mintaka in through the narrow door.

'There will be guards standing over you day and night,' Heseret warned her. 'Should you try to escape I will have one of your feet cut off, to discourage further attempts.'

FROM THE WATCHTOWER above the fort at Ismailiya the sentry shouted the warning, 'Pharaoh! The pickets are coming in!'

Nefer sprang up from the table under the awning in the courtyard where he and Taita were eating the midday meal. He climbed swiftly up the ladder to the platform and shaded his eyes. Through the yellow glare he made out the chariots of his forward pickets. As they drove down the bank of the wadi, the guards threw open the gates and allowed them to enter the fort.

'The enemy comes on apace!' the sergeant of the pickets shouted up to Nefer.

'Well done, sergeant,' Nefer called back to him, and then to the trumpeter on the wall above the gate, 'Sound the call to arms!'

The ram's horn blared out across the plain, and the entire army encamped down the length of the broad wadi began to stir. Soon lines of marching men and columns of chariots were moving forward to their prepared positions.

Taita clambered up onto the high platform, and Nefer smiled at him. 'So, even deprived of his water, Naja has not turned back.'

'We never though he would,' Taita said softly.

In the east the horizon started to darken, as the dust cloud of the advancing enemy army boiled like a brewing thunderstorm.

'Will you ride out to meet him with me, Old Father?' Nefer asked, as he strapped on the sword-belt that his orderly handed to him.

'No, I will overlook the battle from here. Perhaps in my own feeble way I might be of more help to you than if I wielded a javelin or drew a bow.'

Nefer smiled. 'Your weapons are sharper and fly more truly

than any I have ever held in my hand. Horus love and protect you, Old Father.'

They watched as the battalions of archers and slingers marched out of the wadi to take up their positions behind the breastworks. Every man among them knew what was expected of him, and had rehearsed this manoeuvre many times. As the last of them disappeared into the ambuscade, the field seemed deserted.

The dust cloud of Naja's advance was less than a league off when at last Nefer embraced Taita and climbed down the ladder. Meren handed him the reins as he leapt up onto his chariot's footplate.

Nefer lifted his right fist high and gave the command: 'March! Forward!'

The ram's horn sounded the advance and he led the van out, rank upon rank in majestic progress, down between the low breastworks from behind which not a single archer showed himself, out onto the open plain. On the markers he had laid out weeks before, Nefer halted his leading squadron, and let the horses rest while he studied the enemy advance.

Meren murmured, 'Sweet Horus be praised. It seems he has committed all his vehicles. He holds no depth of chariots in reserve.'

'They must be desperate for water,' Nefer answered. 'His only chance of survival is to break our ranks with a frontal charge and win through to the wells.'

Closer and closer came the enemy, until two hundred paces away the mighty host rolled to a halt. A vast silence settled over the brooding landscape, broken only by the fretting susurration of the wind. The dust settled like a falling curtain.

From the enemy centre a single chariot pulled forward. Even though dust coated the coachwork the gold leaf gleamed through, and the royal pennant flew above the driver's head. Naja halted less than a hundred paces to the front, so that Nefer recognised the cold, handsome face under the blue war crown.

'Hail, Nefer Seti, puppy of the dog I slew with my own hand!' Naja called and Nefer stiffened to hear him confess so openly to regicide. 'Upon my head I wear the crown I took from Tamose as he was dying. Will you claim it from me, puppy?'

With a huge effort Nefer kept his face expressionless, but his voice rang like metal on stone. 'Make ready!'

Naja laughed, wheeled his own chariot and drove back to his place in the centre of the opposing line.

'March! Forward!' Naja raised the blue sword. His front ranks gathered momentum, rolling towards Nefer's line. 'At the gallop! Charge!' They surged forward in a solid mass.

Nefer stood his ground and let them come on. Then he lifted his sword again and described three flashing arcs with the blade above his head. His legions responded instantly, turning as though possessed of a single controlling mind, and racing away over the plain, back the way they had come, drawing together from extended order into a column of four.

Naja tore after them, but within three hundred paces his flanks came upon a low stone breastwork that slanted across their front. They could not stop now, so they veered left and right towards their own centre. Like the current of a wide river forced suddenly into the mouth of a narrow rocky gorge, they were squeezed together. Wheel snagged wheel, and horse teams were forced to give way to each other. The charge wavered and slowed as chariots and horses jammed into a solid mass.

At that fatal moment, the rams' horns brayed across the field, and at the signal the heads and shoulders of the archers and slingers rose from behind the breastworks on either hand. The slingers whirled their weapons on high, and the archers held their aim a moment, choosing their targets with care. The first volley was always the most telling.

The slingers loosed their missiles and the archers their arrows in a single concerted volley. They had been ordered to aim for the horses, and to pick out the enemy captains. The first rank of Naja's charge was shot down, and as the horses fell the chariots piled up over their carcasses, swerving out of control into the stone walls on either hand, or capsizing and rolling.

The vehicles that followed were unable to stop the charge, and crashed into the wreckage of those in front. Wheels shattered and were torn from their axles. Men were hurled from their cockpits and trampled under the frantic hoofs of the rearing, milling horses.

At the head of his squadron, Nefer gave the hand signal that the men following him were expecting, and a swarm of foot soldiers leapt out of hiding and dragged away the thorn bushes that concealed the openings that had been left in the walls on either hand. In quick succession Nefer's chariots swerved through them and into the open ground beyond the walls. No longer constricted, they doubled back, circling in behind Naja's trapped squadrons, and falling on their rear echelons.

Now both armies were locked together. Not all of Naja's vehicles had been lured into the trap between the walls. These chariots now came rushing forward to engage Nefer, and a traditional chariot battle swiftly developed. The squadrons broke up into smaller units, and across the plain single vehicles viciously engaged each other, wheel to wheel, and man to man.

Despite the frightful losses he had inflicted on the enemy in the opening phase, Nefer was still heavily outnumbered. As the advantage swung back and forth, Nefer was forced to call in more and more of the reserves he had been holding concealed in the wadi behind the fort. Now he signalled in the last of them. He was fully committed. But they were not enough. Slowly his horses and his men were being ground down by the sheer numbers of his enemy.

In the dust and clamour and turmoil, Nefer knew that his army would soon be in rout, and he shouted encouragement to the charioteers close enough to hear him.

Then beside him Meren shouted, 'Look, Pharaoh!' and he pointed to the east out into the desert. With the back of his hand Nefer wiped his sweat and splashes of enemy blood from his face, and stared out into the glare.

He knew then beyond all doubt that it was over, and that they had lost the battle. A fresh mass of enemy chariots was tearing in towards them. He had thought that Naja had committed all his vehicles. That did not matter now, for the battle was lost.

'How many?' Nefer wondered, black desolation filling his soul.

'Two hundred,' Meren guessed. 'Maybe more.' His voice was resigned. 'It is all over, Pharaoh. We will die fighting.'

As the enemy closed they saw that the leading enemy chariot flew the pennant of a general, a centurion.

'By Horus, I know him,' Meren cried. 'It's Prenn—and he flies the blue!'

Prenn's pennant was streaming back, directly away from them, which was why Nefer had not noticed it until this moment, but

Meren was right: Prenn was flying the blue of the House of Tamose, and all his chariots with him.

Now Prenn slowed, held his right arm across his chest in salute to Nefer, and shouted in a great voice that carried above the rumble of the chariot wheels, 'What are your orders, Pharaoh?'

'What strange business is this, General Prenn? Why do you call on me for orders?' Nefer called back.

'The Princess Mintaka delivered to me your message, and I have come to place myself under your command.'

'Mintaka?' Nefer was confused, for surely she was still closeted in the sanctuary of the temple in Avaris. But his warrior instincts took over and he thrust aside those thoughts. 'Well met, General Prenn. You arrive none too soon. Lay your chariot alongside mine and we will sweep this field from end to end.'

They charged side by side, and Nefer's broken and scattered legions saw the blue pennants coming and took new heart. The red squadrons of Naja Kiafan were in hardly better case and could offer only scant resistance as Prenn's fresh troops charged into them. They fought on for a while, but the heart was torn out of them.

Nefer quartered across the field with Meren, searching for Naja. He reached the stone breastworks and looked over the low wall into the narrow defile where he had trapped the forward legions of Naja's army. Around each smashed chariot lay the dead and the wounded. Some were still moving and weeping, calling to the gods and to their mothers. Others sat dazed with the agony of their wounds. Nefer looked for Naja's body among the dead, but all was confusion. Then he picked out a flash of gold leaf, and the royal standard of Naja Kiafan lying in the dust.

'I must find him,' Nefer told Meren. 'I must know he is dead.' He jumped down from the chariot.

'I will help you search.' Meren tethered the horses to the walls.

Nefer vaulted over the breastworks and scrambled over the other wreckage until he reached the golden chariot. It lay on its side, but the cockpit was empty. Suddenly Meren shouted and stooped to pick up something from among the debris. He lifted his trophy high, and Nefer saw that he had found Naja's blue war crown.

'His body must be close,' Nefer called to him. 'He would not have discarded that. It means too much to him.'

At that moment Nefer caught a flash of movement from the corner of his eye. He ducked and whirled about. Naja had risen from where he had been crouching behind the dashboard of the chariot. He still carried the blue sword of Tamose and he launched a double-handed blow at Nefer's head, but Nefer ducked under the hissing blade and drew his own sword.

Naja stepped back and looked about him. He saw Meren coming to Nefer's aid and he saw the empty chariot hitched to the wall. He drove Nefer back with another thrust of the blue blade, then whirled and sprinted away. As he jumped over the wall he cut the horses free and leapt up onto the footplate. Startled, the pair lunged forward together and within half a dozen strides were both at full gallop.

Behind them Nefer jumped to the top of the wall and saw Naja being carried away across the plain. He drew a long breath and whistled, the high piercing blast his horses knew so well. He saw their heads go up, their ears prick and swivel towards him. Then they changed gait and swung into a tight turn. The chariot was flung hard over in the turn, and Naja had to clutch at the dashboard to prevent himself being hurled overboard. The pair of horses came pounding back towards where Nefer stood poised on the wall. Naja recovered his balance and held the blue sword at guard, ready to strike out at Nefer as soon as he came within reach. Nefer knew that his own bronze could never stand against that terrible blade. It would be certain death to throw himself on top of a swordsman of Naja's calibre armed with that weapon.

As the horses swept by below him, Nefer leapt lightly onto one horse's back, and with his knees steered it onto the open plain, still at full gallop. He glanced back and saw Naja climbing out of the cockpit, then edging along the drive shaft to get at Nefer.

Nefer leaned down and with his own blade sliced the leather rope that hitched the horses to the shaft. Running free, the chariot veered off to one side. The shaft dug into the soft earth, flicking the vehicle over, and Naja was thrown clear. He struck the ground with his shoulder and even above the sound of hoofs Nefer heard the bone break.

Nefer charged at him. Naja had climbed painfully to his feet and stood swaying, clutching his damaged right arm across his chest. In his fall he had lost his grip on the hilt of the blue sword. It had spun out of his hand, and ten paces away from where he stood the point had pegged into the earth. The blade still quivered from the impact. The wondrous blue metal threw slivers of blue light, and the jewelled hilt whipped from side to side.

Naja staggered towards the weapon, but then he saw Nefer bearing down on him, and an expression of utter terror turned his face the colour of cold ashes. When Nefer leaned down and plucked the sword from the sand, Naja knew then that he could not escape his terrible vengeance. He fell to his knees and lifted both hands in supplication, as Nefer jumped down and stood over him.

'Mercy!' Naja sobbed. 'I yield to you the double crown and all the kingdom.' He crawled pitifully to Nefer's feet.

'I already have that. I lack only one thing. Vengeance!'

'Mercy, Nefer Seti, in the name of the gods and for the sake of your sister, the goddess Heseret, and the infant in her womb.' Suddenly there was a dagger in his right hand, and he stabbed up viciously at Nefer's groin. Nefer had almost been taken in, but he twisted away just in time, and struck the weapon out of Naja's grasp with a flick of his blade.

'I admire your consistency. To the very end you are true to your base nature.' Nefer smiled down on him coldly. 'You I grant the same mercy that you showed my father, Pharaoh Tamose.' He drove the point of the blue sword into the centre of Naja's chest, and it came out between his shoulder blades.

Naja toppled face first into the dust, and drew one more ragged breath, but the air from his lungs bubbled out of the wound between his shoulder blades and he shuddered and died.

Nefer hitched Naja's body by its heels to the traces that dangled from the horse's harness, then mounted and dragged it back across the field. Cheering followed him as he rode up to the gates of the fort. He cut the rope and left Naja's bloody corpse lying in the dust.

Then he looked up to the figure who stood high upon the watchtower of the fort, and raised the blue blade to him in salute. Taita lifted his hand in acknowledgment.

He was on the tower through the whole day. What part did the Magus play in the battle? Nefer asked himself. There was no answer, and he put the thought aside. He mounted the ladder to the top of the tower and stood beside Taita. From there he spoke to his men. He thanked them for their duty and their bravery. He promised them their rewards, a share of the plunder to all, and the honours of valour to the captains and centurions.

By the time he had named them all the sun was sinking through a low bank of purple thunderclouds towards the horizon. He ended his speech with a call to prayer: 'I dedicate this victory to the golden Horus, the falcon of the gods,' he cried, and as he prayed there was a strange omen. A fleeting ray of the last sunlight broke through the cloud bank. It glinted on the blue war crown on Nefer's head and on the blue sword in his hand.

At the same moment there was a wild cry from above. Every head lifted and every eye turned towards the sky. A great murmur went up from the multitude. A royal falcon hovered in the air above the head of Pharaoh, and as they stared in wonder it uttered that strange, haunting sound again, then circled three times, and at last shot away in a straight line on rapid, incisive wingbeats into the eastern sky and was gone in the gloom.

'A blessing from the god,' the soldiers chanted. 'Hail, Pharaoh! The gods salute you.'

But beside him Taita spoke softly. 'The falcon brought a warning, not a blessing.'

'What is the warning?' Nefer demanded.

'When the bird called, I heard Mintaka cry out,' Taita whispered.

'Mintaka!' Nefer had forgotten her in the exigencies of the battle. 'What did Prenn tell me about her?' He turned to the ladder and shouted down to the guards. 'Prenn! Where is the centurion Prenn?'

Prenn came at once, and knelt before Pharaoh. 'You have earned our deepest gratitude,' Nefer told him. 'Without you we could not have prevailed.'

'Pharaoh is gracious,'

'At the start of the battle, you spoke of the Princess Mintaka. I thought that she was safe in the temple of Hathor in Avaris. Where did you last see her and when?'

'Pharaoh, you are mistaken. Princess Mintaka is not in the temple. She came to me with your message. I could not bring her into battle with me, so I left her two days ago in my camp in the desert.'

A foreboding seized Nefer. 'Who else is in the encampment?'

'Some of the other royal women. Her Majesty Queen Heseret—'

'Heseret!' Nefer wrung his hands. 'Heseret! If Mintaka is in her power, what will she do to her when she hears that I have slain her husband? We must ride at once.'

HESERET AWOKE IN THE DARKNESS and chill of that dread time before the dawn when the human spirit at its lowest ebb. At first she was uncertain of what had interrupted her sleep, but then she became aware of the sound of many voices, faint but growing stronger. She sat up and tried to make sense of the distant hubbub. She was able to make out words now: 'defeated' and 'slain' and 'flee at once'. She called for her maids and two stumbled in.

'What is going on?' Heseret demanded.

The eldest maid was breathless. 'They say there has been a great battle at a place called Ismailiya, Majesty.'

Heseret felt a great surge of joy. Naja had triumphed: in her heart she was certain of it. 'What was the outcome of the battle?'

'We don't know, mistress. We did not ask.'

Heseret seized the girl nearest to her by the hair, and shook her violently. 'Have you not a speck of brain in your thick skull?' She slapped her across the face, and left her lying on the floor of the tent. She grabbed a lamp and hurried to the door.

The guards were gone, and she felt the first pangs of fear. She ran to the cage outside and held up the lamp, peering into the pig cage. Part of her anxiety was allayed as she saw that Mintaka was still pinioned and tied to the struts at the back of the cage.

Heseret left her and ran to the gate of the stockade. In the starlight she made out a dark cavalcade streaming past. She saw the loom of carts and wagons being drawn by teams of oxen. Some were piled high with bales and boxes, others were crowded with women clutching their children. Hundreds of soldiers hurried past on foot and Heseret saw that most had thrown away their weapons.

She picked out a soldier in the passing throng, who wore the collar of a sergeant. 'What news of the battle? Tell me. Oh, please tell me,' she begged.

He peered into her face. 'The most dire news, Majesty.' His voice was gruff. 'There has been a terrible battle and our army has been defeated. The enemy will be upon us soon. You must flee at once.'

'What of Pharaoh? What has happened to my husband?'

'Pharaoh Naja Kiafan is slain, cut down in single combat by Nefer Seti himself.'

Heseret let out a keening wail. She gathered up a double handful of dust and poured it over her head. Still wailing she clawed her face with her fingernails.

Her handmaidens came out of the stockade to fetch her in, but she screamed incoherent obscenities at them. She ran to the pig cage on the cart, and screeched at Mintaka through the bars: 'My husband is dead. Slain by my own monstrous brother.'

'Praise be to Hathor and all the gods,' Mintaka cried.

'You blaspheme!' Heseret raved. 'Naja Kiafan was a god.' She turned to the captain of her guards. 'Drag the sow from her cage.'

The captain hesitated. Nefer and his captains would be here soon.

Heseret grabbed a spear out of the hand of the nearest soldier and struck him across the back. 'I order you, Captain, to obey me.'

The man backed away. 'You are mad. What punishment would Nefer Seti heap upon my head?' He turned suddenly and bolted from the stockade to join the flood of fleeing refugees in the roadway. His men hesitated only a moment longer, then rushed to the gate hard after him.

Heseret ran after them. 'Come back! I order you!' But they mingled with the crowds and were gone. Dazed as a sleepwalker she went to her tent. She picked a robe at random from the pile in the corner, and pulled sandals onto her feet. 'I am going to find Naja,' she said. Then with new determination she headed for the door.

As she stepped out into the early sunlight, Mintaka called to her from the cage. 'Please release me, Heseret. In all charity, let me go.'

'You don't understand.' Heseret shook her head wildly. 'I have to go to my husband, the Pharaoh of all Egypt. He needs me.'

She did not glance at Mintaka again but hurried out of the stockade, shaking her head and muttering incoherently to herself. She turned towards the west, in the opposite direction from the flood of terrified humanity, and started to run back towards Egypt.

MINTAKA STRUGGLED against her bonds, twisting and tugging, bracing her bare feet against the struts of the cage to give herself better purchase. She felt the skin smearing from her wrists, and warm blood dripping down her hands, but the leather thongs were tight and strong and she could neither stretch nor snap them. She felt her hands becoming numb from lack of blood.

Once Mintaka heard a stealthy scuffle at the entrance to the tent and saw Heseret's two maids creeping out, each carrying a large bag crammed with valuables they had looted. Mintaka called to them, but they glanced at her with startled, guilty expressions and scurried from the stockade.

At last the only sound was the soughing of the desert wind through the branches of the scrawny thorn tree at the gate.

Then she heard something else, hoofbeats and the sound of men's voices growing stronger, and stronger still, until she could recognise one. 'Nefer!' She tried to scream his name, but her voice was a draughty whisper. 'Nefer!'

She twisted her head and saw Nefer storm through the gateway, Meren and Taita close behind him.

Nefer ran to the cage. He tore the gate off its hinges with his bare hand and pulled his dagger from its sheath to slash loose the leather thongs from her wrists. Gently he drew her out of the stinking cage and held her to his chest. Mintaka shut her eyes and slumped into unconsciousness. Nefer was weeping as he carried her into the tent.

MINTAKA CAME AWAKE slowly as though she were rising up from the depths of that dark and terrible pit where demons live.

When she opened her eyes she saw with immense relief the two most beloved faces in her world. Taita sat at one side of her couch and Nefer at the other.

'How long?' she asked. 'How long was I gone?'

'A day and a night,' Nefer answered her.

'You are not angry with me for disobeying you?'

'You have given me a crown and a land.' He shook his head and one of his tears fell upon her face. 'Above that you have given me your love, which is more precious to me than all of that. How could I ever be angry with you?'

Taita rose softly and left the tent, and they stayed together all the rest of that day, speaking softly together.

In the evening Nefer sent for two priestesses from the temple of

Hathor. 'You have come to see justice done,' he told them, then turned to the guards at the door.

'Bring in the woman named Heseret,' he ordered.

Mintaka started and tried to sit up, but he pushed her gently back upon the bolster.

'Where? How did you find her?'

'Our pickets found her wandering in the desert on the road back to Ismailiya,' Nefer explained. 'At first they did not recognise her or believe her claims to be a queen. They thought her a madwoman.'

Heseret came into the tent. Nefer had allowed her to bathe and provided her with fresh raiment, and Taita had treated the cuts and grazes on her face and body. Now she shrugged off the hands of her guards and looked around her with a regal lift of her chin.

'Prostrate yourselves before me,' she ordered. 'I am a queen.'

No one moved, and Nefer said, 'You are a queen no longer.' He stared at her so coldly that Heseret started to weep.

'I am your own sister. You would not harm me.'

'You are right, Heseret. I will not harm you.'

He sighed and turned to the two priestesses. 'I give into your keeping the body and the life of Heseret Tamose, who was a princess of the royal House of Egypt.'

Heseret began to scream but no one took notice of her cries as gently they dragged her blubbering and wailing from the tent.

They sat in silence, and through the linen walls listened as Heseret's wailing, entreaties and blandishments faded into the distance. Then Mintaka covered her face with both hands and Nefer made the sign against evil with his right hand.

WHEN MINTAKA HAD RECOVERED sufficiently to begin the long journey back to Avaris, Nefer insisted that she be carried in a litter to ease the jolting and lurching over the rough road that lay ahead. They travelled slowly, and it was fifteen days later that they reached the escarpment and looked down from the arid wastes upon the wide green valley of the Nile.

Nefer helped Mintaka from the litter, and together they walked a short way from the road, so that they could be alone and savour this joyous moment of homecoming. They had not been there long when Nefer stood up and shaded his eyes.

'What is it, my heart?' Mintaka asked.

'We have a visitor,' he said, but when she exclaimed with annoyance at the intrusion he went on, 'This visitor is always welcome.'

She smiled then as she recognised the figure approaching them. 'Taita. But what strange attire is this?'

He was dressed in a simple robe and sandals, and slung on his back he carried the leather satchel of a holy man on a pilgrimage.

'I have come to take my leave of you,' Taita explained.

'You will not leave me now.' Nefer was dismayed. 'Will you not attend my coronation?'

'You were crowned on the field of Ismailiya,' Taita told him gently.

'Our wedding!' Mintaka cried. 'You must stay for our wedding.'

'You were married long since,' Taita smiled, 'perhaps on the day of your birth, for the gods intended you for each other.'

Nefer knew that there was nothing further to say, that more words would degrade this moment. He did not even ask where Taita was going. Perhaps he did not know.

He embraced Taita, then he and Mintaka stood and watched him walk away, and his distant shape slowly dwindle in the shimmering wastes of the desert wilderness, and they shared the same deep ache of regret and bereavement.

'He has not really gone,' Mintaka whispered, when at last he had disappeared from view.

'No,' Nefer agreed. 'He will always be with us.'

WITH THE HIGH PRIESTESS and fifty acolytes from the temple of Hathor preceding her, the Princess Mintaka Apepi came for her marriage to Pharaoh Nefer Seti.

They stood together on the terrace of the palace of Thebes that overlooked the broad brown floor of the Nile in flood, in the season most propitious to all living things in the land of Egypt.

It seemed that all of Egypt had come to bear witness to the nuptials. The crowds stretched back along both banks of the river as far as the eye could see. When the couple embraced and broke the jars of Nile water, the shout that went up to heaven must have startled the gods themselves. Then Nefer Seti led his new queen out by the hand and showed her beauty to the populace, who fell to their knees and wept.

Suddenly a silence fell over this vast congregation. Slowly every eye turned upwards to the tiny speck in the vaulted sky above the palace.

In the silence there was the wild, lonely cry of a royal falcon, and the bird began its stoop out of the high blue. Just as it seemed it must come into violent collision, the falcon flared its wings wide and hovered over the tall figure of Pharaoh. Nefer lifted his right arm and held it out, and softly as a feather the magnificent bird alighted upon his fist.

A sound like the sea on a stormy day rose from ten thousand throats as they greeted the miracle. But Nefer's eyes fell on the loop of gold that was fastened about the bird's right foot. Engraved into the precious metal was a symbol that made Nefer's heart race as he recognised it.

'The royal cartouche!' he whispered. 'This was never a wild bird. This is Nefertem, my father's falcon. That is why it came to me so often in times of greatest danger, to warn and guide me. It was my father's spirit.'

'And now Nefertem has come to affirm before all the world that you are king indeed.' Mintaka stood closer to him and gazed into his face with eyes that glowed with pride and love.

WILBUR SMITH

Since breaking into print with his hugely successful first book, *When the Lion Feeds*, an epic of 19th-century South Africa, Wilbur Smith has written a string of best-selling novels, most of them about the continent where he was born and brought up, the continent that has always inspired him. He was born at Broken Hill, Zambia (in those days Northern Rhodesia) and educated in South Africa, where he still lives today. As well as his house in Cape Town he has a large ranch where he indulges his love of African wildlife—a passion that comes across in his books.

In the wake of *Sunbird*, a novel set in ancient Africa and published in 1973, fans badgered Wilbur Smith for another story with an ancient setting. Eventually, in 1993, they were rewarded with a stunning Egyptian saga, *River God*, and then in 1995 with its sequel, *The Seventh Scroll*. *Warlock*, the author's latest blockbuster, builds on the stories told in those two books, and many readers will enjoy reacquainting themselves with the extraordinary character of Taita.

Much of the history of Ancient Egypt is known from the research of archaeologists, but Wilbur Smith was drawn to a particularly troubled period—that of the Hyksos invasions—precisely because the history of that time is very confused and obscure. His books are always an inspired mixture of fact and imagination and he wanted to have the freedom to write creatively and to be able to say to any Egyptologists who tried to attack his writings for historical inaccuracy: 'You don't know for certain either.'

Between them, *River God*, *The Seventh Scroll* and *Warlock* form a memorable and dramatic trio of novels that succeed in transporting readers back to a fascinating time and place.